ZAHHN'S MATE

A Dark Sci-Fi Alien Romance

Worldship Brides
Book 4

SUE LYNDON

Zahhn's Mate: A Dark Sci-Fi Alien Romance

Contact: suelyndon@suelyndon.com

Editing by Celeste Jones

Cover design by Sylvia Frost of The Book Brander
romancepremades.com

Published in the United States of America
Sue Lyndon
www.suelyndon.com

Chapter 1

LEONA

I awake drenched in sweat, convinced I'm not alone. Yet a glance around the brightly lit room reveals no one. I sigh with relief and place a hand over my racing heart. Inhuman growls echo in my mind, a remnant of the strange dream that just ripped me from sleep. Each time I blink, I see a pair of purple eyes set in a face obscured by shadows. It's the same thing every night, the growls and the purple eyes and the overwhelming masculine presence.

What's causing the dreams?

Am I actually communicating with some kind of creature?

Knowing I won't be sleeping anytime soon, I take a deep breath, slip out of bed, and get dressed. Then I depart my quarters and slink through the corridors of the *Jansonna*, the worldship that houses the last of humankind.

After climbing down the tubes to Deck Nine, I head for my favorite viewing alcove. I draw the curtain shut, perch on the bench, and proceed to gaze at the Darrvason fleet. Awe fills me as I study the fifteen massive ships.

It's not lost on me that the odd dreams began shortly after the Darrvasons made contact with my people. And if the dreams aren't enough to make me question my sanity, my growing fascination with the alien fleet is.

Ever since the Darrvasons showed up, I've found myself sneaking off to privately gawk at their vessels every chance I can get. Morning, noon, and night. At present, it's past curfew and I shouldn't be outside my quarters, but I can't resist. There's a pull inside me, something inexplicably strong that draws me to the viewing alcove multiple times a day.

I'm most captivated by the *Haxxal*, the lead ship in the Darravson fleet. It's as though I'm missing something important, a vital piece of myself, and if I don't go searching on the *Haxxal*, I very well might go mad.

I sigh and run a hand through my hair as I consider the tension on the worldship as of late. I was born on the *Jansonna* and I've lived here for my entire life, yet I cannot recall a time when so much fear has permeated the vessel.

Waiting. It's like we're waiting for something big and terrible to happen.

The *Jansonna* is *dead in the water*, so to speak, to

borrow an old Earth phrase. Nearly out of fuel, we're unable to make the jump to hyperdrive. The water filtration system also keeps breaking down, environmental controls constantly malfunction, and an uncontained gas leak has rendered the five lower decks uninhabitable. Water and food are being rationed at historically reduced levels, and only the wealthiest on the ship—elderly Founders and their descendants—are able to receive medical care.

And in our time of need, the Darrvasons just happened to show up. I know the aliens have already met with Captain Warren and the rest of the human worldship's command team, but beyond that it's difficult to decipher which of the wild rumors I've heard about the Darrvasons' continued presence might be true.

It's obvious that negotiations of some sort are taking place. Humankind needs help and clearly the technologically advanced Darrvasons can provide it, but at what cost?

What sort of payment are the aliens demanding in return for their help?

Shivers rush through me as I think about the rumors. I've heard everything from the aliens wanting to keep humans as slaves, to the aliens being a vampiric race that craves our blood, to the aliens wanting human women for breeding purposes.

This last rumor causes me to flush and squirm in my seat, though I'm not sure why. I've never engaged in the act of physical congress. I don't know what it feels like and whether it's a pleasurable experience.

On the *Jansonna*, fornication has been outlawed for decades, and we're all given hormone suppression shots to keep us from having *urges.* Whatever that means. Rather than being conceived the old-fashioned way—the dangerous way, or so we're told—babies are conceived in a fertility lab. Reproduction is strictly controlled, and couples who desire a child must submit an application.

Yes, *couples.* We might not be allowed to consummate our relationships, but couples still get married on the worldship, whether for companionship, tradition, or to seal alliances between families.

I cover a yawn, but despite my growing fatigue, I don't depart the alcove. My gaze remains riveted to the *Haxxal* as the longing seems to pulse harder inside my chest, and for a reason I can't fathom, my upper arms feel warm and almost itchy.

Just another hour, I tell myself. Then I'll go to bed.

As I scoot closer to the viewscreen, footsteps abruptly sound in the corridor. I freeze and hold my breath, praying whoever it is will walk by the alcove without peeking behind the curtain. My heart races and my palms become sweaty.

As the footsteps grow nearer, murmuring voices reach me as well. Shit. Multiple people. If they're walking in a group after curfew, they must be security officers.

Relief swarms me when they move past the alcove, and I slowly, very quietly, release a long breath.

Close. That was too close.

Given how I spend my evenings—managing an

illegal bar on Deck Twenty-Two known as Leona's Speakeasy—I really should be more careful. The last thing I want is to run afoul of the law and draw unwanted attention to myself. Being out after curfew is generally considered a minor offense, but I can't afford a fine and I dread the prospect of spending even one night in the brig.

Just as I refocus my attention on the *Haxxal*, the alcove's curtain is pulled back with a flourish. I gasp and spin to face the intruder.

Cold shock grips me. It's not a security or morality officer. Oh no, it's so much worse than that.

Commander Hampton, the first mate of the *Jansonna*, looms above me wearing a menacing smile. Given his reputation as a corrupt asshole, he's the absolute last person on the ship by whom I'd want to be caught.

"What do we have here?" A dark chuckle escapes him.

I summon my bravery and meet his eyes, not wanting him to discern the true depths of my fear. The more frightened I appear, the more guilty I'll look. As far as he knows, I'm just a regular citizen of the *Jansonna* who happened to stay out after curfew to admire the majestic view of open space and the Darrvason fleet. It's a plausible excuse. Non-Founders like me don't have viewscreens in our quarters, so we're only able to glimpse open space when we visit an alcove, a mess hall, or a recreation room.

"Good evening, Commander Hampton." I force a smile. "If you wish to sit in this alcove, it's all yours. I was just leaving." I rise to my feet and try to walk around him, but he snatches my arm in a painful grip.

He leans closer and scoffs. Spittle flies from his mouth. It's all I can do not to flinch. "It's hours past curfew and well after midnight. 'Good morning' is more like it." His gaze brims with violence as he looks me up and down, causing a fresh shiver to rack my body. "What is your name?"

Somehow, I manage another polite smile. "Leona Zimmerman." I don't want to reveal my last name, but if I don't immediately disclose it, I know he'll ask. A quick scan of my palm would reveal my identity anyway.

"Zimmerman?" Disgust fills his visage. "Any relation to Harris Zimmerman?"

I swallow past the dryness in my throat. "He's my father."

The commander's grip on my arm tightens. He whistles, and footsteps once again echo in the corridor. Two security officers approach to stand on either side of him, and my dread promptly deepens. My father has been a thorn in the command team's side for years. He's also spent time in the brig.

"Tell me, Leona, is your father planning to incite any rebellions in the near future?"

"My father has never incited a rebellion." That's probably not true, but there's never been enough evidence to keep Dad in the brig for long.

Commander Hampton rolls his eyes. "If he weren't such a skilled engineer, I think we both know he would've met with an unfortunate accident years ago."

His gaze briefly darts to the alien fleet. "But perhaps our worldship won't need him for much longer."

"So, it's true then? It's true that the Darrvasons are going to help us?" I think of the *Haxxal* and my intense but inexplicable desire to board the alien vessel. "What do they want in exchange for their help?" The *Jansonna* gives an ominous shudder, and the lights in the corridor flicker, a reminder that the Darrvasons haven't helped us *yet*. The worldship is still in a perilous state.

The commander's grip turns bruising, and I can't restrain a gasp. He doesn't answer my questions. Instead, he yanks me out of the alcove, then tosses me toward the security officers. The uniformed men catch me, and before I draw my next breath, they secure my wrists in manacles behind my back.

Oh God. My stomach flips and I shoot Commander Hampton a pleading look. Not that begging will have any effect. The commander has a reputation for arresting and even torturing people without cause. The rumors about him are horrifying, and I pray I'll end up in the brig rather than his private quarters.

What if he sees capturing me as an opportunity to learn more about my father's alleged rebellious activities? What if he tries to torture information out of me? The truth is, I suspect my father is involved with at least a few rebel groups who would like nothing more than to overthrow Captain Warren and the rest of his command team, Commander Hampton included, but I don't have any proof, nor do I know any helpful details.

"The fine for being caught in the corridors after curfew recently increased tenfold, and I doubt you can pay it. Such a pity. Guess you'll be spending two weeks in the brig." Commander Hampton's eyes glitter with malice. "Take her away, gentlemen."

"Wait!" I struggle in the security officers' grasp. Though I'm wearing restraints, they still have an iron grip on my arms. "You can't just keep me in the brig for two weeks. I-I'm entitled to a trial." This being my first offense, surely a judge would only impose a one-night sentence in the brig. Not two freaking weeks. Guilt ravages me as I consider all the people I'll be letting down if I disappear without warning for an extended period of time. My friends and my coworkers. Not to mention the patrons who frequent the speakeasy.

"A trial?" The commander laughs. Then he withdraws a clear vial filled with tiny pink crystals from his pocket. He holds the vial in front of my face. My blood runs cold. "Very well. You may have your trial. Such a shame that not only were you caught out after curfew, but we also found drugs in your possession. Tsk tsk, Leona Zimmerman. What a naughty girl you've been." He passes the vial to one of the officers. "Please log this evidence once you reach the brig."

Disbelief clutches me. The curfew violation is suddenly the least of my worries. A drug charge will result in *years* in the brig. Five at minimum.

"If you're doing this to try to get a confession out of me, Commander, it's not going to work. I don't know anything." Though we share the same quarters, my father barely speaks to me, and he sure as hell has never confided in me about his alleged involvement in any rebel plots.

"Do you know how many rumors I've heard about your father over the years?" He steps closer and brushes my hair behind my ears, allowing his fingers to trail down my neck. I shiver at his touch, repulsed by his nearness. "Some say he was the mastermind behind the Deck Five Massacre twenty years ago. We lost thirty-nine security officers that day."

"As far as I know, my father is just a regular, boring engineer who's had the misfortune of befriending people who later turn out to be rebels. Just because a few of his friends and acquaintances have been charged with treason over the years doesn't mean he's guilty by association." Though I've always believed my father to be cold and distant, I find myself wondering if perhaps his parental detachment is a survival mechanism. If I don't know anything concrete, I can't blow his cover.

The commander smirks. "I hope you enjoy your time in the brig, *Leona*." The overly intimate way he utters my name sends a jolt of terror through me. "Perhaps I'll come visit you. You'll be there for a few years," he says, once again brushing my hair behind my ears, "and I would hate for you to get lonely."

"You can't do this!" I thrash in the security officers' hold while the commander continues stroking my hair. It's perverse, the way he's touching me. He's doing it just because he can, a sick display of power. "I didn't do anything! I-I'll prove you planted the drugs on me. I will. I'll expose your corruption!"

Commander Hampton throws his head back and laughs. He knows my threat holds no merit. Even if I had definitive proof he'd committed an atrocity, the evidence would be tidily swept under a rug. He wouldn't face any consequences. Captain Warren needs someone to do his dirty work. From what I've heard, the more clandestine tasks, including off-the-record interrogations, usually fall to the first mate.

Grinning like a fiend, he pats my cheek before stepping back. He makes a sweeping gesture toward the nearest elevator. "Take her away."

The security officers are quick to comply. Seconds later, I find myself in an elevator headed for the brig. The men don't release me, no matter how much I plead. Neither guard speaks, and I soon give up trying to reason with them.

Years. I can scarcely fathom it. I'll be sentenced to years in the brig. And once I'm released? I'll be assigned to perform the most dreaded, backbreaking tasks on the worldship.

What will happen to my bar?

Tears burn in my eyes as I imagine the patrons and volunteer workers who'll show up at Leona's Speakeasy tomorrow evening to find I'm not there. Eventually, word will get out that I was arrested. People will be too scared to visit the bar, even if the charges against me are completely unrelated to my management of a speakeasy.

I enjoy everything about running the bar, but my favorite part of all is creating a welcoming atmosphere where the regular citizens of the *Jansonna* might socialize and unwind. The command team, security officers, and descendants of Founders reportedly have their own illicit meeting places, underground bars where they might go for an evening of forbidden fun. Illegal or not, why shouldn't the regular citizens of the *Jansonna* enjoy the same type of respite?

My speakeasy is a labor of love. I brew the beer and distill the stronger spirits myself, using materials and credits secretly donated by my regulars. Each day, the minute my shift at my official job as a mess hall worker ends, I always head straight for the bar.

I'm not stupid. I'm fully aware that rebels frequent my bar, and I know I'm providing them with a place they might congregate in secret. But most of my patrons are regular citizens like me who simply want a cheerful place to spend their evenings. A place where they can forget about the constraints of life on the *Jansonna*.

My best friends in the universe help staff my bar, volunteering to serve drinks, provide security, and clean up after closing time. Ellen, Angelo, and Michaela, to name a few. God, they're going to be worried sick when I'm a no-show tomorrow evening. My co-workers in the mess hall will likely be frantic over my absence too. I started working there when I was fifteen, and during the last twenty years, I haven't missed a single day of work.

The elevator comes to a stop and the doors jolt open. I'm greeted by the dimly lit corridor of the brig's entrance, as well as a gust of frigid air. I shiver and wish I were wearing something more substantial than threadbare pants and a thin t-shirt. My teeth practically chatter as the security officers lead me deeper into the brig, past several stern-faced guards and through three bolted doors.

Panic descends and dark spots mar my vision. This

can't be happening. I take deep breaths and pray I don't faint from fear.

In all my life, I've never been so afraid.

I've heard the brig is an awful place, though this is my first time here. Whenever my father was detained, he always forbade me from visiting. Once, he'd even gone so far as to threaten to tell the authorities about Leona's Speakeasy if I dared to visit. To say our relationship is a bit complicated would be an understatement.

I can't help but wonder if he'll visit me. Will he try to help? Will he attend my trial and speak on my behalf? I doubt it would make a difference. The drugs, after all, are about to be logged as evidence. Even if I call Commander Hampton out for his treachery, it will be my word against his. But if my father attempts to help me, it will mean he cares. Knowing he cares, even a little, will bring me comfort.

The guards lead me past several occupied cells, but the light is so dim that I can't glimpse the faces of the prisoners. All I see are dark forms huddled against walls or curled up on the floor. Some cells contain over a dozen people, while others only contain one or two.

Please don't let them toss me into a cell by myself.

I'm scared shitless and could use some companionship right now. Especially in the dimly lit brig. I'm not proud to admit it, but I'm used to sleeping with the lights on, and the thought of being tossed into a dark cell all alone causes worry to clench in my stomach.

To my great relief, I'm taken to a cell at the end of the corridor that contains six women. The security officers remove the manacles from my wrists, then unlock the cell door and shove me inside. The force of the push sends me sprawling on my hands and knees. I hiss in pain and turn on my side, gasping for air. The men chuckle as they walk away, and their cruelty sends a wave of despair through me.

I exchange curious glances with the six women. One of them, a young blonde, scoots closer and places a gentle hand on my shoulder. She gives me a sympathetic look, and it does me in. I burst into tears. Though we're strangers, she gathers me close and hugs me.

"There there," she says in a soothing tone. "It'll be all right."

"It won't be all right." I sniffle and try to get my emotions under control. "Commander Hampton planted drugs on me. I'm so incredibly fucked." I peek up to find the other women moving closer, all wearing looks of concern.

A woman with curly dark hair clears her throat. "I'm so sorry. If it makes you feel any better, we're all here on falsified charges too. Drugs. Theft. Fornication. Curfew violations."

"Thanks, but… I feel bad for all of us," I say. "If we didn't do anything wrong, why waste the worldship's resources keeping us here? At least if we're free, we're working and contributing. I must've counted over two hundred other prisoners in the brig."

"More than that," replies the blonde who'd comforted me. She sits back on the floor and sighs. "There are three additional wings. I overheard the guards talking the other day and it sounds like there are over five hundred prisoners down here. Most are being held on suspicion of rebel involvement. I'm Sheila by the way."

"Hi, Sheila. My name is Leona."

The other five women give me their names. Erin, Nancy, Isabella, Karlie, and Camilla. I briefly study each woman's face and commit their names to memory.

"There's been a surge of arrests since the Darrvasons showed up," Erin says. "People are scared and worried that whatever deal is being brokered with the aliens won't serve humankind very well. So, naturally, there's been an increase in rebel activity. A lot of people think they could do a better job of commanding the *Jansonna* than Captain Warren and his minions."

"Human females," says Nancy, the one with the curly dark hair. "My brother is a guard, and he witnessed the first few meetings between *Jansonna's* command team and the alien leaders. The aliens want human women between the ages of nineteen and twenty-five for breeding purposes, and they're demanding a minimum of two thousand of us in exchange for their help."

My mind reels. Holy shit. The Darrvasons want two thousand women? I can scarcely fathom it. Only about fifty thousand people call the *Jansonna* home. Losing two thousand women of childbearing age will be a huge loss.

I peer more closely at my cellmates. At thirty-five, I'll be safe from the aliens. But my present companions are younger than me. If I had to guess, I'd say all are within the age range the aliens are seeking. My heart goes out to them.

"Try not to worry," I whisper, giving each woman a

comforting look. "Maybe the deal won't happen, and even if it does, that doesn't mean all of you will be taken."

"I work in engineering. The *Jansonna* is just days away from a complete systems-wide failure," Camilla says. "Well, we have a week and a half left at most, if we're lucky. Captain Warren will have no choice but to accept the deal. And look at us. We're in the brig. We're considered expendable. It doesn't take a genius to figure out how this is going to go down."

A week and a half left at most? I don't volunteer that my father is one of *Jansonna's* top engineers. That'll only invite questions for which I don't have answers. I can't help but wonder why he hasn't breathed a word about the seriousness of the worldship's predicament to me. Does he know about the trade the aliens are trying to make with humankind?

My heart sinks as I peer at my frightened cellmates. I try to think of something comforting to say, but nothing comes to mind. Camilla is right. If the captain agrees to give two thousand human females to the Darrvasons, he'll likely pillage the brig for women first.

A long silence ensues, and we eventually situate ourselves against the cell walls. I lean back on the cold, hard surface and wonder if this is the type of cell I'll be kept in during my years-long incarceration. A cell devoid of furniture and blankets. The only item in this small, chilled space is a toilet that's tucked into a back corner.

Will I spend years sleeping on a hard surface with nothing but the clothes on my back?

Guilt visits me a second later. Because what these six women are facing will be so much worse than my fate. A race of barbaric aliens wants to use them for breeding purposes.

At some point, I drift to sleep. The purple eyes set in a shadowed face feature prominently in my dreams. I also dream that I'm trying to reach the *Haxxal*, that I've commandeered a transport vessel so I might board the lead ship in the Darrvason fleet. I awake an indiscernible time later to discover several security officers standing outside the cell.

Commander Hampton steps into view from behind them, and his sinister smile causes cold fear to drench me. "Good morning, ladies. Sleep well, did you?"

A quick glance around the cell shows my companions are awake, each displaying varying expressions of dread.

I lift my chin and meet the commander's eyes. "Good morning, gentlemen." Somehow, I keep my voice steady and infused with confidence, though inside I'm quaking with terror. "Come to serve us breakfast in bed?"

The commander snorts. "Not quite. I need five of you for a little science project."

"That doesn't sound ominous or anything." I glare at the commander as my anger toward him starts to outweigh my fear. Because of him, I've lost everything. My freedom, my friends, and my bar. My whole life and all I care about, gone.

His eyes narrow on me. "I'm supposed to collect five women between the ages of nineteen and twenty-five for the Darrvasons to poke and prod, but since you're being such a goddamn delight this morning, *Leona*, consider yourself drafted." He steps back and nods at the guards. "Grab the mouthy one and four others. And put the mouthy one in restraints."

Chapter 2

ZAHHN

AGITATION GNAWS AT ME AS I PEER AROUND THE inadequate, painfully low-tech medical bay of the human worldship. I don't want to be here. I long to be back in my private laboratory aboard the *Haxxal*, conducting important research that will better the lives of my people. Any Darrvason physician capable of holding a medical scanner could've come in my place. Yet Emperor Radakk had ordered me to join the team of doctors who are scheduled to examine a small group of human females.

I suppress a growl. Even though I'm sterile, an unfortunate effect of the Haflassan Flu, the high-handed emperor believes I should take a mate from among the humans. That's why he ordered me to come here. To tempt me into accepting a human female. He thinks my scientific achievements warrant a reward. He believes I deserve a human female solely for companionship and pleasure, never mind that the entire purpose of the Darrvason-human alliance is to prevent the extinction of our race.

My blood heats with anger. The emperor is perhaps the closest thing I have to a friend, yet there are times I want to pummel him bloody. Would I like to possess a human female? Of course I would. But it wouldn't be logical when I cannot impregnate a woman. As I've already told him numerous times, a female would be wasted on me.

Though the terms of the alliance have already been settled, the exams are necessary so we might discover the full extent of our intimate compatibility with the humans.

In a matter of days, the first wave of human females will be handed over to my people. A group of thirty. After the handover, a team of our most skilled engineers will board the *Jansonna* and begin repairs on the dilapidated worldship.

Once repairs are complete, the humans will give us one hundred additional females.

Eventually, after my people help locate and guide humankind to a habitable planet, a final wave of two thousand human women will be surrendered.

I have no intention of claiming a female from any of the waves. The emperor can attempt to meddle in my life all he wants, but I will never accept a mate. I might endure a lonely existence, and I suspect I'll experience jealousy toward my peers who do claim females from among the humans, but I have my research to keep me busy.

It's a great shame of mine that I've never succeeded in curing my own sterility, nor the sterility of the other Darrvason males who suffered from the Haflassan Flu. Despite the illogicalness of my claiming a mate, perhaps this failure of mine is an indication that I don't deserve a female. Or maybe it's a sign from the Star Gods that I should focus on my research. If I took a mate, surely the female would be a distraction.

I glance at the four Darrvason doctors who accompanied me today. All appear eager and impatient for the arrival of the human females. They keep glancing toward the door and fidgeting with their medical bags.

The five of us will each be given one patient to examine, a female between the ages of nineteen to twenty-five, the age range at which we believe the women will be most fertile. DNA samples we received in advance already confirmed that Darrvasons and humans can propagate, in theory, but we aren't yet sure if we'll be able to physically copulate with the females to accomplish pregnancy. If our sexual organs aren't compatible, conception will have to be achieved in a laboratory.

Several human doctors huddle on the other side of the medical bay, whispering amongst themselves and occasionally glancing our way. I try but fail to keep from staring at the female doctors as I wonder how many orifices they have for claiming. Do they have two slick holes to accommodate the dual appendages our males possess?

At last, the main door zips open. I watch as security officers escort five trembling human females into the medical bay. Our patients have arrived. It's my understanding that the women were taken from the brig, and I can't help but wonder about their crimes, especially when I notice one woman's wrists are bound behind her back.

I study the petite dark-haired female who's wearing manacles, my curiosity growing. Her curvy form is pleasing, and her bosom is enticingly plump. My scrotum commences a slight vibration, and my dual shafts harden as I imagine taking her to an exam room and stripping her naked.

When our gazes collide from across the medical bay, a fierce sense of ownership for the small female steals through me.

Mine mine mine.

Her dark eyes are enchanting and soulful, and no matter how hard I try to tear my gaze from hers, I'm unable to look away.

For the first time in my life, I find myself utterly entranced by a female. I take a deep breath and filter out the various scents in the room until I detect hers. Star Gods, how her sweet scent calls to me.

To my utter shock, the ancestral markings that cover my chest begin to tingle. It's an odd sensation, one I've never experienced before. *Mine. My female.*

More than getting her alone in an examination room, I want to abscond with her back to the *Haxxal.* I want to keep her away from all other males. I want to rut her and make her mine. Though I know I cannot impregnate her, I still want to pump her full of my seed. I want to erupt in her nether orifices, however many she has, as well as in her mouth.

Fluxx. It's preposterous, these urges I'm having. Not to mention, highly illogical.

Focus, I tell myself. I must focus on the task assigned to me and try not to derive any pleasure from the experience. Perhaps it would be best if I selected a different woman to examine. Taking the beautiful female into a room alone might be a bad idea. My shafts are already so engorged that I suspect I'll have trouble walking. And I haven't even touched her yet.

But when one of my colleagues, Doctor Ammdox, approaches the females and reaches for the dark-haired beauty, a snarl rips from my throat. I dart in front of the younger doctor and grab the object of my desires before he can dare touch her.

The female gasps, and terror brims in her eyes. But I don't release her. I won't risk another doctor trying to select her for the examination.

Doctor Ammdox gives me an annoyed look before choosing a different woman, but I barely spare him a glance.

My focus remains on the female I wish to claim. If only it were possible. But even though she can't become my mate, I can't fathom the prospect of another male touching her. Not even for a moment. I glare at the male human guard who'd escorted her into the medical bay, rage pumping through my veins as I imagine shattering his skull. The tiny man grows pale and takes several steps back.

From my peripheral vision, I'm vaguely aware of my colleagues selecting their respective females for the examinations. Am I the only one who feels so on edge and consumed with desire? Am I the only one ready to commit murder just to keep another male away from my patient?

I wrap an arm around the pretty creature and angle my nose closer to her neck, taking another deep inhale. Beneath the obvious coldness of her fear, I detect the floral fragrance of soap, as well as something pungent yet sweet and enticing to my libido. Desire? I remind myself that once I get her alone, I'll be able to discover if she's becoming wet between her thighs.

Her trembling increases. I give her a look of concern, then slowly move my hand up and down her back. For a reason I can't fathom, I long to bring her comfort.

"You needn't fear me, little human," I whisper in her ear, careful to speak in perfect Galactic Common, though it's been ages since I conversed in the universal language.

Her breath catches, and she turns her head to peer into my eyes. My male appendages throb harder as I study her features up close. She's achingly beautiful, and I can't help but count the flecks of gold in her otherwise dark brown eyes. I want to memorize everything about her so I might paint an accurate picture of her in my mind later.

A lock of hair has fallen across her forehead, and I'm about to brush it to the side when a voice booms through the medical bay, interrupting the intimate moment we're sharing. I glare in the direction of the voice.

"Welcome to the *Jansonna*, doctors," says a human man who emerges from behind the guards. He speaks in Galactic Common. "I'm Commander Hampton, *Jansonna's* first mate." He attempts a smile, though it doesn't reach his eyes. Duplicity emanates from him, and I instantly dislike the short puny human.

Being the most decorated physician in the Darrvason Empire, the duty of conversing with the commander unfortunately falls to me. I sigh inwardly as I recall Emperor Radakk's request that I *attempt* to be friendly.

"Thank you for the cordial welcome, Commander Hampton," I force out, though I don't bother to smile. "I'm Doctor Zahhn. My colleagues and I are eager to complete the examinations of the human females as quickly as possible. If you show us the way to the private exam rooms, we will get started."

A tiny, pained whimper escapes the dark-haired female, and I glance down at her bound hands. I frown as I realize the manacles are so tight they're cutting off her circulation, and I feel guilty for not having noticed sooner. Her hands are turning an alarming shade of purple compared to her otherwise light brown skin.

The commander makes a sweeping hand gesture and says, "Follow me," as he heads toward a narrow corridor within the medical bay, but I don't follow.

"Wait!" I glare at the guard who'd escorted *my female* into the medical bay. "You. Unlock these restraints immediately. And do it without touching the female."

The guard peers at me with wide eyes, then he looks to Commander Hampton as though for confirmation.

"I'm the doctor who'll be conducting her exam today. That makes her my patient, and it means her wellbeing is my responsibility. Unlock. The. Restraints. Do it *fluxxing* now." So much for friendliness.

"Do as the good doctor says," the commander barks with annoyance, and a moment later, the guard approaches and quickly removes the manacles from her wrists.

I immediately examine the red marks surrounding her wrists and gently massage the area to help her circulation. The rest of the group moves ahead of us down the corridor, giving us a small amount of privacy. I place a finger beneath the female's chin, forcing her gaze to mine. "I have a dermal regenerator in my bag, and I will use it to heal your wrists, as well as any other injuries you have."

Her eyes widen and fill with tears, then she blinks fast. I'm not an expert on human expressions, but I think she appears stunned, yet also emotional. Perhaps she thought me nothing but an unfeeling beast. I am, after all, about to violate her in ways she will no doubt find humiliating. The examination must be thorough.

"Thank you," she finally whispers, still blinking fast.

I place a hand at the small of her back and guide her toward the narrow corridor. "Come. Let's get you situated in a private room. There will be no witnesses to your exam. It'll be just the two of us."

Chapter 3

LEONA

My head keeps swirling with disbelief. Surely this can't be happening. Surely this is just a crazy dream. Yet the huge alien's touch feels so very real, and his masculine scent tantalizes my senses. I can't believe he's about to examine me in private. *Just the two of us.*

His eyes. My heart races faster.

His eyes are the exact shade of purple I've seen recently in my dreams. I don't understand it, and it's a little bit too strange to write off as a coincidence. Especially considering the strong pull I've felt toward the Darrvason fleet, the *Haxxal* in particular.

I want to ask the Darrvason doctor if he lives on the *Haxxal*, but I'm frightened of the answer. If he says yes, what will that mean?

I remind myself I'm too old to be claimed by a Darrvason. The aliens want human women in the nineteen to twenty-five age range. That means I won't be considered for breeding purposes.

Why doesn't this knowledge bring me relief?

My pulse accelerates when the doctor guides me into an exam room and no one follows us. Holy shit, we really are going to be alone. How much poking and prodding does he plan to do?

The huge alien male steps away from me and sets his medical bag on a counter. As I stand awkwardly in the room, my gaze snags on the exam table. It doesn't look like an ordinary exam table. There are lights coming down from the ceiling, and the table itself features the kind of stirrups that are used during a gynecological exam. I swallow hard and absently rub at my chafed wrists.

Will he actually take a peek at me *down there*?

I flush and press my thighs together as a heated pulsing sensation affects my core. Why am I so breathless? Why do I feel achy and unsettled between my legs?

As I study the alien doctor, the same longing that reverberates through me every time I gaze at the Darrvason fleet surges through me. I watch as he opens his medical bag and sets several items on the counter, two of which appear to be large, silver phallus-shaped objects.

But surely those two objects can't be what I think they are. I mean, what kind of doctor carries around replicas of male appendages in his medical bag? I almost laugh at the absurdity of the idea. I remind myself that I'm unfamiliar with Darrvason technology.

For all I know, the objects could be dermal regenerators or some kind of sanitation devices.

The doctor turns to face me, and I notice he's holding a small flashing device in one of his large, six-fingered hands. I take a moment to admire his features. He stands over seven feet tall, and he's wearing black, form-fitting pants and a long-sleeved shirt over his well-muscled body. The flesh that is visible is dark and textured. The hair atop his head, as well as his facial hair, is black but peppered with strands of white, giving him a distinguished look. He's the most handsome male I've ever encountered, and I flush anew as he approaches me.

"What is your name, little human?" he asks in a deep rumbling tone that incites more heated pulses between my thighs. I can't be sure, but I think I'm becoming wet *down there*, and I can't fathom a reason for it.

My mouth goes dry, but somehow, I manage to reply. "Leona."

"Lee-oon-ahh." He says my name slowly, as though he's savoring each syllable. "I am Doctor Zahhn."

I blink, unsure how I should respond. Given the circumstances, 'It's nice to meet you, Doctor Zahhn', doesn't feel quite right. I stare at him stupidly as my body seems to come alive in his presence. I have the sudden urge to rub myself against him and tear off his clothes. God, what is wrong with me?

I can't help but wonder if the last hormone suppression shot I received was defective. I'm no expert in matters of fornication, but I'm starting to worry that the breathlessness and heated pulses afflicting me might be desire.

Doctor Zahhn taps the surface of the white, padded exam table. "Please remove your clothing, Leona, and have a seat. I would like to get started immediately."

I wrap my arms around my center and take two steps back. Before I realize what I'm doing, I'm shaking my head in refusal. "No, I… there's no need for me to remove my clothes. Please, I would prefer to remain dressed." I can't fathom getting naked in front of this handsome alien male. What will he think when he discovers the moisture I feel gathering in my panties? Shame heats my face, and I take another step back.

His visage becomes stern, and I get the vibe that he's not used to being challenged. Well, too bad. Because I'm not taking my clothes off.

"You must be fully naked during your exam, human female." He taps the surface of the exam table again. "We were promised our patients would be compliant. It's my understanding that your sentence in the brig will be significantly reduced in exchange for your cooperation. I suggest you obey my instructions and be a good little patient, Leona."

"What?" Shock ripples through me. "No one told me any of that. Are you certain my sentence will be reduced?" Not that I've been formally sentenced yet. But maybe that's why Commander Hampton arrested several women on bogus charges recently. So he would have a ready supply of female patients for the aliens to examine.

"Yes, I am certain. Emperor Radakk has ordered

your captain to release the females we examine from the brig very soon, within the next few days. He intends to check back in with Captain Warren to ensure his orders have been followed." Doctor Zahhn looks me up and down, and though I can't be sure, I think I glimpse a spark of heat in his eyes.

"Well, that's a relief." I try but fail to suppress a shudder. "I was facing at least five years in the brig."

"Five years? What did you do?" Doctor Zahhn closes the distance between us and reaches for my forehead. Trembles besiege me as he brushes an errant lock of hair behind my ear. His touch is everything and I cannot get enough.

What would it be like if he... hugged me? The longing inside me soars, and I close my eyes briefly as I imagine him wrapping me in a tender embrace.

"Leona?" he prompts, his deep voice threaded with the barest hint of impatience. "What did you do to warrant at least five years in the brig?"

I exhale slowly. Should I tell the truth? But if I reveal the truth, will Doctor Zahhn think I'm lying? For a reason I can't fathom, the idea of him thinking I'm dishonest makes my stomach twist.

"I didn't do anything," I finally say. Oh, how I wish he would brush another lock of hair behind my ear. I resist the urge to step closer to his muscular form. "Well, technically all I did was remain in the corridors after curfew, but after Commander Hampton caught me, I suppose I became a tad too argumentative for his liking, and he planted drugs on me in retaliation. Getting caught after curfew only warrants a night in the brig. Or it used to. The drug charge, however, would've seen me locked up for years." Though I'm exceedingly nervous about getting naked in front of Doctor Zahhn and allowing him to examine me, it's a tremendous relief to know I'll be going home soon. Back to the quarters I share with my distant father, and back to my usual routine of working in the mess hall followed by spending my evenings managing the speakeasy.

Life will return to normal soon. I just have to endure a medical exam performed by a sinfully handsome alien doctor who makes me feel warm and tingly all over.

"I will inform Emperor Radakk that Commander Hampton is corrupt and not to be trusted. Thank you for sharing that information, Leona, however I am sorry about what he did to you." A frown creases the doctor's brow, and he appears deep in thought for a few moments.

"Maybe you shouldn't say anything to the emperor. I don't want to cause any trouble. If Commander Hampton finds out I blabbed, he might retaliate. Please don't say anything." My throat nearly closes up as I await his response.

A low growl rumbles from Doctor Zahhn's chest, then he gently cups my face and trails his thumbs over my cheeks. Goosebumps erupt on my arms, and the back of my neck prickles with sensation. I feel pleasantly delirious, and I don't pull away from the alien's touch.

"Very well," he says after a minute. "I will remain silent on the matter." He removes his hands from my cheeks, only to commence stroking his long fingers through my hair. Oh God. I bask under his attentions and soak up the intimacy of the physical contact.

"Thank you," I whisper. Gratitude wells within me. He's planning to keep a secret just because I asked him to. As he continues petting my hair, a warm itchiness skitters over my upper arms. I resist the urge to scratch, however, not wanting to do anything to cause him to stop caressing me.

Is he touching me as part of my examination? Or is he stroking me simply because he desires to feel the texture of my hair? What would he think if I followed my present desires and ran my hands up and down his muscular chest?

"You're becoming flushed, little human." He rests his hands on my shoulders and peers at me intently. "Furthermore, I detect a sweet but pungent aroma emanating from you that I suspect is arousal. Remove your clothing at once so I might examine the area between your thighs." He steps back and lifts his eyebrows, an expectant look coming over him.

I open my mouth, preparing to refuse once again. But then I remember what he revealed about Emperor Radakk's orders. The women who are being examined today will be released from the brig *soon*. Surely that means I won't have to spend five plus years imprisoned. I hope it means I'll be released in a day or two.

Okay, I can do this. Besides, the sooner I get naked, the sooner my exam will be over. I can only hope Doctor Zahhn will be quick about it.

"I've never… never taken my clothes off in front of a male before." I reach for the hem of my shirt, draw in a deep breath, and pull it over my head. I toss the garment onto a chair near the exam table. "I must confess that I'm very nervous."

What sounds like an appreciative growl leaves Doctor Zahhn's throat. His nostrils flare and his body becomes tense. I also notice a massive bulge in his crotch area. It appears his pants suddenly aren't quite large enough. I stare at the bulge as I consider why his male appendage might be getting bigger. How very strange.

"There's no need to be nervous, little human," he says in a comforting but strained tone, as though he must force the words out. His expression almost appears pained as his gaze roams over my body. "I am a doctor, and you are my patient. My job is to examine you and your job is to be compliant for the duration of the inspection." He draws himself up taller. "Continue undressing."

I struggle for air as I slip my shoes and socks off, then unfasten my pants and start pushing them down. I soon find myself standing in the middle of the room wearing nothing but a bra and panties. A sense of vulnerability steals through me, and the same dark heat from earlier sparks in Doctor Zahhn's eyes. He emits another satisfied growl that echoes off the walls.

Does he find my body pleasing? Will he like what he sees when I finally remove my undergarments? It shouldn't matter to me what he thinks of my body, yet I yearn to please him, and I ache to feel his hands skimming my flesh.

"Show me what a good little female you can be,

Leona, and finish getting undressed." His nostrils flare wider. "Be obedient."

A whimper builds in my throat, but I remain quiet. I lower my gaze, unable to meet his eyes for a second longer, and unhook the front clasp of my bra. I let it slide down my arms and toss it toward the chair that holds my clothes. A quick glance at Doctor Zahhn shows he's gripping the edge of the exam table, and his muscles are more tense than ever.

"Continue." His tone is raspy, and he soon turns his back to me and rummages through his medical bag again.

I take the opportunity to quickly remove my panties as his back is turned. My heart thumps rapidly as I wait for him to face me. As I wait for him to spin around and glimpse my total nakedness.

He finally finds what he's looking for in the bag, pulls it out, and turns to meet my eyes. But he doesn't hold my gaze for long. He soon stares openly at my nether area, the part of me I desperately wish I might hide from him. No male has ever looked at me down there, and I don't understand why his gaze feels like a physical caress.

When his scrutiny becomes too much, I place one hand in front of my crotch, and another over my bosom, drawing my breasts together so I might shield my nipples from his view.

"Sit on the exam table, little human. *Now.*"

I peer with curiosity at the two devices he's holding, but I suppose I'll soon discover their purpose. I pray whatever he's about to do won't hurt. Summoning my courage, I climb on the table, trying my best to shelter my private parts in the process. Once I'm seated, I keep my thighs pressed together with one hand resting atop my nether area and another hand covering my nipples. I cast a worried look at the stirrups and hope he doesn't order me to place my feet inside. The last thing I want to do is spread my legs wide for the doctor.

Doctor Zahhn moves in front of me, sets the smaller device aside, then holds the second one up. The lights on the thin, wide contraption flash blue and green intermittently, and there are numerous tiny buttons covered in unfamiliar symbols. "Give me your wrists, Leona, and I will heal your chafing."

Oh. *Oh.* I'd forgotten about his promise to heal my injuries. Still, I hesitate to comply. Because if I give him my wrists, I won't be able to keep my privates covered any longer. But when his eyes flare with impatience, I find myself obeying his order as a wave of submission courses through me, that odd urge I have to please him.

He takes my right wrist in one hand and turns it slightly as he runs the dermal regenerator over my marred flesh. I watch, shocked to my core, as my chafed skin heals before my eyes in mere seconds. Once he finishes with my right wrist, he moves on to my left wrist, healing the marks left by the too-tight manacles. The pain also vanishes.

"Why were you wearing restraints but not the other females?" He's leaning down and standing so close that his warm breath dances across my face, and his nearness makes it difficult to form a coherent thought or even breathe. Being close to him feels dangerous yet so very right.

I clear my throat. "I pissed Commander Hampton off."

"Ah, I see." He sets the dermal regenerator aside and commences rubbing my freshly healed wrists. The pads of his fingers are rough, and I suspect the rest of his skin is harder to the touch than a human's due to its unique, almost rippled texture, but I don't wish for him to stop. "Do you have any additional injuries?"

"No." I swallow hard. "Thank you for healing my wrists."

He cups the side of my face in one hand. "You're welcome." His eyes search mine, causing my cheeks to grow warm. My gaze lowers to his lips, and for the first time in my life, I wonder what it might be like to kiss a male.

Feverish. I've felt feverish in his presence since the moment he grabbed me before the other doctor could. Why did he growl and push his associate out of the way just to claim me first?

"When did you last receive a hormone suppression shot?" His question takes me by surprise.

"You know about that?" Despite myself, I squirm in place as the heated pulses between my thighs become more urgent.

"Yes. Your captain mentioned something about it to the emperor. I also know that fornication is outlawed on the human worldship and that your people use fertility labs to achieve pregnancy. I know your population is strictly controlled." His caressing hands move to my thighs, and he rubs slow circles on my flesh. I nearly release a moan, though I stop myself just in time. Oh God. What is wrong with me?

"I last received a hormone suppression shot about six months ago," I say. Should I admit I don't think the shot is working? I peer into his eyes as if searching for guidance.

"Six months? Are you certain?" He inhales deeply and a faint rumble emits from his chest and vibrates through me.

"Yes, I'm certain."

"Well, before we begin your examination, Leona, I must administer a hypospray to counteract the effects of the hormone suppression shot. It's necessary so that I might determine your capacity to experience arousal."

Before I can respond, he places the hypospray to my neck.

Chapter 4

ZAHHN

Leona. I keep repeating her name-sound over and over in my head. Why am I so drawn to her? Why am I consumed with thoughts of ravishing her?

But my feelings for her go beyond carnal need. I also long to protect the pretty female, as well as to exact vengeance on her behalf. I want to storm through the *Jansonna* and slaughter the guards who'd put her in manacles as well as Commander Hampton for his role in her captivity. I'm still reeling from the revelation that the first mate framed her. I want to wrap her in my arms and promise nothing bad will ever happen to her again… yet I can't.

Because after I complete her examination, I will never see her again.

My heart becomes heavy at the thought. But it's for the best. I'm more valuable to the Darrvason Empire if

I'm wholly focused on research and scientific advancements that will help my people, including my most important endeavor to date—finding a cure for a hereditary disease called *forlonggsa*.

Also known as the great madness, the disease emerges later in life and afflicts far too many Darrvason males, and it unfortunately runs in the royal family. Emperor Radakk's father perished from the condition, and I'm in a race against fate to ensure the same doesn't happen to my friend.

If I took a mate, the distraction might affect my work. I might not be able to think clearly enough to make a breakthrough in my research. The weight of my responsibilities combines with my shame over my inability to sire offspring, and I find myself glaring down at Leona as though it's her fault. She squirms in place, then casts a wary glance at the hypospray I just used on her.

Fluxx, I want her. Badly. I fight the urge to roar with frustration.

She struggles to keep her bosom concealed from my view, as well as the sweetness between her thighs. Though I caught brief glimpses of her nether area, which is covered in a small amount of dark hair, I am still unsure how many orifices she possesses for claiming. I glance at the placements for her feet that extend from the table, concluding that I must use them so I might better view her feminine attributes.

Little tremors afflict her body as she continues trying to conceal her nudity. I meet her eyes and reach for her hands, then guide them to rest at her sides. Her breath hitches. She appears panicked for a moment, but she closes her eyes briefly, takes a deep breath, and exhales slowly.

"Good little female." I reach for her soft locks, unable to resist stroking my fingers through her glorious mane. Her dark, luminous waves reach her lower back, and I delight in combing my digits through it again and again. "Your hair is like a waterfall illuminated by a full moon." Where those flowery words come from, I'm not certain, but a thousand similar compliments spring to mind as I admire her ethereal beauty.

"Thank you." Her eyes flick to mine and she blushes.

The enticing scent of what I'm confident is her arousal deepens. Heat envelops me as my dual shafts harden further and my scrotum vibrates faster.

Focus. I almost give my head a shake. I need to concentrate on her examination rather than her loveliness and my desire to rut her until she's sore and dripping with my seed.

I retract my hands from her hair and step back. "Lie down and put your feet in the placements." I gesture at the two extensions.

"Placements? You mean the stirrups?" She gives them a dubious look.

"Whatever you wish to call them," I reply. "Lie down and put your feet in the *stirrups*. Be sure to scoot your buttocks to the table's edge and keep your thighs parted wide. The inspection will be easier and go more quickly if you cooperate by giving me unhindered access to your private parts."

Her eyes widen, and as she turns on the table, her hands tremble. She pauses, closes her eyes, and takes another long breath. As she exhales, she opens her eyes and finally lies down. She scoots to the table's edge, and when she struggles to place her feet in the stirrups, I dart around the table to assist. I grasp her left ankle and guide her petite foot into the placement, then do the same with her right foot. Rather than immediately glance at her nether area, I peer in shock at her feet, not quite believing how small they are. She has the tiniest toes I've ever seen.

Finally, my eyes roam upward, over her quivering thighs, until I'm staring directly at her spread center. The sight of her womanly folds, parted slightly to reveal the slick pinkness within, causes a scorching wave of heat to pummel me. My senses scatter until there's only instinct—the overwhelming urge to bury my face in her nether area and taste her essence.

I stand between her thighs and push the stirrups wider apart, which forces her legs to spread further. *Fluxx*. There's even more pinkness within, and it looks so very slick. One hole. I think she only has one slick hole for claiming. Unless of course, a Darrvason male might also make use of the tiny dark pucker that's nestled between her ass cheeks. Perhaps with proper training, it would be possible.

I glance at the metallic phalluses I'd set on the counter earlier. The larger phallus is the average size of a Darrvason male's lower appendage, while the slightly smaller phallus is the average size of a Darrvason male's upper shaft.

"Please," Leona whispers. "Are you finished? You've seen me naked now. Is the exam over?" She tries to put her feet closer together, but I place a hand on her leg, not allowing her the movement.

"Little human," I say in a voice thick with desire, "I am just getting started." Though protocol dictates I ought to wear protective gloves, I hesitate to put them on. In the end, the urge to feel her feminine slickness with my bare fingers prevails, and I reach out with one hand to trace her delicate folds.

She gasps and her center lurches upward, as though she's seeking more of my touch. Wanting to get a closer look at her nether area, I sit on a chair with rolling wheels and move back into place, directly between her spread thighs. Except this time my eyes are level with her pussy. Again, I reach out to stroke her nether parts, so pink and enticingly slick. A keening moan erupts from her throat as a shiver quakes through her body.

"You are very sensitive to my touch," I say, though there's nothing clinical about the observation. I'm deeply pleased that she's trembling and moaning on the exam table, all because I'm caressing her intimate parts.

I continue the light strokes as I peer at an engorged button that's peeking out from between her folds. I suspect it's a bundle of nerves to enhance her pleasure during coitus, as Darrvason females possess a similar feature. When I gently trace a finger over the swollen bit of flesh, her hips jerk upward and she cries out, emitting a wanton noise that heats my blood and causes my shafts to harden further. Confusion and alarm fill her eyes, and she stares at me with a thousand questions brimming in her dark gaze.

"Very sensitive to my touch," I repeat, my voice coming out raspy and thick. What I wouldn't give to bend her over the exam table and impale her with my dual appendages. A growl rumbles from my chest. I can't help it. Everything about this female is a temptation to my senses. I give my head a slight shake, trying to concentrate on the task I must accomplish—I must determine her capacity to physically mate with a male of my kind.

"What are you doing to me?" She whimpers and her center undulates against my caressing digits. The wetness escaping her core increases, as does the delicious aroma of her need.

"Determining your ability to experience arousal. The more I touch you, the slicker you become. The more responsive you become. I believe your body is anticipating the physical act of mating. I suspect what you're experiencing is the craving to be filled up with an erect shaft."

Her eyes widen. She shakes her head. "No, no, that's not what's happening to me. There must've been something in that hypospray to make me feel like this." Another whimper. Another quick lifting of her hips. She flushes and glances quickly around the room, as though she's searching for an escape. When her gaze lands on the door, she tenses and grips the edge of the table, and there's a moment where I know she's tempted to flee.

"The hypospray didn't contain anything that might unnaturally stimulate arousal, little female. Only a compound to counteract the hormone suppressants that remained in your system." I give her swollen clit a brief pinch, then lightly stroke my finger in a circle around the pulsing button. She sucks in a rapid, shaky breath and her thighs quiver harder. Again, she peers hopefully toward the door.

"If you attempt escape, Leona, I will have no choice but to handle your disobedience myself." An image of the pretty female draped over my knee while I smack her buttocks speeds through my mind, and *fluxx* how it makes my scrotum vibrate.

"Handle my disobedience?" She props herself up on her elbows. "What, like… you'll ask for another *volunteer* for your little science experiment?"

"No." I remove my hand from her center and straighten as I meet her gaze. "I will punish you, Leona, and I will make you obey."

She gapes at me for a long moment, then says, "How dare you threaten me. I-I demand another doctor perform my exam. One who's less arrogant and beastly."

"Arrogant and beastly?" I grin and rise to my feet. For a reason I can't fathom, I find her defiance invigorating. If she were mine, I would savor the process of training her.

I move to stand over her, and I trail a hand along her right breast. She attempts to shield her bosom from my touch, but I grasp her wrists in my free hand, preventing her attempt at modesty.

I lean down and place my lips to her ear. "I am the only doctor who will be examining you today. I claimed you, and *you're mine.*" I force in deep breaths as I try to calm the possessiveness that surges through me. "And if you attempt escape or prove uncooperative during your exam, little female, I will show you just how arrogant and beastly I can be."

She turns her head away from me, her entire body trembling. Whether she's shaking from fear or need, or perhaps a combination of both, I am uncertain. But maybe she's right. Maybe I am beastly. Because having her at my complete mercy sends a thrill rushing through me.

Still keeping her wrists held tight, though not tight enough to cause the same sort of damage as the manacles, I allow my free hand to travel down her stomach and lower, until I'm once again stroking her wet folds. She quivers and jolts and whimpers. I'm even rewarded with a brief moan. There's no denying it. She's aching to be filled up, to be penetrated and ridden hard to completion. I'm soon rewarded with a fresh surge of her feminine essence in the air, and my digits glide more easily through her core.

"I need to get a better look at your orifices, little human." I release her wrists and remove my hand from her center, then resituate myself on the stool between her thighs. She peers at me in shock, though surely she must've realized I would be thorough in my endeavors. "I need to spread your nether area very wide, little female, so I can determine how many holes you possess for mating."

Chapter 5

LEONA

Disbelief seizes me. He wants to know *how many* holes I possess for mating. What the fucking fuck? I draw in a deep breath, ready to blurt out that I have one hole for coitus, thank you very much, but before I can speak, he spreads my center shamefully wide. The words catch in my throat, and I release a strangled moan, much to my mortification.

I'm about to retract my feet from the stirrups and jump off the exam table, but then I remember his threat to handle my disobedience himself, and I freeze in place. What did he mean by that, anyway? Surely he wouldn't strike me, would he?

Fear coils low in my belly, merging with the warm pulses that can't seem to stop afflicting me. I remind myself that once this is over, I'll be released from the brig. Despite my embarrassment, freedom is a powerful motivator, and I strive to hold still as he continues spreading my nether folds wider apart.

"Hm." There's a note of scientific interest in his voice, and I'm not certain whether he's speaking to himself or me. "It would appear human females only possess one main orifice for mating."

I snort. "I could have told you that." I sigh with frustration as the achiness in my core mounts. God, I wish I weren't so breathless. I also wish I could stop trembling. Suddenly, a thought occurs to me. A horribly frightening thought. I stare at Doctor Zahhn as my suspicion grows, as well as my worry for the women who'll be given to the Darrvasons for breeding purposes. "Were you hoping we would have more than one… *mating orifice*?" I whisper the last two words, then flush as he gazes intently at the area between my thighs.

Finally, he lifts his head, and his purple alien eyes flick to mine. He doesn't blink very often, I realize, and it gives him a preternatural quality. It also makes me feel like I'm his prey and he's a ravenous predator intent on sizing me up.

"Female Darrvasons possess two mating orifices which, naturally, accommodate our males' dual appendages." He says it so casually, yet the information he's just revealed comes as a shock.

Two cocks. Darrvason males have two cocks.

He removes his hands from between my thighs and stands suddenly, and I can't help but glance at the immensely large bulge in his pants. Shame heats my face and I just as quickly look away, but the deep chuckle that vibrates from his chest reveals he noticed my gawking. He's aware of my curiosity, the arrogant bastard.

Naked. I can't believe I'm lying on an exam table with my feet in stirrups, legs spread wide, my private parts on display. All while a huge beastly alien touches me and observes my reactions.

But maybe… maybe he's done. He just figured out how many vaginas I have, and I see no need for the exam to continue. I clear my throat and say, "It would seem we're finished here. May I get dressed?"

His eyes twinkle as though I'd just told the funniest joke, though he doesn't laugh again. Instead, he stands between my spread thighs and inserts the tip of one thick finger into my core. I gasp and tense, not quite believing what he's doing. The fullness is overwhelming. It's shocking. It's also… deliciously intense. The achiness in my center mounts, and I can't restrain a whimper as my hips jerk upward.

"We are not finished here, little female. Not even close." As he presses deeper inside me, his thumb grazes a very sensitive part of me. My clit, I realize, though I can't recall where I learned the word for that part of my anatomy. Probably something I picked up from a drunk customer at my speakeasy.

I swallow hard as my gaze lands on the phallus-shaped objects he'd set on the counter. Realization dawns, and my legs fly out of the stirrups. Need to run. Need to escape. I couldn't possibly endure either of those huge objects in my *mating orifice*. But before I'm able to make it off the table, Doctor Zahhn grasps my upper arms and blocks me with his huge body. I push at his chest, but my efforts to move him prove futile. He glances over his shoulder at the phalluses, apparently having noticed the reason for my sudden fear.

"Please." I tremble in his hold. "Those phalluses, they won't fit. Please don't. My people, our females, we aren't physically compatible with the males of your kind. Trust me on that. You're too big. We'd likely die if you tried to physically mate with us." Either of those phalluses would surely break me in two. My trepidation deepens.

He grasps my face, forcing my gaze to his. "I don't plan to force the phalluses inside you. I simply intend to determine how much you can accommodate, particularly when you're in a heightened state of arousal. Perhaps you'll manage half a phallus, but perhaps your body will surprise you and you'll manage the entirety of the largest one. But there is no need for fear. I plan to take my time and prepare you for this portion of the examination."

God, I hope he's telling the truth. I hope he really won't force the largest phallus inside me, heedless of how much it hurts and how much damage he's inflicting. I peer into his eyes as I search for any signs of deceit. His gaze isn't as warm as I would like, but it's not mean or evasive. If he were human, I would probably trust him based on his earnest expression alone. But he's not human, and he has all the power in this interaction, while I have none. I'm completely at his mercy, and I need to keep my guard up.

"Please be gentle." The plea escapes my lips before I can stop it, and I nearly cringe at how weak and pathetic

I sound. Dammit. Most of the time, I have no difficulty projecting an aura of confidence, even when I'm not feeling brave. Fake it until you make it, right? It's a coping mechanism, one that makes me feel safe on a worldship that's anything but. Doctor Zahhn, however, has stripped away my protective armor, leaving me exposed and vulnerable.

A strange shudder vibrates through the alien physician, and he steps closer and leans down to bury his face in my hair. He draws in a deep breath, then an inhuman growl reverberates from his chest. My heart accelerates, and I'm not sure what's happening. If I possessed more knowledge about the act of sexual congress, maybe I would know for certain whether Doctor Zahhn is attracted to me. He seems to be enjoying the act of examining me on an intimate level, but perhaps I am mistaken.

He's smelling me. I flush and wonder if he likes the way I smell. Well, if he didn't, I suppose he wouldn't keep doing it. Nor would he keep growling and shuddering against me. Waves of heat envelop me, and I find myself suppressing the urge to touch him. To run my hands up and down his muscular chest, or maybe stroke his arms or even cup his face and feel the texture of his facial hair.

As I squirm in place, I become aware of the increasing wetness between my thighs, and I flush anew. Oh God. Pretty sure I'm going to leave a wet spot on the exam table. How humiliating.

Doctor Zahhn eventually pulls back, straightens a bit, and gazes into my eyes with a look I can only describe as hungry. For a few seconds, I fear he might pounce on me. Or kiss me.

I study his full lips and realize I wouldn't be averse to the idea. I've gone my entire life without experiencing the urge to touch or kiss a man, yet with Doctor Zahhn, I'm having the most exciting yet shameful urges. The type of urges I've been taught are dangerous. Fornication leads to disease and injury and unsanctioned pregnancies. That's why it's been banned on the *Jansonna* for several decades.

Yet as I hold Doctor Zahhn's gaze, I find myself wanting to break the laws of my people and willingly surrender myself to the handsome but strict alien doctor's scandalous attentions.

He nudges my thighs apart and strokes a digit through my immense moisture. I gasp and jerk against his touch, eager for more, wondering if there is some way he might caress me that will help me feel more settled and less breathless. There's a deep nameless yearning inside me, and if those strange and entirely new desires aren't quenched, I think I might cry and beg him for help.

And yet I don't know *what* I could ask of him. What sort of help he could render to stop the incessant ache between my trembling thighs. My frustration grows and I release yet another whimper.

He presses down on my clit and swirls, and I finally take hold of his arms, needing something to grasp for support. His huge biceps bunch under my hands. "I will be exceedingly gentle with you, Leona, as I attempt to fit a phallus in your mating orifice. In fact, I will endeavor to make the experience as pleasurable for you as possible. But you must be a good female and obey my commands. If you are insubordinate, I will not hesitate to discipline you."

"Discipline me?" I gulp past the abrupt dryness in my throat, and I don't understand why his vague threats of punishment make the warm pulses in my core come faster.

"If you prove uncooperative, little female, I will give you a sound thrashing on your bare bottom. As I said previously, I will make you obey."

A sound thrashing. My mind reels. I know I should be outraged. I should tell him to fuck right off. Yet I can't find my voice.

Doctor Zahhn glances at the stirrups. "Return your feet to the placements. Do it now."

Chapter 6

ZAHHN

I WATCH AS LEONA, MY BEAUTIFUL LITTLE PATIENT, slowly assumes the ordered position. She lies down, situates her bottom at the table's edge, then sets her feet in the placements. Such an obedient female.

Pleasure hums through me, and I'm certain I've never felt so feverish in my life. My scrotum vibrates steadily, and my dual shafts threaten to burst out of my pants. Not for the first time in her presence, the ancestral markings on my chest tingle. It's alarming, the level of possessiveness I feel for her. The need that burns in my soul. The desires that invade my senses.

Her fragrance keeps calling to me, so pungent and sweet. Sometimes, if I listen carefully enough, I can hear the rapid beating of her heart. I imagine it beats only for me, and maybe mine beats only for her.

Fluxx. I need to maintain control of myself. I need to

banish thoughts of claiming the pretty human. I yearn for her to belong to me, yet it isn't possible. I'm destined to be alone. I'm fated to devote my life to scientific advancements, not a woman I cannot impregnate.

"Good little female." I brush a hand through her hair, eager to feel her soft locks again. Everything about her is soft. Her hair and skin, even the area between her thighs that I long to plunder.

I can't be certain, but I think she blushes because of the praise I bestow on her. How very interesting. I make a note to test this theory later during her examination, just to see if her face turns dark pink while she shyly glances away.

I place a generic medical scanner atop her lower stomach, which will record her responses as I strive to bring her pleasure and push a phallus in her slick mating orifice. She peers at the scanner but says nothing, and I turn to retrieve the smallest phallus from the supply table. I half expect her to bolt off the table, yet she remains in place, my compliant little patient.

"Copulation is very natural," I tell her in what I hope is an assuring tone. "There is no good reason why your people have ceased the practice that I can surmise. It's my opinion that outlawing fornication is one of many control tactics employed by the *Jansonna's* command team."

She shoots me a dubious look. "Fornication leads to disease, injury, and unsanctioned pregnancies. I'm not defending the command structure of the *Jansonna*, but our ship has limited resources, and we must control our population as a result." She appears troubled for a brief moment, then sighs and gives a slight shake of her head. "I-I have never experienced any unlawful urges until now. Until I met you. I don't understand what's happening to me. I am very embarrassed, but also… excited." Her cheeks flame dark pink, and her eyes sparkle and reflect the overhead lights. She's breathtakingly gorgeous and so sweetly innocent, and I cannot look away.

Yes, she's innocent, and I'm about to defile her.

Perhaps I should feel guilty for what I'm about to do, but I don't.

I'm eager to shove a phallus into her slick core, eager to test how much of the object she can withstand. I'm also eager to watch her moan and writhe upon the exam table as I bring her to the heights of pleasure. Yes, I'm certain I will make her reach a climax. She's in possession of a clit, after all. Surely if I coax her with careful ministrations, she will cry out in a release as she gushes moisture and accepts the metallic shaft.

"I am going to touch you and attempt to bring you pleasure, little female. When I think you are ready to accept the phallus, I will begin inserting it. Do you understand?"

Eyes wide, she nods. I tear my gaze from hers and study her spread center. The insides of her thighs gleam with wetness that's trickled out from her core. I breathe deep of her feminine essence and don't bother restraining an appreciative growl. The sudden urge to bury my face between her thighs and taste her almost prevails. Almost. But I summon my self-control and place the tip of the phallus at her gaping entrance. Her legs tremble harder, but she doesn't move or protest in the slightest.

"Good little female." This time, not only does she flush under my praise, but her eyes dilate, and her breath catches in her throat.

Though I hold the tip of the metallic shaft at her core's entrance, I don't yet attempt to penetrate her. I only apply the tiniest amount of pressure. As I hold the phallus in place, ready to thrust inside when the time is right, I spread moisture from her core over her pulsating clit. The distended bit of flesh swells larger as I pay it attention, and Leona occasionally lifts her center and mewls deep in her throat as I tend to this sensitive part of her nether region.

"Doctor Zahhn?"

"Yes, human female?"

"If Darrvason males have two shafts, how will physical copulation with human females even work? I am not trying to argue or be uncooperative, but I am truly curious, and I'm also worried for my friends who might be claimed by your people." Her eyes flutter shut as I press harder on her clit while swirling moisture atop it.

"If the one mating orifice your females possess is able to accommodate a Darrvason shaft, our males could still claim your females and impregnate them without having to resort to the use of fertility labs. We could simply drive one appendage into your one hole, then switch and claim you a second time with the unspent appendage." I gaze at the tiny pucker nestled between her cheeks. "However, I suspect that with proper training, you could withstand a shaft in your bottom hole, which could make traditional Darrvason mating methods possible."

Her mouth drops open, and she shakes her head so fast her dark locks bounce over her shoulders. "Absolutely not. That doesn't sound possible. I could never take one of those huge phalluses in my… *bottom hole*. I still don't believe it's possible that one will fit in my… *mating orifice*."

It hasn't escaped my notice that she has a tendency to whisper words she deems scandalous, nor that she flushes profusely when she utters them. I think it's a charming habit, and I cannot wait to make her blush even more.

"We will see what is possible very soon, won't we?" I finally reply.

Then I recall something else she'd just said. About her worry for her friends who might be claimed by Darrvason males. It's an odd comment, one that doesn't quite make sense. Why would she worry for her friends but not for herself? I peer at her intently as I try to unravel this mystery.

Her *age*. The answer practically screams at me.

If she's worried for her friends but not for herself, perhaps it means she's not in the nineteen to twenty-five age bracket. Older. She must be older. It makes sense, especially since she'd recently pissed Commander Hampton off, a repugnant male who seems to thrive on framing citizens of the *Jansonna* and meting out revenge.

The prospect of Leona being too old to be claimed by one of my people's males causes relief to rush through me. Yes, I want her for myself, never mind that it's not possible. But knowing another male won't be able to claim her is a calming thought.

If another Darrvason male were to take possession of her, I fear I might go mad with jealousy and challenge the male to *lahhkda*, a fight to the death for the ownership of a female.

I exhale a long breath as I study the petite woman, trying to determine if she looks older than the other four female patients who were brought to the medical bay. In truth, I'd barely glimpsed the faces of the other females, for I'd been so taken with Leona's beauty.

"How old are you?" I ask, pausing in my caresses to her engorged nubbin.

The alarm that fills her eyes confirms my suspicions. She's above the age of twenty-five. Not that I care. Whether she's among the most fertile of her people's females or not, I feel fortunate to have met her, and I still can't push away the fervent need to claim her. I still want to rut her savagely and spill my seed in her tight depths. I want to watch my blue essence trickle from her core and down her inner thighs, a mark of my ownership. Proof of our mating.

Fluxx. I need to regain control of my urges lest I bend her over the table, push her thighs wide apart, and ravish her in a moment of lust-fueled madness.

Crazed. Being in her presence makes me crazed with desire.

It's true. If Doctor Ammdox had tried to take her to an exam room, I would've fought that *shoggra* to the death, never mind that we weren't claiming mates, only patients for a private examination.

"How old are you, little female?" I ask again. "Tell me the truth and no harm will come to you."

She blinks fast. "Thirty-five."

"Let me guess. Commander Hampton selected you despite your age just because you'd pissed him off." I push the phallus a bit more firmly to her core, and her legs quiver as a rapturous look overtakes her. She appears to struggle for air. All the while, I continue my assault on her swollen button, spreading moisture over it and circling it with increasing pressure.

"Something like that," she says on a quick exhale. "But please, don't tell anyone." She grips the sides of the table, and her sudden whimpering moan echoes off the walls. I think it's the most enticing sound she's made thus far, and I long to hear it again.

"I vow to guard your secret, little female."

She shudders and her center lurches upward. "Thank you, Doctor Zahhn."

I like hearing my name on her lips, though I can't help but fantasize about her simply calling me *Zahhn*. If she were my mate, she could follow the custom of my people and address me as *Zahhn* when we were alone.

If she were my mate…

Star Gods, I rage that it cannot be so.

Even if I decided to accept Emperor Radakk's offer and claim a mate of my own, a reward for my long years of service to the Darrvason Empire, Leona would not be an option due to her age. I can't fathom claiming a different female. Only her.

I silently curse the details of the blasted treaty between my people and humankind. The particulars have already been finalized, and though I'm an asset to the empire, I'm not arrogant enough to believe I could personally request a specific female from the *Jansonna* who happens to be outside the predetermined age range.

My gaze sweeps over Leona as I once again try to memorize everything about her. I also inhale her scent, wanting to remember the deliciousness of her budding arousal.

I study her center. More slickness has escaped her core to trickle onto her thighs. I finally nudge the tip of the phallus into her chasm, and her mouth parts on a huge gasp. Quivers assail her as her back arches, drawing my gaze to her bosom. Her nipples remain ever hard, firm little peaks that are begging to be sucked.

Fluxx. I'm on the verge of losing control. All I can think about is leaning down and taking one ripe berry in my mouth. I tear my gaze from her chest and return my eyes to her nether region, though that does little to help calm my desires. I switch from thinking about suckling her bosom to feasting on her pussy.

If I ran my tongue over that sensitive, distended button of hers, would she shatter directly against my mouth? All the blood in my body rushes southward and I become momentarily dizzy. I'm so utterly intoxicated by Leona that I fear I'm losing my sanity.

I increase the pace of swirls to her clit and nudge the metallic shaft a tad deeper, and though it's a tight fit, her mating orifice stretches around the object. I stare, enraptured, at her center, then push the phallus forward, until it's halfway submerged in her chasm. Her breath hitches and she continues moaning and whimpering, though none of the noises escaping her sound pained.

Her sensual excitement, the copious slickness in her core that only keeps increasing, helps the metallic shaft glide deeper… until I'm suddenly unable to easily push it further.

I peer at the readings on the medical scanner, as well as the live feed that's playing on my wrist comm which shows the other physicians' current results. Two of my colleagues have encountered the same fleshy blockage when attempting to penetrate their patient's mating orifice with a phallus, though the readings show the fleshy blockage is quite small and the channel continues beyond it, as though it's a minor obstruction that's meant to be breached. A barrier of innocence, I realize, as I recall that Darrvason females possess something similar. Not that I've ever examined a woman of my kind, as there are only a handful of Darrvason females left in the universe, but I've done plenty of reading on the subject.

"Are you in pain, Leona?" I don't cease strumming her clit, and I revel in her struggle to open her eyes and answer my question. Though she might be experiencing some discomfort from the phallus, I suspect she's close to a climax. Her nubbin has never appeared so swollen.

"There's a lot of pressure all of a sudden. Perhaps a slight sting."

As I inspect the readings on the medical scanner, I debate whether I ought to proceed. Yet I must perform my duty to the Darrvason Empire and determine the full extent of her ability to physically mate with a male of my kind. Truly, I'm about to steal what's left of her innocence, but it can't be helped.

I increase my efforts to bring her to a release, spreading more moisture over her throbbing button. I also withdraw the phallus slightly from her core only to push it back inside, and I repeat this motion over and over, mimicking the movement of a plunging shaft in the act of mating.

Just as her body tenses and her face contorts with euphoria, I shove the phallus beyond the fleshy barrier, then immediately withdraw the object and push it even deeper, continuing to drive in and out of her chasm.

She cries out and shudders almost violently, but the blissful look remains on her face, and she continues undulating her hips in a rhythm that mirrors my plunges. A quick glance at the scanner reveals the fleshy barrier is gone.

I wait until her hips cease moving and she settles on the table, panting breathlessly as she peers up at me, her visage once again showing her shock and confusion. I suppose given her upbringing in a sexually repressed society, she likely doesn't comprehend the significance of what just transpired.

"What," she gasps, "what was that? That feeling. That intense quaking I just felt. I've never... *what*..." Her voice trails off and she appears dazed.

Satisfaction swells inside me as I realize the gravity of her statement. Not only did she just experience her first climax, but it was I who brought her to the heights of pleasure.

Carefully, I withdraw the phallus from her center

and set it aside. Then I brush a hand down the length of one slender thigh. Her legs continue trembling, and she hasn't quite caught her breath. Questions still brim in her eyes, and I suppose I ought to enlighten her.

"You just experienced a climax, little female."

"A what?"

"An orgasm," I clarify. "A perfectly natural response to the pleasure that was winding up inside you as I stroked your clit and penetrated you with the phallus." I tilt my head to the side as I study her. "You truly have never touched yourself before and felt any such sensation?"

She flushes profusely and shakes her head, appearing scandalized by the very notion of self-pleasure. "No. Never." Once again, confusion flits through her gaze, and her mouth opens and closes a few times as she struggles for words. "It, well, I have never had the urge, nor did I know it was possible." She peers down at her nether area, and I follow her gaze and take in the sight of her quivering thighs and the slick arousal that coats her flesh.

I move to her side and caress a hand through her hair. Soft. So soft. I could spend days on end just touching her and memorizing the texture of every tiny part of her body.

"I will help you get cleaned up and allow you to rest for a moment, Leona. Then we will continue with the exam."

Chapter 7

LEONA

My face burns with shame as Zahhn cleanses the sticky wetness from my inner thighs. He also runs a damp cloth gently over my nether folds. I strive to remain still as he tends to me in a way no male ever has before.

Shuddering breaths escape my throat as residual pulses from my climax affect me. Or perhaps my excitement is returning. I can't be certain, and I don't like not feeling in control of my own body.

Hell, I could scarcely control the whimpers and moans that Zahhn drew from me as he plunged the phallus in and out of my center while strumming my clit.

I eye my clothing, wondering why I can't get dressed. Why does he want to continue examining me? He's just determined that I, a human female, am quite capable of arousal and able to physically copulate with a Darrvason. What more does he need to learn?

After Zahhn finishes cleaning me, he tosses the cloth into a bin, then turns to focus his full attention on me. I immediately flush, and I can't help but wonder what I must look like. Surely my face has turned bright red. I still feel feverish, and it's not just my face but my entire body. Heat thrums through me in a rhythm that matches my racing pulse.

"How do you feel?" His gaze dances up and down my prone form, lingering on my heaving breasts and the area between my thighs that is suddenly pulsating anew with need.

I swallow hard. "Breathless. Shaky. Tired. Blissful. Confused." I pause as I take a quick inventory of my senses. "And thirsty," I finally add.

To my surprise, concern darts across Zahhn's face. He removes the scanner from my stomach, then retrieves a bottle from the side of his medical bag, places it in my hand, and helps me sit up. "Drink. It's just water."

I study the bottle. It's cold and heavy, though I suppose that's because it's Darrvason-size.

"How do I know you aren't trying to poison me?" Though I'm desperate to quench my thirst, I can't claim to trust the handsome alien who incites my desires. I remind myself that I need to keep my guard up. "How do I know this won't render me unconscious?"

Amusement flickers in his eyes, but only briefly, and his expression once again turns serious. He stands taller as he peers down at me. "I much prefer you awake and alert while I torment you, my little patient. Now drink."

I sigh, perhaps a bit dramatically, then lift the huge bottle to my lips and take a sip. Mm. The water is clean and crisp and the perfect temperature. As it glides down my throat, I eagerly swallow more. Due to problems with the water purification system on the *Jansonna*, it's been a long time since I've enjoyed such a refreshing drink.

Once I'm finished, I pass the bottle back to Zahhn. He returns it to his medical bag, and I watch as he riffles through the bag and withdraws a small clear bottle that contains some kind of liquid, which he promptly sets on the counter. He peers at one of his medical scanners and taps at the screen a few times.

Is he making notes about my exam?

"Return to your previous position on the table with your feet in the placements, your thighs spread wide. Comply," he orders without so much as a glance upward.

I bite the inside of my cheek as annoyance flares in my chest. Yet I cannot defy him. The urge to obey swells inside me, and I soon find myself moving back into the previous position. A shiver courses through me.

He leans against the counter and continues tapping away. Meanwhile, I remain in the awkward, vulnerable position on the table with my legs spread wide, my feet planted in the stirrups. I want to get up and I long to cover myself, but I don't want to interrupt his train of thought and end up pissing him off.

A quiver races across my bottom cheeks as I recall

his threat to spank me if I prove disobedient. Yes, I'd better stay in this awkward position until he tells me otherwise, even though I feel exposed and utterly defenseless.

But if I start to become slick between my thighs again, he'll likely see it immediately, and I try very hard not to entertain any thoughts that might lead to such an outcome.

I study Zahhn as he works. How old is he? If he were human, I might say he's in his late forties or early fifties, given the white streaks in his otherwise dark hair. His visage is marred by thinking lines as he concentrates on the device in his hand, and for some reason, my heart skips a beat as I continue my observations. Raw masculine power emanates from him. Maybe he's the lead physician on whatever ship he calls home in the Darrvason fleet. At the very least, he must command respect among his people. After all, he was the sole doctor to converse with Commander Hampton. I also remember how he pushed one of his comrades aside so he could reach me first, and a warm tingly sensation suffuses my body.

Handsome. Powerful. Highly intelligent. Dominant. My heart beats faster as I can't help but admire the tall muscular alien who just gave me my first climax.

Why am I so drawn to him?

I absently scratch at my upper arms. They're itching again and I don't know why. Perhaps I'm allergic to something. Maybe it's because the recirculated air in the *Jansonna* isn't as clean as it's supposed to be due to issues with the filtration system.

Zahhn's nostrils flare and a low growl emanates from his chest. He glances up from the device and gives me a knowing look. He takes a deep breath, then exhales slowly, another growl leaving him.

Heated pulses swirl in my core, and I can't help but squirm in place as he stares down at me. I grip the edges of the table and feel his eyes on my center as though he's physically touching me there. The throbbing of my clit becomes so intense that I find myself fighting the urge to reach between my thighs and caress the sensitive spot.

He takes another leisurely inhale, and his eyes flick to mine. "You're becoming aroused again, little female. I can smell it." He pushes away from the counter and comes to stand directly between my spread legs. "I can see it too. There's a fresh glimmer of wetness coating your pink parts."

"Why am I still here?" I blurt, unable to keep the frustration from my tone. "You already succeeded in shoving a phallus inside me. You also learned I can have a cli-climax." I flush. "What more do you want from me?"

He gestures to the larger phallus, which is still sitting upright on the counter. I'm not sure where the slightly smaller one went after he finished using it on me. I guess he shoved it in his medical bag when I wasn't paying attention. "I confirmed you could take a shaft which corresponds to the average size of a Darrvason male's upper appendage, but I have yet to determine whether you're able to accommodate the larger phallus, which of course corresponds to the typical size of a Darrvason male's lower appendage. And then there is the matter of learning how much of an intrusion, if any, you can withstand in your bottom hole. We still have more work to do. Your exam isn't even halfway over yet." He picks up the large phallus and gives me an expectant look.

Chapter 8

ZAHHN

Trepidation glimmers in Leona's dark eyes, yet the delectable scent of her arousal keeps heightening in the air, and the gleam of moisture between her thighs increases as well. She's nervous, but she cannot hide the true level of her growing excitement from me.

As I stand over her, another thought enters my mind. How easily could she accept a Darrvason-size cock in her mouth? I glance at the large phallus I'm holding and move to stand next to her head. She side-eyes the phallus as her legs tremble in the placements that keep her wet center spread wide.

"Before I attempt to penetrate your core with this object, I would like to see how easily you can take it in your mouth. Please open." I place the tip of the phallus at her lips, but she wrenches her head away and emits a little squeak of outrage. "Leona." I utter her name in the most scolding tone I can muster, but it doesn't encourage her to obey.

She closes her eyes and shakes her head slightly, all while keeping her lips pressed tightly together. Another outraged noise leaves her throat. Impatience sears me. Surely accepting a phallus in her mouth would be easier than taking it in her pussy. Why is she resisting? I clear my throat, making an outraged noise of my own, a growl of warning, yet it doesn't prompt her to obey.

"Very well." I set the phallus aside. Then I shift position, lift her feet from the placements, clasp her ankles together in one hand, and immediately deliver two hard slaps to her bottom.

She gasps and squirms and tries to escape, but I don't release my hold. "I'm sorry! Please." She whimpers as I apply two additional firm smacks to her cheeks.

"You had your chance to obey, little female. Perhaps once you have a sore, stinging bottom, you will be more cooperative." Ignoring her protests, I set a quick pace of spanking. The rapid blows echo in the exam room, alongside her gasps and whimpers.

"Please stop! You must stop!" Her face contorts with pain, and she makes another attempt to hurl herself off the table.

I tighten my grip on her ankles and spank faster, intent on making a lasting impression. Perhaps she thought my threat to punish her was nothing but a bluff. I continue peppering her buttocks with quick slaps, paying particular attention to the area where her thighs merge with her cheeks, as I notice the blows to this region prompt her to gasp louder.

As I punish my naughty little patient, I can't help but admire the sight of her exposed nether area. In this position with her legs held high, her pussy is on full display. I can even see her clit poking out from between her folds.

My scrotum vibrates and my dual shafts throb hard inside my pants. *Fluxx*, I'm so eager to rut her. So eager to make her take my larger, lower appendage rather than the phallus. For a moment, I consider stopping her punishment so I might ravish her to completion.

A deep growl leaves me, one borne of frustration and lust. Inhaling a deep breath, I attempt to get my desires under control. Taking a deep breath, however, only causes me to fill my lungs with the sweet, pungent scent of Leona's arousal.

A glance at her nether area shows she's soaking wet, moisture coating her inner thighs. I imagine I can see the pulsing of her clit as she writhes on the table. She's no longer trying to escape, but she's not remaining still either. No doubt the sting of the spanking makes it difficult for her to remain unmoving.

I apply ten additional smacks to her bottom, then pause to admire my handiwork. The globes of her ass are dark pink, and the backs of her upper thighs show some color as well. Beautiful.

My shafts lurch in my pants. Primal need surges in my veins. Yet, somehow, I resist the urge to rip my clothing off and plunge into her wet mating orifice.

Focus. Focus on the details of her examination. You must report your findings in a manner befitting a decorated physician and admired researcher.

Reminding myself of what's at stake seems to calm the worst of my urges, though my shafts don't soften, nor does my scrotum cease vibrating. But my blood cools just enough that I'm no longer on the verge of claiming the pretty little human.

Fluxx, that was close.

Still holding her ankles, I straighten and peer down at her. She blinks fast against a sheen of moisture, though no tears have fallen. I haven't spanked her to the point of crying, but it was close. A few more hard smacks and no doubt tears would stream down her face.

If she continues to resist me and refuses to suck the phallus, I resolve that I will resume her thrashing with renewed vigor, even if it causes her to break down sobbing. I won't abide her disobedience.

I stroke a hand over her punished flesh, and her breath catches as the scent of her excitement swells in the air. It's apparent that she became exceedingly wet as I chastised her, despite the pain of the spanking. What a treasure she is.

Though she has a rebellious side, I suspect there's a part of her that longs to submit to my authority, a part of her that can't help but quiver and ache as I exert my control over her. The immense slickness between her trembling thighs is evidence enough.

Not for the first time, I find myself regretting that I cannot take a mate. Furthermore, I regret that Leona's not in the age range decreed by the newly sealed alliance. No matter what, it wouldn't be possible for us to join. I wouldn't lawfully be permitted to claim her.

Still holding her legs high, I meet her eyes. "Will you

be obedient and demonstrate your ability to suck on the phallus, or shall I turn your bottom an even brighter shade of pink?"

A shaky breath escapes her. Then she says, "I'll be obedient. Just please… no more spanking. *Please.*" While there's a definite note of defeat in her voice, she doesn't sound downtrodden. A spark of her vivacious personality remains. She's submitting to me, but she isn't entirely happy about it.

Hearing her beg, however, stirs something deep and primal inside me.

I continue to admire the sight of her punished cheeks as well as the wetness between her thighs. *My mate. Mine.*

Fluxx. Though I know it's impossible for us to become mates, I cannot stop the word from echoing in my psyche.

A wave of possessive desire steals through me, but I attempt to tamp it down. Once again, I remind myself of my responsibility to my people. If I go rogue and physically claim my human female patient, I might single handedly endanger the Darrvason-human alliance.

"I am pleased that you have agreed to comply," I finally say, and my voice comes out strained. I lower her legs and assist her in returning her feet to the stirrups. She winces as she assumes the original position, though she says nothing. There's no doubt in my mind that she'll be sore for days and likely have difficulty sitting.

Will she think of me each time she experiences a twinge of pain and winces? I rather like the idea of her thinking of me in the days to come, even if she's harboring unkind or angry thoughts.

Once she's settled to my liking, I stroke the backs of my fingers down her cheek and neck, gently caressing her as if she's a skittish animal I wish to calm. I muse that if I were to make the comparison aloud, she would likely try to bite my hand off. She's nervous and aching to submit—I can sense it—yet there's a fire of defiance burning inside her.

Star Gods, how I would love to be the male to tame her.

If she were my mate, I would teach her to serve and obey.

I would punish her insolence, and I would reward her submission. Either way, she would be perpetually sore. Sore from a recent thrashing, or sore from a recent mating session during which I would make her climax repeatedly.

I reach for the larger phallus, and this time my subdued patient doesn't turn away when I place it at her lips. Progress, I decide, though she hasn't yet opened her mouth. I wait and watch, wondering if she'll require additional punishment. But finally, she parts her lips and allows me to slide the phallus inside. Her cheeks bulge from the intrusion, and her eyes water.

"Good little patient." I withdraw the object from her mouth nearly the entire way, then plunge back inside. Repeating this motion over and over, I continue as I train her to accept the phallus more deeply with each thrust. "That's it, Leona. Show me how you would obediently suck your mate's appendage. Very, very good."

Perhaps it's due to the praising tone of my voice, or perhaps it's because she's embarrassed or angry, but she blushes a shade of pink so bright it rivals the hue of her punished buttocks.

Eventually, I nudge the phallus against the back of her throat, which causes her to gag. Her eyes go wide and she whimpers, but she remains compliant and doesn't try to withdraw from the demonstration. Pride swells in my chest, an emotion that's almost tender.

To my shock, I have the strangest urge to lean down and press a soft kiss to her forehead. But I don't follow the urge. Every muscle in my body tenses as I resist.

Fluxx, what utter madness is clutching me?

I try to focus on the practical implications of this demonstration—I'm showing that human females will be capable of pleasuring their Darrvason mates with their mouths. After administering a few more plunges of the phallus, I remove the object from her mouth and move to stand between her spread thighs.

It's time. Time to learn whether Leona can withstand a larger Darrvason male's appendage in her mating orifice. As though on cue, my lower shaft throbs against the front of my pants. Heat engulfs me, but I ignore my spiraling lust and position the phallus at her drenched core.

I capture her gaze as I place a thumb on her clit. She shudders as the tiny, distended bit of flesh pulses under my touch. Her back arches slightly and a whimpering gasp drifts from her lips. Such a lovely, responsive little female.

"You did an excellent job sucking the largest phallus. Even though it proved a challenge for you, and you gagged several times, I believe that if you were given the opportunity, you could successfully bring a Darrvason male to completion with your mouth alone." I try not to imagine her kneeling on the floor to take my appendages in her mouth, one after the other, but it's suddenly the only thing I can think about. I picture her peering up at me with wide eyes, then shyly leaning forward as she parts her lips to accept one of my erect shafts in her mouth. *Fluxx*, what an experience it would be.

She tears her gaze from me and studies the wall, though I notice she's not immune to my touch. It appears she's trying not to be affected by the swirling pressure I'm enacting on her clit, but I glimpse the slight tremors running through her body, and there's no hiding the immense moisture that gleams between her thighs.

She gasps as I push the tip of the phallus into her pussy. I commence a steady thrusting motion. In and out, and in and out. I go deeper with each drive. Her whimpers and moans reverberate in my head, encouraging me to continue. Every now and then she winces as though I've hit a sore spot, but each time the pained look fades and is replaced by a look of rapture as I tend to her clit.

Pleasure. I'm striving to bring her pleasure. Even if she can't manage to take the entirety of the largest phallus, I intend to make her shatter again on the exam table. I want to watch her face contort with ecstasy as she reaches the heights of bliss.

"Good little female." I lean closer and inhale her pungent arousal. Then I increase the pace of swirls to her sensitive button. Her eyes meet mine just before she starts writhing and moaning. "That's it. Come for me, Leona. Be obedient and come."

Chapter 9

LEONA

I CRY OUT AS THE WAVES OF PLEASURE CONSUME ME. God, I can't believe he's doing this to me a second time. As I climax, my insides clamp down on the huge phallus, reinvigorating my soreness from the session with the first one. The euphoria goes on and on, until I'm left panting on the table as little twinges of sensation jolt in my center.

Good little female.

I flush. Why do I feel all warm and tingly when he utters those three words in a praising tone? Why do I long to hear him say it again? A wave of submission courses through me, and not for the first time in Zahhn's presence. Though part of me wants to defy him, even if it results in pain and humiliation, a much larger part of me wants to surrender. To kneel at his feet in supplication.

I give my head a shake. Where are these thoughts coming from?

And why the fuck are my upper arms itching again?

Before I can start scratching, there's a sudden tug between Zahhn and I, as though we're being physically pulled toward one another. He rises and abruptly comes to stand at my side, and I flush as I realize he's left the phallus submerged in my depths, filling me up and stretching me wide.

Alarm tinged with wonder sparkles in his gaze, and he places a hand to his upper chest and massages the area. I can't be certain, but I think I see something glimmering beneath his black shirt. Something blue just under the neckline of the garment, right where he's caressing. His eyes flare as he peers down at me. With a growl, he tears his hand from his chest and grips the exam table. His muscles bunch and his breaths increase.

Without warning, pleasure jolts through me and my inner walls clench the phallus. I whimper low in my throat and wiggle on the table. My hips jerk upward and my clit throbs, desperate to be stroked. I'm hovering on the edge of a thunderous release, if only Zahhn would resume tending to my center. I ache for him to start plunging the phallus in and out of me, going deep with each thrust as he rubs my throbbing nubbin with the perfect amount of pressure.

"What are you doing to me?" The alien doctor whispers. He slowly peruses the length of my body, moving from my face down to my toes, then back again. "What the *fluxx* are you doing to me?" Accusation tinges his deep voice, but he doesn't sound angry. Surprised, maybe. And curious.

But I'm not entirely certain what he's talking about.

He moves between my thighs, and I almost shed tears of relief when he commences toying with my clit. He rubs and circles it with precise motions.

Zings of sensation affect me, skittering throughout my body, making me hyperaware of every little action he takes. Every brush of skin, every deep exhale as he leans closer and his breath drifts across my naked flesh.

His lips hover so close to my upper thigh that for a moment I think he might kiss me there. Constant growls rumble from his throat, and the noise vibrates through me, enhancing my pleasure.

He straightens, grabs hold of the phallus, and begins to withdraw it from my pussy. A second later, he drives it back inside, going so deep that I fear he might break me. I'm still a tad sore from the first phallus, the smaller one, yet he seems determined to force this larger one to the very depths of my core.

"You're so close to taking the whole thing. Good, good little female." The praise in his tone warms my heart in a way I don't want to think about. My head prickles with sensation as goosebumps skitter down my back, followed by a deep throb in my center, the most delightful physical response to his voice yet.

What are you *doing to* me*?* I almost ask him.

Why do I feel frantic and saddened by the idea of never seeing him again? It's preposterous. I should be relieved by the knowledge that after he finishes my exam, he'll return to his ship, and I'll return to the brig.

I should be relieved I won't have to worry about seeing him again, and I should be buoyed by the knowledge that I'll be released from the brig soon. I'll be free, and I need to focus on forgetting and putting this experience behind me.

But how can I forget Zahhn?

Fuck. So much for keeping my guard up.

What if I'm drawn to the alien doctor because of what he's physically doing to me? I remind myself that he removed all traces of the hormone suppressants from my system. He's also touching me in shamefully intimate ways I've never been touched before. He gave me orgasms, shoved two huge phalluses in my core, and made me suck on one of those fake appendages.

Oh, and let's not forget the embarrassing and painful spanking he gave me. I flush as a tremor dances across my sore bottom cheeks. Yes, I'm simply confused by my physical response to his ministrations.

How much longer does he plan to drive the largest phallus inside me?

"Almost there." He works circles over my clit, occasionally pausing to drag moisture from my core atop the nubbin. Tingles sweep over me as the throbbing heat coils tighter in my center. My toes curl and I tense, ready to combust. He pushes the phallus deeper, until I'm stretched impossibly wide and filled up.

Then it happens. I cry out as another pulsating release steals through me. Gasping for air, I writhe on the table, gyrating my hips against Zahhn's expert ministrations.

"There." He gives a final push of the phallus that

sends a shockwave of delicious sensation spiraling outward from my pussy. "Good little female. You've managed to fully accommodate the largest phallus, as I suspected you could."

Good little female. There it is again. Those three little words that sort of feel like an endearment. I can't help but flush as he meets my eyes and gives me a nod of approval. I shouldn't like that I pleased him, but I do.

Heat flares in his gaze as he studies my center. I think he's about to remove the phallus, but he leaves it submerged. I watch in confusion as he withdraws a protective glove from his pocket and places it on his right hand.

"Please." I wiggle on the table. "It's so big. Please take it out."

"Just a moment." He grabs the small bottle I'd all but forgotten about and pours a copious amount of clear liquid on his gloved fingers. Before I can ask what he's planning, he reaches between my thighs, draws my butt cheeks apart, and places a lubricated finger at my anus.

I gasp and go tense, shaking my head as I clutch the sides of the table. But every little movement I make increases the fullness of the phallus that's still submerged in my depths, and he seems determined to slip that gloved digit into my bottom hole.

Oh God. He'd mentioned that he wanted to learn whether I could withstand an intrusion in my ass. *I suspect that with proper training, you could withstand a shaft in your bottom hole, which could make traditional Darrvason mating methods possible.*

My stomach flips, and I pray he won't attempt to shove either of the phalluses in my anus. I'm fairly certain he's only slipped the tip of his finger inside thus far, and I can't fathom the discomfort of something the size of a Darrvason cock.

"I want to test whether this delightful puckering hole of yours could stretch to withstand the pounding of a shaft during a mating session. But," he says, shoving deeper and causing me to gasp again, "you are very tight back here, so I will only invade you with a finger or two. Try to relax, little female."

I whimper and almost ask him to remove the large phallus from my core, but he shoves deeper in my ass and the abrupt fullness makes speech impossible. Despite the immense discomfort and my utter embarrassment, I can't claim it hurts. Heated waves continue throbbing outward from my center, and the unexpected pleasure only increases as he shoves deeper in my bottom hole.

He emits a noise of approval, a rumble that makes my pussy clench on the massive phallus. Perspiration runs down my temple and I blink fast as my eyes water. What he's doing to me… it's overwhelming. I cannot form a coherent thought, and I still can't manage words.

"So very tight, yet I suspect with consistent training, perhaps with a set of plugs in incremental sizes, you could eventually take an upper Darrvason shaft in your bottom hole." He growls and starts pumping his digit in and out of my snug, private hole.

I lurch upward on the table with a keening moan, seeking relief that I'm not sure will come. Because my clit is suddenly throbbing but he's not touching it. He's too preoccupied with keeping my ass cheeks spread while he drives in and out of my tightness. I'm sorely tempted to reach down and stroke my clit, but I promise myself I'll resist the urge. I don't want him to know just how breathless and achy I'm becoming, or how desperate I am for another release.

"Your clit is becoming hugely swollen, Leona." Still working his long, thick digit in and out of my asshole, he gives me a satisfied look. I whimper and cover my face with my hands, feeling vulnerable and ashamed. But also excited, exceedingly so.

"*Please*," I whisper, finally managing a single word, though I could be begging for anything. For his touch, or perhaps for him to withdraw the phallus and his finger from my orifices.

In truth, I'm not certain what I want. I only know that I cannot endure the deep plunges in my ass for much longer unless he pays my clit some attention. A few quick rubs and surely I'll shatter, and the relief will make this experience a bit more tolerable. Well, maybe.

A dark chuckle leaves him, and as he withdraws his finger partially from my ass, he shocks me by adding a second one during the next plunge inside. My strangled groan echoes off the walls, and my center keeps undulating, my hips shifting up and down of their own accord. The fullness in my ass causes the phallus to feel larger in my pussy, and vice versa. I don't know how he's managed to fill both my holes at the same time, and I'm stunned that I'm capable of such an indecent feat.

Breathless and moaning, I have no choice but to

endure the double invasion. Just when I think I cannot withstand another thrust, he slowly withdraws his fingers from my bottom hole. I exhale quickly as a shudder winds through my body, watching as he removes and disposes of the protective glove.

He glances at something on a device he wears on his wrist, and a deep frown suddenly mars his visage. A communication device of some sort, I realize, perhaps one that allows him to receive news from his people. I want to ask what's caused him to appear so upset, but I remind myself that we are strangers and I'll never see him again. I shouldn't care why he looks so frustrated and perhaps a bit angry. Whatever the cause, I don't think it's because of me, and that brings me some relief.

He growls and turns to face me more fully, then reaches for the large phallus that's still submerged in my pussy. With careful movements, he pulls the object from my center and sets it aside. When his gaze collides with mine, the lines on his face soften, and he parts his lips and draws in a deep breath, as though he's preparing to say something. But just as quickly, he presses his lips together and turns away. My heart sinks, though I'm not certain why, and I chide myself for being affected by his apparent rejection.

"Are we finished?" I ask in a shaky tone. "Is-is it over?"

He nods. "Yes. I will clean the wetness from between your thighs, then you may get dressed. The other exams are over, and your fellow prisoners are in the main area of the medical bay waiting to be returned to the brig."

"Oh," is all I say. I don't understand the panic that

abruptly swells inside me. Nor do I comprehend the immense, gaping sense of loss. The thought of being parted from Zahhn is alarming, yet I don't know why. The strange tug between us remains, and my upper arms won't stop itching. His dark purple eyes mesmerize me as he once again stares at me as though he wishes to say something profound.

Finally, he retrieves another damp cloth and commences dragging it over my slick folds, cleaning away the evidence of my arousal. The evidence of the transformative experience we just shared. Well, I don't know about him, but it was transformative for me.

Because I will never be the same.

Chapter 10

ZAHHN

THE DAYS PASS IN A BLUR, BUT I KEEP BUSY, AND I continue to achieve numerous scientific advancements that better my people.

After the first wave of thirty females is handed over, a young human woman named Sheila injects her male with a dangerous virus. Apparently, she concealed a hypospray filled with the substance between her thighs, then injected her mate, a male named Paddax, just as he was about to claim her.

While my colleagues focus on treating Paddax, it takes me less than a half day to formulate an inoculation that will counteract the virus. All males who came into contact with Paddax after the attack are given the vaccine, myself included.

The day after the attack, Emperor Radakk pays me a visit. He reeks of feminine arousal and male seed, leaving me in no doubt that he successfully claimed his mate. He, along with Admiral Tornn and many other Darrvason males of importance, took a mate from among the first wave of thirty human females yesterday. I fight back a pang of jealousy.

I stand in the middle of my laboratory, watching the leader of the Darrvason Empire carefully for any signs of active *forlonggsa*, though he doesn't appear afflicted yet. His movements are natural, and his eyes don't glimmer with any hints of madness. His speech also sounds normal. It's a relief to know I have more time to help him, though I resolve that I will redouble my efforts.

"It's been over a moon cycle since I last visited you, Doctor Zahhn," he says. "I thought I would visit you and personally thank you for your help with the quick development of the vaccine. Once again, the Darrvason Empire is in your debt." He tilts his head to the side, and I sense there's another reason for his visit, and I bite back a groan of frustration as my suspicion grows.

I wave a hand in the air. "It was my pleasure. Gave me a nice distraction. Didn't even take up half the day." I chuckle, but it feels too forced. "The humans who created the virus made several errors that made it easy to combat. Idiots."

He attempts to restrain a smile. "Nevertheless, your service is much appreciated. When we finally settle on a planet, your house will be among the first that will be built."

I lean against a table and cross my arms, an image of a sturdy abode entering my mind. A house. A house that will belong to me. After twenty-five years spent aboard the *Haxxal* in open space, I long for fresh air and a real home. "I expect a grand house." I grin. "Perhaps not as grand as whatever palace you intend to build for yourself, but a large house in an elevated location, if that is possible, with a majestic view of the landscape." *Alone.* I'll live there alone. I'm careful not to let my arrogant smile falter as I hold Emperor Radakk's gaze. I don't want him to know the depth of my despair over never claiming a female. Not just any female, but a certain little dark-haired patient I still cannot banish from my mind. Leona. Beautiful, trembling, defiant Leona.

"What about a mate?" he asks. "You declined a female from the first wave of women, but the second wave will likely be delivered in a few moon cycles. Would you like a female of your own?"

My mood darkens. "As you know, Emperor, I am sterile. A result of the Haflassan Flu I had as a young male. I would not be able to procreate. A female would be wasted on me." I draw in a long breath, frustrated that we must have this argument again. But the leader of the Darrvason Empire is nothing if not persistent.

"You have saved our people many times over, Zahhn," he says, and I'm stunned that he omits the title of Doctor before my name. It's a sign that he truly considers me a friend, though if we were in the presence of others and he addressed me without my title, it would be considered rude.

"Just because I've saved lives doesn't mean I'm owed a mate." I straighten as pain and self-loathing fill me. I think of Leona and mourn the loss of what I can never have. "The purpose of the Darrvason-human alliance is to procure females for breeding purposes. If the next generation isn't born soon, the survival of our people remains at risk. It would not be logical for me to claim a female. As I've already said, a female would be wasted on me."

"A female would not be wasted on you. Please promise you'll consider it. If a female would make you happy, if you desire to claim one, I would be honored to arrange that for you." He gives me an overly serious look.

I release a long, dramatic sigh, but it's a cover. I must conceal my longing for a mate from the emperor. Even if I accepted, I wouldn't be given the female I desire. Leona. She's not in the age range decreed by the alliance. I would be given an alternate woman, and I cannot fathom claiming any female but her. "May the Star Gods save me from officious emperors," I finally say. I clear my throat. "Very well. I will consider it." I *won't* consider it, but I'll say anything to shut him up.

"Thank you."

"No, no, thank you." I force another cocky grin. "I love it when my superiors meddle in my life."

"You do realize if anyone else talked to me like that, I would have their head, don't you?" The emperor attempts to look stern, but there's no hiding the smirk that twitches his lips.

I snort. "But then who would solve all your problems, my dear emperor?"

He growls. "Speaking of problems, my uncle is getting worse, and so are many others who are suffering from *forlonggsa*. Last time we spoke, you mentioned a possible treatment that you were almost ready to test. Any update on that?"

"Tests will begin in a few days, and I will be living on the *Rorrsa* while the tests are conducted," I say, referring to the Darrvason ship that houses those afflicted with *forlonggsa* in a specialized medical unit. "I will keep you apprised of the progress, Emperor Radakk, but even if this test fails, we still have many more years."

"Eight years," he blurts. "Only eight years." He appears suddenly haunted, and I know he must be thinking about his father. About how utterly mad and violent his father became during his decline.

"Your father first showed signs of *forlonggsa* far earlier than most males do. He was a special case—not only did he show symptoms earlier than usual, his decline was also more rapid than usual. Even if you are stricken with the disease, you likely won't show signs for fifteen years or more. Also, I would like to remind you that it's not a certainty that you'll fall ill. I've sequenced your genes, Emperor, and while you have a genetic predisposition for *forlonggsa*, it's not an inevitable diagnosis. There is still a twenty-eight percent chance you'll live a long, healthy life without any medical intervention."

The haunted look doesn't leave him. I know he's still remembering the sheer madness of his father. I can remember only too well. I was a physician-in-training at the time his father first showed signs of *forlonggsa*, busy with treating our males who became wounded during the war with the Yelltzins, a terrible war that claimed the lives of nearly all our females and too many children.

A pained spasm afflicts me as I recall the fateful day the Yelltzins destroyed our homeworld, slaughtering millions, and the horrible retaliation Emperor Radakk's father took against our enemies. Rather than plunder the Yelltzins' homeworld for their females, of which we were in dire need, Emperor Radakk's father ordered the destruction of their planet and everyone on it. Emperor Radakk was still a child at the time, but surely he must've realized the imprudence of his father's actions. I swallow hard as I think about my parents and sisters who died during the war.

"Thank you," Emperor Radakk finally says, "for devising a method to remove the genetic markers for the disease in-vitro. Knowing my sons won't be afflicted is a great comfort." He straightens and peers toward the door. "I must return to my mate now, but I hope you'll give some thought to accepting a female of your own. Whether you can sire offspring matters not. You are a living legend among our people, Zahhn, and no one would begrudge you for choosing to mate."

I give a brief nod, then lift a finger. "Before you leave, can you tell me if you've learned anything about Sheila's attack on Officer Paddax? Why she did it? Who helped her and whether the human worldship's command team might be involved? The reason I ask is because I've been tasked with developing strict protocols for us to follow when the next wave of females arrive, to ensure another virus doesn't find its way onto any of our ships. Or another sort of weapon."

He shakes his head. "We haven't learned anything yet. Sheila remains in the brig, and she's refusing to talk.

But the admiral and I believe it was likely a rogue attack orchestrated by a group of rebels aboard the *Jansonna*. Captain Warren is a moron who's clearly unfit for leadership, but I don't believe he's stupid enough to provoke us to war. Admiral Tornn is directing the investigation, and I will let you know if I learn anything that might be helpful to you."

"Thank you, Emperor."

We exchange a quick farewell, and I watch as he departs my laboratory, observing for any signs of *forlonggsa*. Thankfully, I glimpse none. The door slides shut as he exits, and I once again find myself alone in the massive space where I conduct the important research that's earned me more accolades than all my colleagues combined.

Leona. I can't stop thinking about her, and I don't like the idea of a meddlesome rebel group aboard the *Jansonna*, the worldship she calls home. I hope whoever was behind the virus is caught quickly—surely the human female who attacked Paddax didn't act alone—and I hope the unnamed rebel group doesn't pose any additional threats to my people or the human worldship. The prospect of the citizens of the *Jansonna* facing danger, Leona among them, fills me with worry.

I want to keep the spirited female I examined safe, yet how can I do so when we don't reside on the same ship? If there was an emergency, what could I do? Could I commandeer a shuttle and attempt to board the *Jansonna*? Not likely. While I'm capable of piloting a shuttle, the docking bay of the *Haxxal* where our smaller transport vessels are housed is heavily guarded. Only authorized personnel are permitted in the area.

I rake a hand through my hair and growl. It doesn't help that not only do my thoughts keep wandering to Leona during the day, but I dream about her every night. Highly erotic dreams that cause me to awake panting and sweating with the bedcovers tangled around my legs, my dual shafts erect and my scrotum vibrating with pleasure.

Fluxx. I turn to the numerous screens that display my progress against *forlonggsa*, trying to banish thoughts of the pretty, dark-haired female. But what I wouldn't give to see her just one more time.

Chapter 11

LEONA

I STAND BEHIND THE BAR, SURVEYING MY DOMAIN AS regulars filter through the door. Angelo guards the entrance this evening, as he does most nights, listening for the secret knock before he admits a patron. I peer toward the entrance as a tall man enters, my heart skipping a beat as my mind briefly plays tricks on me and I think I see purple eyes and dark, textured alien skin. But I blink and the image is gone. It's just another human man. It's not a Darrvason. It's not Zahhn. I sigh with disappointment.

It's been over two weeks since my brief stint in the brig and the embarrassing medical exam performed by Doctor Zahhn, but I still find myself looking for him, half convinced he might walk through the door and lay claim to me.

It doesn't help that there are about two dozen Darrvason males currently roaming the *Jansonna*. Engineers who are stationed here to help make repairs to the worldship. They boarded the *Jansonna* on the day the first wave of thirty human women were handed over to the aliens. Every day as I'm walking to and from work in the mess hall, I glimpse the aliens as they go about their business. And when I first see one of the huge males, there's always a split second during which I'm convinced it's Zahhn.

I also still feel a strong pull to the Darrvason fleet, though strangely, my focus has shifted to one of the smaller ships lately, a vessel I recently learned is called the *Rorrsa*. Clearly, I'm losing my mind.

I blink and a familiar pair of purple eyes flashes in my vision. Not only have the dreams gotten worse since my encounter with Zahhn, but I sometimes glimpse remnants of those dreams during the waking hours. My blood heats as I recall every detail of the shameful examination, from the moment he ordered me to strip off my clothing, to the moment he rubbed me to my first climax, to the moment he shoved two fingers into my bottom hole while the largest phallus was still submerged in my pussy.

The hum of conversation in the bar fades into the background as I become further lost in thoughts of the handsome alien doctor. His touch electrified my senses, causing me to soar through the stars. His deep voice vibrated through me, jolting my insides as I ached and throbbed for relief.

His aura of power also made me melt. Made me feel submissive.

The sharp commands he issued prompted me to obey. Well, most of the time. I was so scandalized when he wanted to shove the metallic phallus in my mouth, however, that I'd defied him and provoked his wrath. I flush as I recall the spanking he'd given me, a punishment that had left my bottom sore for days. I'd been helpless to escape the smacks as he held my legs high in the air and swatted my exposed buttocks. And the wetness between my thighs… well, my excitement only grew as he thrashed me, much to my astonishment and shame.

Arousal. For the first time in my life, I experienced arousal. Even before he'd administered a hypospray to counteract the effects of the hormone suppressants, I'd found myself aching for his touch. Being in the authoritative alien male's presence had rendered me wanton and breathless. I couldn't help it. Even now as I think about him, I feel myself growing wet and achy between my thighs.

I cast a quick glance around the bar, fearful that someone will notice I'm entertaining forbidden thoughts. It shouldn't matter in Leona's Speakeasy, as this is a laid-back place where rebellious activity sometimes occurs, but I still fear someone will notice I'm flushed and aroused. I turn around briefly to face the wall of liquor, then snatch my water bottle and gulp down the last of my daily water ration, needing to cool my temperature. Feverish. Whenever I think about

Zahhn, I become so feverish and unsettled, that I don't know how to handle it.

If I were alone in my bedroom, perhaps I would attempt to caress myself, but I can't very well do that in public. Maybe later tonight. Ever since my encounter with Zahhn, I've been tempted to try self-pleasure. Perhaps a climax will alleviate my aching discomfort and help banish my constant thoughts of Zahhn. I can only hope.

Voices near the entrance catch my attention, and I turn to see Angelo speaking with Jenny, a young patron who frequents the speakeasy and often provides entertainment in exchange for free drinks. She plays the keyboard and has an amazing singing voice, and my spirits brighten as I watch her smiling at Angelo. Given recent events, I hope she's okay. She hasn't visited the bar in about two weeks. Not since the handover of the first thirty women. Her older sister, Ellie, was among the women who were given to the Darrvasons. I imagine Jenny's been grieving the loss of her sister and spending more time with her mother in recent days.

To make matters more complicated, Jenny happens to be Captain Warren's niece, as well as a descendant of Founders. But she's not a snitch, and even though most of my patrons are non-Founders, I welcome her all the same.

As she looks in my direction, I start drying a bin of freshly washed glasses, needing something to keep my hands busy. I force a bright smile as Jenny heads my way. The last thing I want to do is look at her with pity. I doubt she would appreciate it very much. People come to the speakeasy to have fun and forget whatever troubles are plaguing them, if only for one night.

"Look what the cat dragged in," I say.

"Lovely to see you too." She slides onto a stool at the bar. "Any requests for tonight?"

"Sing whatever your heart desires." I flash another smile. "It's good to see you again, kid."

She nods and glances at the stage with a look of longing, then she slips off the stool. I continue drying glasses as she makes her way to the stage. Normal, I muse. This feels somewhat normal. It's a regular night, and though the speakeasy isn't crowded, there are enough patrons here to keep me busy. Plus, a performance from Jenny is always appreciated. She never fails to lighten the mood and bring the crowd together with one of her songs.

As she takes her place behind the keyboard, the murmur of conversation halts, and there's a swell of excitement in the air. I exchange a smile with Angelo. Yes, nothing but a normal night, I remind myself again.

But I don't feel normal. I still feel… transformed.

Enlightened.

My encounter with Zahhn has changed me irrevocably, and I fear I'll never return to the person I once was. The person who was completely and blissfully ignorant about fornication and breeding and orgasms.

My gaze sweeps around the bar, and not for the first time I worry that someone might know the truth about what happened to me. Gossip and rumors spread like wildfire on the worldship. If one of the guards who escorted me to the medical bay blabs, everyone on the *Jansonna* will discover my secret.

Thus far, I haven't admitted to anyone why I missed two days of work in the mess hall and one evening managing the speakeasy. After being released from the brig, the very day after my embarrassing medical exam, I simply told everyone who cared to ask that I'd suffered from food poisoning.

I think of the six women I'd met in the brig. All of them were included in the group of thirty, and guilt ravages me that I only escaped that fate due to my age. I'm not much for praying, but I've sent a few beseeching requests to whatever higher power might be listening for their wellbeing. I hope they aren't suffering terribly at the hands of their Darrvason masters.

Jenny starts playing the keyboard, a catchy tune I recognize as a favorite among the bar's patrons, and her beautiful voice soon echoes off the walls. The song is an ancient rock 'n' roll piece from Earth, and the theme happens to be fighting back against government control.

Well, this is an illegal bar, so the song is nothing if not fitting. Most of the songs Jenny sings are about rebellion, and as I watch her perform, I can't help but wonder if she's involved with any rebel groups.

She clearly despises Captain Warren—I've heard her talk shit about him before—and the captain obviously holds no love for his late brother's widow or her two daughters either. Is that why he selected Ellie, his own niece, to be among the group of thirty? Out of hatred or spite?

Well, if Jenny is part of a rebel group, she's a

goddamn genius. Because here she is, in an illegal bar, performing a song about fighting government power while the crowd cheers and sings along. One could argue she's trying to incite a rebellion, just like it could be argued my father does when he holds secret "talks" with citizens who are concerned about the decisions made by Captain Warren and his command team. Talks that sometimes coincide with attacks on guards and even riots in the corridors.

I decide if Jenny is a rebel, I don't want to know. The less I know, the better. I think of Commander Hampton and suppress a shiver. I consider myself lucky that the bastard didn't try to interrogate me, though I can't help but worry for my father. The Darrvasons are repairing the extensive damage to the *Jansonna*, and they're supposedly going to lead us to a habitable planet. My father might not be needed anymore, and someone like Commander Hampton could quietly order his execution.

Suddenly, there's a collective gasp, and people start turning toward the entrance. Jenny's eyes widen. Her voice trails off mid-song, and her fingers go still on the keyboard. My stomach flips as I glance to the door, praying we haven't been set upon by security or morality officers.

I'm only partially relieved by the sight that greets me: A huge Darrvason male stands several feet inside the speakeasy, waving a keycard in Angelo's face as they exchange terse words. And yes, there's a split second where I think it's Doctor Zahhn. But it's not him. I don't know this alien's name, but I've seen him around the ship lately. I don't think he's an engineer, however, since he's usually following Captain Warren and other members of the command team around.

Why is he here?

I notice he keeps looking at the stage. At Jenny, to be precise. They're staring at one another in a way that tells me they aren't strangers.

In the crowd, people are keeping their heads low and whispering amongst themselves, as though trying to obscure their faces from the alien male. No one can flee the bar easily. Not without running past the Darrvason male. I shake away the feeling that we're trapped and all I've worked for is about to come to an abrupt end.

Well, time to find out what the hell's going on. This is my bar, after all, and it's ultimately my responsibility to keep my patrons safe.

I draw in a deep breath, summon an aura of confidence, and sashay over to the entrance where Angelo is still arguing with the Darrvason male. As I approach the door, I notice several patrons leaving their tables to hide behind the bar. I pray I'm able to diffuse the situation quickly and keep everyone protected.

I reach the scene and immediately place a hand on Angelo's arm, hoping to calm his agitation. He has a tendency to be a hothead, and I draw him closer to my side. Meanwhile, I gaze at the tall alien while wearing the politest, most welcoming smile I can muster.

"Greetings and salutations, sir," I say. "I'm Leona and I manage this bar. Who might you be?" I keep my voice level and carefree. If I sound or look scared, I'll appear guilty. We all will. I'm really hoping this Darrvason, whoever he is, doesn't go blabbing to the command team.

The alien growls and casts another glance toward the stage. "I am Officer Brute and I demand entry." He holds up the keycard he'd previously waved in Angelo's face. "I have full security clearance on this vessel, meaning I am permitted to go anywhere I wish." His gaze narrows on me. "Even illegal bars."

Well, he's just confirmed that he's familiar enough with our laws to know this place is an underground establishment. Still, as I stare up at him, I don't allow my smile to falter. "Well, Officer Brute, we are honored by your visit, and I do hope you'll sit down and enjoy a drink." I give him a playful wink.

Unfortunately, Angelo chooses this moment to act like an idiot. He stiffens and takes a menacing step toward the alien. "You need to leave. Now. This establishment serves humans only."

Officer Brute snarls and practically shoves his keycard, which I'm now realizing he must've used to open the door, rather than the secret knock, in Angelo's reddening face. A full-blown argument erupts, during which the alien threatens to rip Angelo's arms and legs off. Wonderful. Each time I attempt to get a word in, the males cut me off and my voice is drowned out by their spatting.

Jenny approaches and shoots Officer Brute a beseeching look. She glances at Angelo, then at me. "It's okay," she tells us. "I know this Darrvason." She grabs the alien's arm and pulls him toward a secluded table. I watch with curiosity as he takes a seat directly beside her.

"What the fuck are you doing? Why are you letting this scum into the bar?" Angelo hisses at me.

I grip his arm and lead him back to his post at the entrance. "We don't have much of a choice, do we? It's best to make him feel welcome and hope he keeps our secret. Promise me you'll behave."

We glare at each other for a few seconds until he finally nods, though he doesn't verbally promise to act cordial. I sigh and head for the bar where I'm quick to grab two large mugs of beer.

I approach the table where Jenny and Officer Brute are sitting. To my shock, the alien is gripping her leg underneath the table, and they appear engrossed in a tense exchange of words. Yes, clearly, they're well acquainted.

As I get closer, I glimpse a spark of heated possessiveness in the Darrvason's eyes. It reminds me of the way Zahhn looked at me during the examination, and I experience a sudden urge to depart the speakeasy to seek out an alcove with a viewscreen that faces the alien fleet. It's all I can do to keep my feet moving forward.

Then the oddest thing happens. *Lee-oon-ahh.* I swear I hear the high-handed doctor uttering my name. I also feel the vibration of his voice, yet when I glance around, he's nowhere to be seen. I concentrate on breathing steadily and putting one foot in front of the other, but it's honestly a challenge to remain upright. Because my entire body is trembling, and my knees feel abruptly weak.

I tell myself it's just my imagination getting the best of me, and the weird auditory hallucination was simply brought on by the sudden arrival of a huge Darrvason male who's similar in appearance to Zahhn, though noticeably younger.

As I attempt to ward off the strange occurrence, I force another polite smile and start humming a cheerful tune, hoping my relaxed demeanor will help ease the tension in the speakeasy.

I place the drinks on the table in front of Jenny and Officer Brute. "Compliments of the house." I wink, spin on my heel, and return to the bar.

Gradually, people start to look up from their drinks and the steady hum of conversation resumes. I exhale with relief, and I go back to drying the glasses, though I keep one eye on Jenny and her alien companion. When Jenny downs her beer and gestures for me to bring another, I'm quick to do so.

After a few minutes, Jenny and Officer Brute depart the speakeasy, and he appears to be escorting her out. My worry grows as I watch them leave. Does she have a choice? Has the alien taken a liking to her? It seems the most plausible explanation, and my heart goes out to her. Considering what happened to her sister, she's probably terrified right now.

In the days since my release from the brig, rumors about the Darrvasons have continued to swirl. Not all the worldship's security officers are loyal to the command team, and those who aren't like to talk. Apparently, the aliens are monogamous and claim one female each. It's also said that they mate for life and are quite possessive of their women.

Lee-oon-ahh.

Good little female.

I flush and start trembling as I hear it again. I place a hand to my head and rub my temple, but it doesn't make the rumble of Zahhn's voice fade. Not in the slightest.

What is happening?

Chapter 12

ZAHHN

Situated in my temporary quarters aboard the *Rorrsa*, I toss and turn in bed, trying to allow sleep to claim me. But my mind keeps drifting to Leona, making rest impossible. With each inhale, I can almost smell the sweet pungency of her arousal. I lift a hand toward the ceiling and feel as though I'm reaching for her dark silken hair. As I move my fingers, I swear I feel the softness of her wavy tresses.

Sweltering need seizes me, and I growl and sit up in bed. *Fluxx*. This is madness. How long has it been since I examined her? About sixteen days, perhaps. It's a struggle to count the days when I can't stop calling her lovely face to mind.

Her name echoes in my psyche, over and over. Eventually, I start uttering it aloud. It's a compulsion, one I'm hopeless to stop. "Leona. Leona. Good little female."

I hear a tiny gasp, and I peer around the darkened room, but I see no one. I'm alone. Of course I'm alone. It's the middle of the night. The scent of feminine excitement fills the air, and my dual shafts become hard as *Rullian* steel. My scrotum vibrates faster with each breath I take. I growl again, depart the bed, and hasten to the small viewscreen in my quarters.

My eyes instantly seek the *Jansonna*, which is situated on the edge of the Darrvason fleet, right next to the *Haxxal*. I can't help but wonder if Leona has spared me a thought since we parted. I know she's been released from the brig, for which I am relieved. I casually inquired about the human female patients, asking a guard who frequently protects Emperor Radakk for information. I couldn't bring myself to ask the emperor directly for fear that he would discern my true motives.

A snarl rips from my throat. What *are* my true motives? It's not as though I'm plotting to break the alliance by stealing away with Leona. I almost laugh at the idea. Me, a sterile but highly respected doctor and researcher, single handedly violating a treaty by absconding with a human female. Not just any human female, but the one I examined, the one who was briefly my patient.

The one I claimed after pushing Doctor Ammdox out of the way.

I groan and bang a fist on the viewscreen. I wasn't subtle in my attraction to Leona. Anyone who was present that day—my colleagues, the human doctors, the security officers, and *fluxxing* Commander Hampton —knows I felt possessive toward the female. If the emperor finds out, he'll likely increase his efforts to get me to accept a mate from among the two remaining waves of females.

I cannot fathom claiming any woman but Leona.

I yearn for her. I see her in my dreams each night, and it would seem I'm now sensing her presence during the waking hours too. The scent of her feminine arousal remains thick in the air, and I keep hearing her tiny gasps and moans.

Turning away from the viewscreen, I run a hand through my hair as I utter curses. How will I endure not seeing her at least one more time? The constant wanting of her is affecting my day-to-day life, making it difficult to concentrate on my important work, the trials I'm running to discover a cure for *forlonggsa*. I resolve that I must put her out of my mind. I must forget her.

I return to bed and get under the covers. Through sheer force of will, I banish all thoughts of Leona from my mind. I visualize an endless expanse of star-encrusted space interspersed with planets as I listen to the steady hum of the hyperdrive bubble that the entire fleet is traveling within.

Finally, I drift to sleep, ensconced in a vision of a beautiful galaxy.

But at some point, the stars fade, and the planets disappear. There's naught but darkness until… a small bedroom illuminates. Somehow, I know I'm on the *Jansonna*.

I approach the bed and notice it's not empty.

Leona. She's tucked beneath the covers, her eyes pressed shut, a look of concentration on her face.

There's movement under the covers near her crotch, and when her lips part on a gasp and the scent of her excitement thickens in the air, I nearly growl at the realization of what she's doing.

She's touching herself.

Shock rises alongside my dark satisfaction at having caught her in the midst of self-pleasure. I stand above her for some time, observing as her hand moves beneath the covers and her breathing increases.

Tiny whimpering moans keep escaping her throat, and she also occasionally lifts her hips as she gyrates against her hand. I imagine she's swirling moisture from her core overtop her pulsating clit, mimicking the very treatment I gave her as I'd brought her to a climax during her medical exam.

"Zahhn… oh, Zahhn."

My name. Star Gods, she's moaning my name.

My shafts harden further, and as I glance down I realize I'm only wearing sleeping shorts. But of course that's all I'm wearing. It's nighttime. I was in bed sleeping only moments ago, yet now I am here. In Leona's bedroom aboard the *Jansonna*.

Confusion grips me as I try to recall what transportation method I used to reach the human worldship —a transport vessel or the docking tunnel?—but I quickly push away the questions.

The details don't matter. All that matters is that we've been reunited.

I clear my throat, and Leona's eyes shoot open. She stares at me in shock, her lips parting on a soundless gasp. "What… how…" Her voice trails off and she shakes her head, as though she can't quite believe I'm here.

"Naughty little female." I cross my arms over my chest as I stand tall above her. "Do you have permission to touch yourself?"

Her face pinkens as she gulps in shaky breaths. She glances around the room and then sits up against the pillows, keeping the covers pulled up to her neck.

Is she naked beneath the sheets? I suppose I'll find out soon enough. And if she's wearing clothing? I'll *fluxxing* rip it off.

"I asked a question and I expect an answer." I step closer to her. "Do you have permission to touch yourself?"

Her wide eyes sparkle with disbelief, but I also catch a glimmer of shame. Yet she lifts her chin in a defiant manner and says, "No, but I don't need anyone's permission. What are you doing here? How did you get inside my bedroom?"

I sink down on the bed beside her, grab the sheets, and wrench the fabric from her hands. She makes a squeak of protest, then shields her breasts with her hands. I allow the covers to rest at her waist. For now. I tilt my head to the side, studying her loveliness. She's adorably flushed and breathless, and so very guilty.

Drawing in a long breath, I savor the scent of her arousal. "If you were my mate, you would not be permitted to touch yourself in my absence. Not without explicit permission." I reach out and stroke a hand through her hair, luxuriating in the softness, as well as the tiny whimper she makes as I finally touch her.

"But I'm not your mate. Therefore, I can do as I please." Though her words are brave, she cannot hide the tremor in her voice. The shakiness that betrays her nervousness.

I tangle my fingers in her hair and give a slight tug, causing her head to tilt back and exposing a tantalizing expanse of her neck. The urge to kiss her there prevails, and as I hold her in place, I lean down to trail my lips over her flesh. She stiffens and attempts to pull away, but I tighten my grip on her hair.

"Perhaps a demonstration is in order. Perhaps I should show you how a Darrvason male would deal with a female who touches herself without permission." A growl vibrates through me, and I revel in the quick intake of her breath even as she tries to shake her head.

"You have no right to be here. I demand you leave at once." As she trembles, the scent of her excitement becomes stronger, so pungent and sweet that I almost grow delirious as I take long inhales of the enticing aroma.

I lean back and capture her gaze. Defiance continues to flicker in her dark eyes. Training. She needs training. If she's to become my mate, I must teach her to serve and obey me.

Yes, there are many reasons I should leave. Many reasons I shouldn't claim her, including the strict terms of the alliance. Yet I cannot resist, and deep in my soul I know she'll belong to me before the night is over.

I will mount her and ride her to completion.

I resume tearing the covers off her. She gasps and tries to grab them, but I succeed in hurling the covers to the floor, out of her reach. An outraged gasp leaves her, and she pushes at my chest, but I don't budge. Doesn't she realize I'm not going anywhere? I'm here to stake my claim on the female who consumes my thoughts.

Desire scorches me as I glimpse her nearly unclothed body. She's only wearing a small covering over her nether area, practically a scrap of fabric. I reach for the undergarment, slipping my fingers into the crotch area, then give a sharp tug. The sound of fabric shredding combines with more shocked gasps.

"That's much better." I grin at her as I toss the remnants of her undergarment to the floor. "Now, lie back and spread your legs, little female, and show me how wet you've become while touching yourself."

She sucks in a quick breath, and her face reddens further. "I will do no such thing."

When she attempts to flee, I grab her arms and hold her in place, not allowing her to leave the bed. I make a noise of disapproval deep in my throat, and I'm pleased when she finally ceases her struggles.

Fear gleams in her eyes, and an almost violent tremor racks her petite body. "Please," she whispers. "Please let me go."

A frustrated growl emits from my chest, and I tighten my hold on her face. The pull between us feels stronger than ever, and my ancestral markings won't stop tingling. Surely it's a sign that we're meant to be together. A sign that I'm meant to claim her.

"You're mine, Leona." Still holding her face, I press my lips to hers, overcome with the need to taste her. To devour her and conquer her no matter how fervently she protests. As I kiss her, the scent of her arousal invigorates my senses, causing my shafts to throb harder and my scrotum to vibrate faster.

She gives a tiny moan, and then her lips part. I sweep my tongue inside to tangle with hers. *Mine mine mine. My mate.* It doesn't take long for her to surrender to the roughness of my kiss, and I pour all my need into her as I clutch her face.

When I finally break away, she's so breathless that her chest is heaving, which naturally draws my gaze to her bosom. Her nipples are hard and ripe, and I reach out to trace one of those stiff peaks, gently circling it with my thumb. She whimpers and arches into my touch.

At some point during the kiss when she ceased struggling, I'd released her arms. But as I touch her, she doesn't make a move to shield her breasts or her pussy. She also makes no move to push me away. Instead, she rests against the pillows, trying to regulate her breathing as she stares at me with an increasingly heated expression.

"You're mine." I caress her hair. "Do you understand?"

Though a small glimmer of fear remains in her eyes, she gives a subtle nod and leans into my touch. Her eyes flutter shut, and she releases a satisfied sigh.

"Spread your legs for me, little female," I say with a growl. "Show me how wet you are."

Chapter 13

LEONA

He's here. In my bedroom. I don't know how it's possible, how he managed to board the *Jansonna* and find me, but *he's here*.

My pussy aches and I can't seem to catch my breath. He's watching me carefully, waiting to see if I'll obey his order to spread my legs. My face flames with embarrassment. Not only did he catch me pleasuring myself, but he probably heard me moaning his name as well. I was touching myself while thinking about him and he knows it.

His eyes darken, his expression becoming stern, and I sense he's growing impatient. Though I'm hesitant to reveal the extent of my arousal to him, I know I don't have a choice. If I refuse, he'll likely punish me. Then he'll force my legs apart and discover the moisture that's gathered in my core. He'll see how swollen my clit is too.

I inhale a shaky breath and lean back further on the pillows. Slowly, cognizant of his unblinking gaze, I bend my knees slightly and spread my thighs. A glance down shows I'm soaking wet, and I flush as a satisfied growl rumbles from his massive frame. His nostrils flare as he leans closer to my center, and his eyes shine brighter.

He's shirtless, and oh what a perfect body he has. His muscles are huge and perfectly defined, and his upper chest is covered in glowing blue symbols. Tattoos, I guess. I study the markings, wondering what they mean.

My eyes drift lower to the colossal bulge in his thin black shorts. As I stare openly at his crotch, I think I glimpse a vibration, and when I hold my breath, I swear I can feel it. I swallow hard as nerves assail me.

Though I'm familiar with carnal pleasure, thanks to the thorough medical exam Zahhn gave me, I've never actually had sex before. Sure, he penetrated me with the metallic phalluses, but I'm not entirely certain what to expect.

What will happen if he claims me? Will he take me back to his ship? Will he keep me as his mate forever? Though I'm aching for his touch, I can't help but worry about what will come later. Despite my intense attraction to Zahhn, I can't imagine leaving my life on the *Jansonna* behind. Troubled ship or not, this is my home and I'm reluctant to say goodbye.

But as I become lost in the alien doctor's heated purple gaze, I also find myself mourning the prospect of being parted from him. There's a sharp tug inside me whenever I look at him, a flowing of power and emotion that feels like a tether between our hearts. A preposterous thought, maybe, but it's the only way I can describe it.

He scoots closer to my spread center and places his hands on either side of my inner thighs, forcing me to part my legs wider. The cool air in the room wafts across my exposed nether parts, and I tremble with need as I await his touch.

Surely he'll reach for my clit and stroke it. Surely he won't allow me to suffer much longer.

I suppress a whimper as I debate whether to beg him for relief. He'd caught me just when I hovered on the edge of a climax, and I'm still on edge. Still aching and quivering for the euphoria I was only seconds away from reaching.

"You're soaking, little female." He delves a finger through my folds, and I buck my center upward as my clit pulses harder. "So wet and so very naughty."

Before I can respond, he rises briefly only to lower himself to the bed and situate his head between my legs. At first, I think he simply wants a closer look at my nether parts, but then his head dips further and he starts lapping at my aching pussy.

For a few seconds, I'm utterly frozen with shock. I stare down at him, not quite believing what he's doing.

As he drags his tongue over my spread center, his growls of pleasure reverberate through me, causing my core to clench under a fresh wave of heated desire.

He focuses on my clit, circling this sensitive part of

me with increasing pressure. Quaking waves of bliss consume me, and I finally shift in place and gyrate against his mouth as a deep moan leaves me.

Oh God. Oh yes.

When he'd mentioned claiming me, I'd expected him to immediately shove one of his male appendages into my pussy. I hadn't anticipated sensual play before the physical act of coitus.

He lifts his mouth from my nether area and shoots me a taunting grin. My arousal gleams on his lips, and while he doesn't seem to care, I still flush at the sight. I'm unable to control my urges and I'm making a mess.

All the bad things I've heard about fornication suddenly resurface in my mind, and though I'm aching and desperate for a release, I reach down and attempt to shield my center from Zahhn. I glance toward the door, convinced morality officers are going to storm into my bedroom at any moment and drag me back to the brig. But the door never opens. I remain alone with the alien doctor who seems intent on taking his time with me.

He doesn't try to move my hands aside like I'm expecting. Instead, he gives me a scolding look, shakes his head in a very human gesture of disappointment, and delivers a firm smack to the inside of my left thigh.

"Oh!" I jolt upward and make to jump off the bed, but he maneuvers me back in place, propped against the pillows with my knees slightly bent and my legs spread wide enough to make my muscles ache. He also forces my hands to rest at my sides.

"I know you're hovering on the brink of a climax, little female. Be obedient and remain still as I tend to your nether parts. If you try to cover yourself again or attempt escape, I will take you over my knee and punish you. You don't want a spanking, do you?"

I whimper. "Please. What we're doing… it's not proper. Fornication is dangerous. You might cause permanent damage to me, or we could both become ill, or I could get pregnant."

He tenses, and a shadow crosses his face. He delivers another swat to my left inner thigh, then proceeds to smack the right one. I hiss in pain and writhe beneath him, wishing I were strong enough to throw him off.

But he's so much larger than me, and he's built of solid muscle. I don't stand a chance against him in a physical fight, and nerves twist in my lower stomach even as the heated pulses in my pussy come faster. He scares me, but he also excites me in ways I don't quite understand.

"You will *not* become pregnant." He practically barks the words at me. His sudden agitation fills me with dejection, and I tear my eyes from his, unable to hold his gaze. He utters a few words under his breath in the Darrvason tongue, and I suspect he might be cursing.

To my surprise, he leans down and places a gentle kiss on each of my inner thighs, directly over the areas he just smacked.

Feeling a tug on the tether I imagine links us, I chance a look at him. His eyes flash with remorse, but only briefly. I sense a secret hovering between us, something dark from his past. I want to ask him about it, but I can't seem to find the words. What if he doesn't feel the tether?

"I am sorry I shouted at you, little female." He sighs and caresses my thighs, rubbing gentle circles over the areas he just spanked and kissed. In a much calmer voice than before, he repeats, "You will not become pregnant. As for illness or permanent damage to your body… well, I promise that won't happen either. You successfully accepted both metallic phalluses during your examination, and I am confident you can withstand the rigors of a mating session with me."

His words help settle the worst of my nervousness, and I find myself relaxing back on the pillows. His expression is earnest and truthful, and the tug between us feels like a constant flow of affection. It's overwhelming, but I can't claim I don't like it.

For the first time in my life, I don't feel adrift and alone. I don't feel the need to put on airs and act like I'm confident even when I'm not. With Zahhn, I can simply… *be*. Tears burn in my eyes, but I'm quick to blink them away.

"Good little female," he says in a praising tone. Then he dips his head between my thighs again and circles in on my clit. A gasping cry erupts from my throat when he prods my aching entrance.

He slips two, or perhaps three, thick digits into my core, gliding in and out as he brings me to the precipice of ecstasy.

A second later, I tumble into an abyss of pulsating sensation. I moan as the waves of pleasure crash over me, writhing on the bed as Zahhn continues his assault on my clit and doesn't slow the thrusts of his fingers into my aching chasm. Dark spots cloud my vision and dizziness grips me, and I finally close my eyes as I gasp for breath.

After the final ebbing pulse fades, Zahhn withdraws his digits from my core and sits upright on the bed. Satisfaction brims in his eyes, and he gives me what could almost be considered a playful look just before he wipes his mouth on the back of his arm, removing the glimmer of my arousal from his lips.

My heart skips a beat as I stare up at him. Zahhn. Is he truly about to claim me? Is he about to make me his mate? I remember the rumors I've heard about his people's mating practices. Darrvasons mate for life. In his culture, there's no separation. No divorce. Mating means forever.

It's a scary prospect because despite my attraction to him, and the intense pull of whatever strange force has linked our hearts, the truth is that I don't know him well. He might possess a cruel side. A dark side. I don't like the thought of being trapped. I swallow past the abrupt dryness in my throat as I await his next move, expecting him to pounce on me at any moment.

A glance at his crotch shows his appendages are about to burst out of his shorts. I don't know what it means that his shafts have gotten larger since he first appeared in my bedroom, nor do I understand the vibrations coming from that area of his body.

He rises to his feet and takes a few steps away from the bed, and I can't help but admire his huge muscular body. His dark, textured skin gleams under the overhead lights, and the tattoos covering his chest glow brighter.

He tenses and his nostrils flare as he inhales a few deep breaths.

As a low growl rumbles from his throat, he removes his shorts, and his massive cocks spring free. He meets my eyes and points to the floor. "On your knees, Leona. I'm going to teach you how to properly suck my male appendages."

Chapter 14

ZAHHN

Leona rises from the bed on shaky legs. I watch her intently, prepared to catch her should she fall. But she soon straightens and appears steadier. Her eyes widen and fill with nervousness, however, when she peers down at my erect shafts. Her legs start trembling again, but she's quick to sink down on her knees before me.

But I didn't anticipate the difference in our bodies. My crotch is much higher than her head while she's kneeling. I walk around her and retrieve two pillows from the bed, place them on the floor in front of her, and help her move to a kneeling position on the pillows. Satisfied that she's now elevated enough to reach my shafts, I stand in front of her again, so close that my cocks are almost brushing her lips.

I nearly growl when her warm breath caresses my

appendages. *Fluxx*, it's going to be ecstasy when she finally takes one of my cocks in her mouth. I grasp my upper shaft and guide it toward her lips.

"Open," I say in a commanding tone. When it comes to training her, I will not be lenient. If she resists, she will pay a steep price for her disobedience.

My palms tingle as I imagine taking her over my knee and smacking her bottom until it's bright red and she's writhing in pain and begging for mercy. My appendages jolt with a surge of pleasure.

"Your shafts, um, are a bit larger than the metallic ones you used on me during the examination." She studies my larger-than-average cocks as a tremor rushes through her body. She gulps hard.

"And yet you will endure," I say with finality. Though I realize she's apprehensive, I won't allow her to stall for a moment longer. "Open and take me in your mouth, Leona. If I must ask again, you will not like the outcome."

She shifts on the pillows and tilts her pretty face upward. I catch a flash of trepidation in her eyes just before she parts her lips and leans closer to my upper appendage. Her nervous whimpers pulse through me as she struggles to take my erect member in her mouth. The feel of her lips closing around my shaft makes me momentarily dizzy. I groan and clutch her head, hold her in place, and jut my center forward, ramming deeper. When she gags as I hit the back of her throat, I pause in my movements, but I don't withdraw from her mouth.

"Not only are you about to learn how to properly

suck my appendages, but you will also learn to swallow my seed." I pat her cheek as she peers upward with wide eyes, though she can't quite meet my gaze because I won't release my hold on her head. She tries to speak around my cock, but her words end up muffled. "Perhaps it will help you to know a Darrvason male's essence is highly nutritious. If we were stranded together in a desolate place, you could survive on nothing but my seed." I chuckle as she whimpers around my cock.

Arrogant ass. I startle as I hear her voice in my head. But that's impossible. She's a human, and I'm Darrvason. Even if I rut her and claim her fully, we could never share a heartbond, the kind of mating bond that would result in a mind-connection. An analysis of human DNA verified that traditional Darrvason mating bonds are not able to form. Though I didn't personally conduct the analysis, I studied the work of my colleagues and determined their methods were sound. I must've only imagined Leona's voice in my head. That is the only explanation.

I withdraw from her mouth partially, then glide forward, once again nudging the back of her throat. I endeavor to be gentler this time, however, and I'm pleased when she doesn't gag. The little noises she makes pulse through my cock and cause my scrotum to vibrate faster.

Heated desire sweeps through me, the fervent need to mount the human female and make her mine. Soon, I promise myself. Though I long to plunge both my appendages deep in her womanly core, the feel of her mouth is delicious, and I'm hesitant to pause her lesson in cock sucking when she's doing such a good job. She's not exactly eager, but she's making an honest effort, and *fluxx* I'm so close to erupting down her slender throat that I can't fathom stopping now.

"Good little female." I stroke a hand through her hair, petting her as she continues sucking my upper shaft. Meanwhile, my hard lower length drags alongside her neck. As soon as I spurt down her throat, I'll instruct her to suck my unspent cock. By the time I'm finished with this lesson, her stomach will be filled with a copious amount of my seed.

The scent of her increasing arousal prompts me to plunge faster and deeper in her throat. Her whimpers and moans and occasional distressed squeaks send me over the edge, and my growls reverberate off the walls as I erupt in her mouth.

"Remember to swallow all that I give you." I tighten my hand in her hair. "Gulp it down like an obedient little female." More spurts of my essence spill down her throat, and she manages to swallow every last drop. "Very, very good. You have pleased me greatly, Leona." I withdraw from her mouth and cup the side of her face, brushing my thumb along the softness of her cheek.

She sucks in a series of deep breaths and collapses on the mound of pillows. She places her hands on the floor and peers up, casting a dubious glance at my lower appendage, which is raging hard and ready to be sucked. "You can't be serious," she whispers.

"Back on your knees," I command. "You still have work to do." I grasp the base of my lower appendage, the largest of my two shafts, and give her an expectant look. "Just remember, you will have one job as my mate: To serve and obey."

Lucky me.

There it is again. Her voice in my head.

Shock ripples through me when my ancestral markings start to tingle. What is happening? Stunned to my core, I stare at Leona as she sighs and returns to her previous position, settling on her knees with her back straight and her face angled upward to receive my cock.

Wet. Oh God, I'm going to leave a damp spot on this blasted pillow. Achy. I'm so achy. Why can't I stop craving him? Will he touch me again? Will he grant me another release?

Fluxx. Am I going mad? Or am I actually hearing her thoughts? I resolve to reevaluate my colleagues' findings regarding the probability of Darrvason-human heartbond formation. Perhaps they made a mistake when they analyzed the DNA samples.

A growl rumbles from my throat as the pretty human parts her lips slightly. Possessive thoughts consume me. *Mine. My female. My beautiful mate.*

"How obedient you are, Leona." I stroke her hair and angle my cock closer to her mouth. "Awaiting a second nourishment session while on your knees like a good little female."

She blushes and whimpers as I grasp her head. Applying pressure to her parted lips, I plunge into her mouth and immediately strike the back of her throat. *Fluxx*. I can't help but be rough this time. I'm ravenously eager to watch her suck my lower appendage, and I'm thrilled by the idea of filling her stomach with my seed again.

Still gripping her face, I commence a rapid drive in and out of her mouth. Though she gags on occasion, I don't show her any gentleness. Not this time.

My vibrating scrotum smacks against her chin and neck with each harsh thrust. Her keening moans and urgent whimpers cause my blood to heat further. I tighten my grip on her hair, holding her in place as I fuck her pretty human mouth.

Star Gods, the aroma of her arousal tantalizes my senses and prompts me to plunge faster and deeper into her mouth. She moans around my shaft, grabs hold of my legs, and digs her nails into my flesh. *Fluxx*, I'm so close to erupting in her mouth… I slow my thrusts for a few moments and take deep breaths, not wanting to ejaculate down her throat just yet.

A glance down shows her cheeks are bulging with the invasion in her mouth, and the sight of her struggling to accept my lower appendage, whether the plunges are rapid or moderately paced, nearly does me in.

Fluxx. I pause my movements, though I remain fully submerged in her mouth, my scrotum pressed snugly against her chin and neck. I pet her hair, gently dragging my fingers through her soft locks. Somehow, I sense she derives comfort from the caressing. It's as though I can sense her emotions, which is another aspect of a heartbond.

I reach out with my heart and mind, searching for fragments of her thoughts and feelings, searching for any concrete proof that a traditional Darrvason heartbond might be forming between us. We haven't physically copulated yet, and I'm stunned that my ancestral markings are continuing to tingle.

Affection brims in my soul as I stroke Leona's dark hair. She draws in a deep breath through her nose and peeks upward. Our eyes meet and my chest tightens with tenderness for her. But my brutish carnal urges remain steadfast even alongside these gentler feelings. Arrogant and beastly. I bite back a smile as I recall the insults she'd hurled at me during her medical exam.

Gradually, I withdraw from her mouth nearly the entire way, then I plunge back inside. Her moans and whimpers vibrate around my cock. I shut my eyes and snarl as the ecstasy quakes through me.

Is it *wrong* for me to claim her? I suppress a groan of frustration as the question zips through my mind. Is it wrong for me to claim her when I cannot impregnate her? And what about the terms of the Darrvason-human alliance?

The blissful sensation of having Leona's lips wrapped around my cock soon helps drown out these worries. Each time my shaft impacts with the back of her throat, my subsequent growl or moan reverberates throughout the room.

There's a sudden cascade of pleasure, then my scrotum tightens and I erupt in her mouth, shooting my seed down her throat as she struggles to swallow. I tighten my grip on her hair, thrusting deep as jets of my blue essence fill her.

Nourishment. I'm nourishing her, just as the males of my kind did for their mates thousands of years ago during a time of great famine. Warmth tinged with possessiveness spreads through me. I want to wrap my arms around Leona in a tender embrace, but I also want to bend her over the bed and rut her until she's so sore she's begging me to stop.

I finish spurting into her mouth and watch as she succeeds in swallowing every last drop. "Good little female." I loosen my grip on her hair and run my knuckles down her cheek as my more primal urges rise to the surface, nearly blocking out the tenderness I'd just felt. "Listen to me very carefully, human. I desire to see how swollen and wet your mating orifice has become." I pause and give her a pointed look. "I want you to bend over the bed, reach back to grasp your buttocks, and draw your center wide apart. You are to keep holding yourself spread until I say otherwise."

Chapter 15

LEONA

I PEER UP AT ZAHHN, STUNNED BY HIS ORDERS. THE sweet taste of his seed lingers on my tongue, and I flush with excitement as I recall how rapidly he'd just plunged his massive shafts into my mouth. There's a twinge of soreness in the back of my throat whenever I swallow, and I can't deny that I already feel thoroughly claimed by him.

And yet… he wants to look at my spread center. My mating orifice. Likely because he's preparing to impale me with his male appendages.

Copulation. My stomach abruptly twists. But not because he disgusts me and I'm averse to fornicating with him, but because I still harbor concerns that we'll be found out. What if morality officers burst into my bedroom and we're caught in the act? What then? Will

Zahhn be sent back to his ship? Will I be taken to the brig?

Or… could we truly become mates?

There's a part of me that's terrified of the prospect of belonging to a Darrvason. But there's another part of me that yearns to experience more of the connection I already feel with Zahhn.

I draw in a deep breath and glance at the bed. My face heats as I imagine bending over, grasping my buttocks, and pulling my center wide for his inspection.

Comply. Be an obedient female.

I gasp. There's no mistaking what I just heard: Zahhn's deep rumbling voice in my head.

Even as I struggle to understand what's happening, my upper arms commence itching full force and a wave of submission crashes over me. Despite my reluctance to assume the embarrassing position, there's a growing compulsion in me to acquiesce to the huge alien's orders.

As I rise on trembling legs, I tell myself that the only reason I'm about to comply is because I want to avoid punishment. A quiver races across my backside. It's been about two weeks since he spanked me during my shameful examination, but I haven't forgotten the sting of his flattened palm descending on my bottom cheeks.

Somehow, I find myself standing at the foot of the bed. Zahhn stares at me unblinkingly and gives a subtle nod. His nostrils flare and he inhales deeply as pleasure flares in his eyes. I emit a tiny squeak of surprise as I realize what he's doing. He's smelling my arousal, the wetness between my thighs that I cannot prevent.

A smirk tugs at his lips. "You smell delicious, human female." He tilts his head to the side and his visage takes on a predatory look.

My gaze soon falls to his appendages, however, and I can't hold back a gasp. Both his enormous shafts are fully erect again, and it's only been a minute or so since he spurted down my throat for a second time. As I continue staring at his male parts, I think about the curious vibrations I felt coming from his scrotum.

How will it feel when this vibrating part of him comes into direct contact with my aching center? Just the mere thought of it causes a spasm of heat to clench in my nether area.

He makes an impatient sound in his throat, and I experience a tug of emotion in my chest. It's the tether, the pull between us. I swear I can feel his dominance as he compels me to obey. Somehow, I become aware that he's not usually a patient male, but he is trying to rein in his annoyance over my failure to comply with his orders immediately.

I begin to lower myself to the bed, bending over as I maneuver my feet a few steps apart. I rest my forearms on the covers and brace myself for the next part. The difficult part.

Not only does he expect me to reveal my wet, swollen center to him, but he wants me to keep holding myself spread until he says otherwise.

How long will I be required to hold the humiliating position?

Good little female. His voice invades my head again. *You're almost there. Just reach back and draw your buttocks apart.*

Be obedient or I will give you a firm thrashing before I ram my shafts into your mating orifice, one after the other.

I gulp hard, noting that my throat is still sore from the rough face pounding he gave me, and the sweetness of his seed yet lingers on my tongue.

Dammit. I need to obey him. I need to reach around, grasp my butt cheeks, and spread myself wide. If I don't, he'll make me regret my insubordination.

He moves around the bed to stand behind me. I know he's staring. I know he's watching and waiting. I whimper as I start inching my arms back. Once I grasp a cheek in each hand, I take a deep calming breath, then I gradually begin spreading my center wide.

"Very good." His tone is praising, and though I'm utterly embarrassed by what he's making me do, I cannot help the rush of excitement that flows through me. The thrill that comes from knowing I've pleased him.

I bask under the feeling and find myself drawing my cheeks wider apart without any additional prompting. The cool air in the room drifts over my unprotected nether parts, heightening my sense of exposure. I hold my breath as I await Zahhn's next move.

The warmth of his body suffuses mine, though he's not touching me yet. I feel his eyes on my pussy, and my face grows warm when I realize my bottom hole is exposed too. As I remain in the uncomfortable position, my core keeps pulsating with need and my asshole occasionally clenches as though anticipating an intrusion.

Look at that. She's aching to be filled up.

She's aching for my appendages.

Hot and flustered, practically feverish, I wait for Zahhn to drag his long, thick fingers through my drenched folds. If he rubs circles over my clit, I'm certain I'll shatter in a heartbeat. Desire swells inside me and I'm mortified when my hips suddenly gyrate against the bed. I didn't mean to make the indecent movement, it simply happened.

I sense a dark chuckle emanating from the Darrvason male, though I don't hear it aloud. But I'm not as surprised as I was the first few times I heard his voice in my head. I suppose this connection we share has been developing for some time. After all, I've been hearing his voice and sensing his masculine presence for about two weeks now.

Of course, there's also the dreams. The dreams started before I ever met Zahhn, as did my fascination with the Darrvason fleet.

Fated. It's as though we're fated to belong to one another.

It's a scary thought, and I instinctively rebel against it. I never planned to marry or belong to anyone, but I cannot surmise another explanation for the strange occurrences involving Zahhn.

Is there a way to make it stop? A way to push the high-handed alien doctor to take another human female? Guilt settles over me when I consider making Zahhn another woman's problem. But alongside the guilt, there's also a surge of white-hot jealousy. I try to ignore it, try to pretend it's not a real emotion. Yet it burns through my insides.

A jolt of pleasure hits me, and I gasp with relief.

He's finally touching me. His steady growls echo off the bedroom walls as he drags moisture from my core atop my pulsing clit. Oh yes. More please.

I lurch upward on my toes as my hips undulate again. Pleasure cascades outward from my center, a constant throbbing bliss that leaves me breathless and quivering in place.

Anticipation skitters through me. When will he claim me? How rough will he be? My pussy keeps clenching, and I can't help but wonder if maybe he's right. Maybe I am aching to be filled up.

Just as I hover on the edge of a climax, he abandons my nubbin and I feel him step back. I whimper and peer over my shoulder, only to notice he's still focused on my spread center. As he stares hungrily at my nether parts, his shafts remain hugely erect, and his nostrils flare whenever he takes a deep breath.

Her bottom hole is so tiny yet enticing. Fluxx, *how I long to thrust an appendage into that delightful pucker of hers. I will train her. Yes, I will train her to withstand the rigors of an ass fucking so she can eventually accommodate my dual shafts at the same time—one cock in her wet mating orifice, and the other in her snug little asshole.*

His thoughts shock me, and I'm tempted to announce that I'll refuse any such training. But then I consider the advantages of knowing his thoughts. I don't think he can hear mine. If he could, surely he would've already made an arrogant comment about it, especially considering I've called him a few choice names in my head.

Okay, fine, I won't tell him. It'll be a secret, one that

will hopefully help me remain one step ahead. Despite my immense attraction to him and the warmth he fills me with, when he's not pissing me off that is, I still don't trust him. How can I trust a male I've known for such a short time?

Just when I think about jumping out of position and attempting to flee the bedroom, he taps one of my hands. "You may let go of your bottom cheeks now, little female. I will take over and keep you spread to my liking."

I release my grip and return to my previous position, resting on my forearms, my hands grasping the covers for support. My arms tingle and itch, momentarily distracting me. I resist the urge to scratch and keep holding the covers.

Expectation surges inside me, the desperate need for him to assuage the fervent aching in my core. I suck in deep breaths and await his next move even as I contemplate escape.

In the end, I don't bolt off the bed. My legs are trembling too hard to make it very far. He would no doubt catch me before I reached the door.

He takes my bottom cheeks, one in each hand, and draws them wide apart. I flush as the cool air once again caresses my nether parts and makes me aware of my total exposure. He presses the tip of one appendage to my wet center. I gasp and tense, and all rational thought flees my mind.

He drags his cock up and down through my moisture, coating his shaft in my arousal. Each time he touches my clit, my hips jerk on the bed as I gyrate wantonly against his huge erect member. Though his scrotum isn't touching me, the vibrations still travel through his cock, causing waves of pulsating heat to steal through me. Pleasure coils in my nether region, and I cannot seem to catch my breath.

"You're mine, Leona. Mine."

He gives a sudden thrust, and then he's inside me, filling me up with a massive appendage. For a few moments, I stop breathing entirely as I attempt to come to terms with the intrusion. He's larger than the metallic shafts he used on me during the examination, and it's a struggle to accept the entirety of him. I can't be certain, but I think he's only about halfway submerged in my depths.

I'm about to protest, I'm about to announce he'll never fit, when he tightens his grip on my spread cheeks and plunges forward. I gasp as his vibrating scrotum finally presses directly to my center.

Oh God. The vibrations to my clit. The coiling pleasure tightens and then snaps, and I cry out as a climax sweeps over me, pulsing through me as my insides clamp down on his cock. He remains still inside me as I gasp and whimper during the throes of the thunderous release.

Good little female. That's it. Climax while the largest of my appendages is buried deep in your tight mating orifice.

My mind reels. I wasn't certain which of his shafts he'd just shoved inside me, but apparently it was the biggest one. As I fill my lungs with air, this knowledge brings me a bit of relief. Because he hasn't split me in two yet, and if I've managed the largest shaft, I'll be able to endure a second pounding with his unspent member. Assuming that's how this plays out.

I've never copulated with a Darrvason before but given that he spurted down my throat twice in quick succession, I assume he'll give the same treatment to my pussy. I try to remember if he's ever told me how our first mating session would go, but my thoughts remain so scattered in the aftermath of my quivering climax that I cannot think clearly.

"Brace yourself, little female." His fingers dig into my flesh. "I'm about to ride you hard. This tight, wet orifice of yours will soon be sore and dripping with my seed."

Chapter 16

ZAHHN

Fluxx. Leona's mating orifice is exceedingly tight, but she's managed to accept my entire shaft—the largest of my dual appendages. Though I hover on the verge of a lust-crazed rutting session, ready to commence thrusting in and out of her almost violently, the same tenderness I've felt for her before swells in my chest.

Dark spots cloud my vision as I slowly withdraw from her pussy. I'm struggling to restrain myself, attempting to tamp down my most barbaric urges. While I have no qualms about rutting her until she's sore between her thighs, I don't want to damage her during our first mating. Even if I'm a physician and I could easily repair the damage, I find myself wanting to earn her trust, find myself thinking about how it's my duty as her mate to take care of her always.

I draw in several deep breaths and wait for my vision

to clear. Then I gradually plunge my cock back into her depths, until I'm once again fully submerged in the exquisite tightness of her slick center. I build a steady thrusting motion, in and out, while she trembles and whimpers beneath me. She lifts her center to meet my drives on occasion, and whenever my vibrating scrotum impacts with her center, I can briefly feel her engorged clit.

I release one of her cheeks and stroke a hand gently down her back, seeking to connect with her on an emotional level. I feel her soften beneath my caresses, and though I don't hear it aloud, I sense her release a long, contented sigh. If I hadn't already heard her voice in my head multiple times, I might say it was a strange occurrence. But it would seem something profound is transpiring between us. Whether it's the beginning stages of a heartbond, I cannot say.

Mating fever, I remind myself. Though I'm sweltering with desire, I'm not out of my mind with the mating fever that strikes a Darrvason male during the formation of a heartbond. I'm still able to form semi-coherent thoughts as I continue driving in and out of Leona's moist chasm.

My scrotum vibrates harder, and I increase the pace of my thrusts, until the sound of flesh slapping flesh fills the room. *Take it. Take my lower appendage like an obedient little female.* With each deep plunge, my upper shaft drags across her bottom cheeks, and I once again find myself staring at her puckering hole. Soon. Soon I will commence training her ass to accommodate my upper shaft, then I will be able to fuck both her orifices at the same time. My blood heats further at the prospect.

I cease stroking her back and resume gripping her buttocks hard, forcing her cheeks wider apart as I drive into her tight depths.

Mine. My female.

Though I would like to draw this experience out, I'm eager to fill her mating orifice with my seed, and I don't hold back when the waves of pleasure start descending. Instead, I fuck her faster. Harder. I growl as I give her the savage rutting I'd promised her.

Then I erupt in her depths in quaking torrents. My animalistic roar reverberates off the walls, a sound I didn't know I was capable of making, as my desire for the human female culminates in a shuddering release that leaves me panting for breath.

As the final gush of seed erupts from my shaft, suddenly her insides contract around my plunging length, and she cries out in the throes of her own climax.

Fluxx. How extraordinary, how thrilling, this first mating session of ours.

I sense her intense need, followed by relief as the orgasm quakes through her. I also sense her blissful satisfaction as she grows still on the bed.

Keeping my gaze on her nether area, I carefully withdraw my lower appendage from her depths. I hold her spread wide, and I observe, utterly enthralled, as my blue essence trickles out of her slick pink core.

Seeing her marked with my seed causes an intense wave of possessiveness to seize me. A fresh surge of desire pummels me, and my upper shaft hardens further. Ready to impale her with my unspent cock, I nudge the tip of my throbbing member inside her.

Her gasps and whimpers delight me, as does the immense wetness in her core. Most of my seed has already trickled out of her, but she's becoming slick all over again, my eager little mate.

Mate. The full impact of what's occurring between us abruptly hits me. I'm breaking the terms of the alliance, while she's breaking the laws of her people simply by fornicating. The illicitness of our coupling adds a measure of excitement to the deed, and I give a quick thrust and seat myself fully inside her.

She's grasping the covers so hard her knuckles have turned white, and every now and then, as I remain buried in her tightness, she writhes beneath me and gyrates her center.

I grip her hips as my need for her rises, and I commence ramming into her with abandon. My growls mingle with the sound of flesh slapping flesh and her urgent moans and whimpers. The scent of her arousal becomes so thick in the air that I can almost taste the sweetness on my tongue.

When she cries out and her insides start contracting around my plunging shaft, I fall into the abyss of pleasure with her. For a second time this evening, I erupt in her tight, slick depths, spurt after pulsating spurt, until I'm finally spent.

Breathless and dizzy, I withdraw my cock from her center and once again hold her spread wide so I might watch my seed gush out of her core. Her inner thighs gleam with a mixture of her own arousal and my blue essence.

A sort of peace settles over me, taking me aback. It's done. She's mine. Come morning, there will be a reckoning as my people are forced to deal with the violation of the Darrvason-human alliance.

According to the treaty, Darrvason males aren't permitted to claim any human females outside the bounds of the alliance. Women who aren't in one of the three groups specifically handed over to my people are considered untouchable.

I lift Leona from the bed and cradle her in my arms. She peers up at me, beautifully flushed, her hair in disarray. My chest tightens and my heart skips a beat as we stare into one another's eyes. The ancestral markings covering my chest tingle more intensely than ever before.

Suddenly, all I can think about is sharing a bed with her. Sleeping with her sheltered in my arms. Whenever I awake in the night, I'll find her right there, pressed close to my body.

Affection brims in my soul and there's a fleeting moment during which I sense warmth flowing *from her.* It's a strange but not unwelcome experience, and I soak it up and pray to the Star Gods that a traditional Darrvason heartbond will eventually form between us. One that will allow us to always sense one another's thoughts and emotions.

Leona covers a huge yawn, and her eyes twinkle as she holds my gaze. "You wore me out."

I grin. "I won't apologize for it. For the rest of our

lives, I intend to thoroughly exhaust you before bed each night. And let's not forget: There's not a rule that we can't copulate during the daytime hours as well." My grin widens. "As my mate you will be perpetually sore between your thighs."

She blushes, but then her eyes glimmer with worry. "What will happen? In the morning, I mean, what will happen? I'm too old to be considered for—"

"*You're mine,*" I say, cutting her off, "and I promise to keep you safe. We are mated, and no one can dissolve our mating union. Not your captain, and not my emperor."

"But the alliance…"

"The alliance can suck my appendages."

She laughs, and it warms my heart. It's the first time I've heard her laughter, and the musical sound becomes immersed in my soul, a treasure I will carry with me until my dying breath.

I sink down on the bed, still holding her in my arms. The small human-size bed creaks under my bulk, and I soon realize there is no way both of us will fit side by side.

I kiss Leona's forehead and gently place her on her feet, then watch to ensure she remains steady. Once I'm certain she won't collapse from exhaustion, I set about creating a sleeping area on the floor using the covers from the bed, as well as all the pillows I can find, including the pillows she kneeled upon as she sucked my shafts.

We curl up beside one another, and I take her in my arms. She stiffens for a moment and glances toward a small door that I assume leads to a bathroom. "Um, maybe I should clean up first. Your seed is covering me. I don't want to get pregnant, and maybe cleaning it off will help that not happen. I'm not sure, but it seems like a smart idea." She attempts to slip out of my embrace, but I tighten my hold and kiss her forehead again.

"No," I say firmly, meeting her eyes. "You don't need to clean up." I sigh and debate whether to admit I'm sterile. It's not something I like to talk about, but I suppose if we're mated, I ought to give her honesty. Especially when I expect honesty from her.

Her gaze turns knowing, however, and I start to wonder if perhaps she can hear some of my thoughts, just as I've heard some of hers.

"Never mind," she blurts. "I'm fine not cleaning up. Let's just go to sleep."

I suppress a growl and resolve to admit the truth soon. It would seem that being mated to me hasn't changed her opinion about having offspring, and perhaps it's a blessing that I cannot get her pregnant. Our mating union will face enough obstacles in the days to come.

I draw the covers atop us and she snuggles deeper in my arms. When I tangle my legs with hers, I feel the stickiness of her arousal and my seed, the proof of the consummation of our mating union.

For the first time in ages, I drift to sleep in a state of utter contentment.

Chapter 17

LEONA

I AWAKE ON THE FLOOR, AND FOR A MOMENT I'M confused. What the hell am I doing down here? The alarm on my bedside table is beeping, and I call out a verbal command to shut it off. I yawn hugely and then wince as I feel soreness between my thighs.

Memories crash over me, and I turn on my side, expecting to find Zahhn asleep next to me, but he's not there. I place a hand on the covers and frown. Still feels warm. And his scent lingers in the air. His discarded underwear is on the floor nearby too.

Maybe he stepped out for a while. Or maybe he went to contact his people. I suppose he'll have to inform them as soon as possible that we've mated.

I sit up and wince again. It's not just my pussy that's sore, but all the muscles in my body as well. I swallow hard. Yep, my throat still hurts too. We shared a few gentle moments last night during our coupling, but for the most part Zahhn was rough and demanding. Especially when he claimed me the second time while I was bent over the bed. I flush in remembrance.

Tossing back the covers, I peer down at the dried blue seed that's covering my thighs. It's all over the sheets as well. I sigh and peer toward the doorway, wondering if I should start getting ready for my shift in the mess hall.

But seriously… what happens now? Will Zahhn take me back to whatever ship in the Darrvason fleet he calls home? Or will he stay on the *Jansonna* with me?

Mated. I can scarcely believe I'm mated to the huge alien doctor.

My breathing increases and panic swirls in my head. I tuck my knees up and place my head between them, trying to quell the sudden attack of anxiety. What will the leaders of the worldship say? How will my friends and coworkers react? What about my father?

Leona's Speakeasy. Guilt flows through me as I consider the true ramifications of what I've done.

What will happen to my bar? I despair over the thought of abandoning it or allowing someone else to take over. Managing the speakeasy has brought me joy and kept me sane during the last fifteen years.

Yes, I founded the illicit meeting place when I was only twenty years old. It started in a small storage room on Deck Nine, only to move to a larger abandoned storage room on Deck Twenty about five years ago. When I think about all the hard work I put into the place, I find myself hoping Zahhn will somehow end up staying on the *Jansonna*. Maybe I could convince him to work in the worldship's medical bay.

But doubts keep plaguing me—this entire situation is complicated—and my worry deepens. Mating with Zahhn was unexpected. I'm still not certain how he ended up on the *Jansonna* and found his way to my bedroom.

I remain on the floor for a few more minutes, trying to decide how to proceed with my day. I'm a bit miffed that Zahhn departed my bedroom without waking me to say goodbye. It sure would be nice to know his whereabouts.

Finally, I decide to shower and get dressed. Maybe I'll encounter my new mate as I'm headed through the corridors on my way to the mess hall.

Once I'm ready, I slip out of my bedroom and shut the door quietly, just in case my father's still sleeping. He keeps odd hours for a variety of reasons, and sometimes he'll sleep during the day.

The sound of a throat being cleared in the living room causes me to freeze in my steps. I peer to the left and discover my father seated on the couch, his face pale, his eyes brimming with fear.

"Jesus fucking Christ, Leona," he whispers. "What the fuck have you done?"

I stare at him dumbly for about thirty seconds. But of course. Zahhn and I weren't exactly quiet last night. I flush as I recall how often he growled, not to mention how frequently I whimpered and moaned. Caught up in the moment, I hadn't stopped to consider that anyone might overhear us.

"Good morning, Dad," I finally say. I cross my arms over my chest and glare at him, annoyed that "Jesus fucking Christ, Leona. What the fuck have you done?" is the most he's said to me in over two months. I fight back a wave of hurt.

"I cannot believe you fornicated with one of those Darrvason engineers. For fuck's sake, have you lost your mind? Darrvasons mate for life, you stupid girl! For life!" His face reddens and he stands up and starts pacing the living room.

"How do you know it was a Darrvason? Did you see him leave?" I swallow hard and wonder if he had an encounter with Zahhn this morning. Oh dear. Even though I'm pissed as hell at my father, a smile tugs at my lips as I imagine the two of them crossing paths in the hallway.

"Humans don't growl like that. The entire deck must've heard you copulating. Shit, I'm surprised morality officers haven't come knocking yet. But no, I didn't see him leave." My father appears flustered. "Isn't he still in your bedroom? I've been sitting here waiting for him to come out so I could give you idiots a piece of my mind."

"He's not in my bedroom," I say, my confusion growing. Where's Zahhn? Why do I suddenly have a very bad feeling?

"Not in your bedroom? How the hell did he get out? I would've seen him leave." My father huffs and stomps into my bedroom. I hear him cursing and cringe as I realize he likely just found the stained covers and Zahhn's underwear. Seconds later, he comes stomping back out, his face twisted with fury and confusion.

"I don't know where he went. He was gone when I awoke this morning. Maybe… maybe you drifted to sleep for a while and you missed him leaving."

The anger doesn't leave my father's visage. "Perhaps." He clenches his jaw and appears on the verge of screaming again, but when he next speaks, his voice is eerily calm. "You must keep it a secret. Do not tell anyone you mated with a Darrvason. I will take care of it. Just give me his name, and I will take care of it. You don't need to spend your life in slavery to one of those barbaric creatures."

"You'll take care of it? What the hell does that mean?" Shock courses through me. Surely he doesn't mean to kill Zahhn. My father might be involved with some rebel groups aboard the *Jansonna*, but I can't imagine him having the power and resources to take out one of the Darrvasons, even if he thinks the Darrvason in question is an engineer who's temporarily stationed on the worldship.

"I will worry about the details." He draws in a deep breath as though summoning patience. "Just give me his name, Leona. I will do whatever it takes to make sure your life isn't ruined."

I shake my head. "No. I'm not giving you his name."

His face twists with disgust. "You stupid girl. I've allowed you to have your little speakeasy, and I've paid off security officers to keep you from being arrested several times over the years. But I won't watch you ruin your life by becoming chained to a Darrvason."

For a moment, the room tilts. Is he telling the truth? Has he actually paid off security officers to protect me? I think about the two days I spent in the worldship's brig. Maybe if I hadn't been released, he would've tried to help me. Though I'm infuriated by his plans to commit murder on my behalf, I'm touched that he's secretly protected me over the years.

"Darrvason males are savages, and they think they have the right to over two thousand of our women just because they're offering us a little help? Fuck that. Tell me this bastard's name."

I take a step backward, then another. I shake my head. "I won't tell you his name."

"Before your mother died, I promised her I would protect you!" he shouts, and it's a low blow.

My mother died shortly after giving birth to me due to complications, and while I know she wanted children and carefully planned my conception in a fertility lab, I still harbor guilt over her death.

"I'm thirty-five years old, Dad. I know what I'm doing." Except that's a big fucking lie. I *don't* know what I'm doing. I still can't believe I mated with Zahhn, and I'm terrified my life is about to change drastically. If I'm forced to live on the *Haxxal* or another ship in the Darrvason fleet, I'll be miserable. I can't imagine not seeing my friends every day and enjoying the cheerful ambiance of my bar. It's who I am—I'm the person who brings everyone together. But what if I'm about to let my friends, coworkers, and patrons down?

My father's agitation mounts. His face reddens further and his nostrils flare. His fists clench as he ceases his nervous pacing. He stands in the middle of the living room, staring at me with a look of utter revulsion. It breaks my heart and chills me to the bone. I don't have any awful memories about my father—he kept me fed and took care of my basic needs as a child—but I don't hold any warm memories of him either. Yet he decrees the Darrvasons to be the barbarians.

"You enjoyed it," he says in an accusatory tone. He shakes his head with an air of disbelief. "At first, I thought he was forcing you and I was about to call security officers to intervene, but then I heard you moaning and having a grand time." He shudders. "Did you fail to get your last hormone suppression shot?"

"I don't want to talk about it." I'm shocked and grossed out that he sat in the living room listening. I wish I didn't know. I wish he'd never told me. It feels wrong and like an invasion of my privacy, never mind that I should've maybe stayed quieter. But during the mating session, all I could think about was pleasing Zahhn, and there were times I had little choice but to obey his commands. Like when he ordered me to suck his appendages, and when he told me to bend over the bed and spread my cheeks wide.

"Very well." My father stands taller and straightens the collar of his shirt. "Even though you won't divulge your alien lover's name, I have no doubt he'll be dead soon." His eyes flash with malice. Then he departs our shared quarters, and I'm left to ruminate over the meaning of his ominous words.

The rebels. Shit. What if he's aware of a rebel plot against the Darrvasons? I run a hand through my hair and wish Zahhn would return soon. I would feel much better if I could confide in him about the conversion I'd just had with my father.

But how would Zahhn respond? My stomach flips.

The truth is, I'm not certain. I don't know for sure that he wouldn't turn my father in to *Jansonna's* authorities for conspiring against the Darrvasons.

I feel torn. Though I'm angry with my father and I don't want him to cause any harm to our new alien friends, I also don't want my father to end up in the brig. There's no doubt in my mind that a threat to the alliance would result in harsh consequences to any rebel groups who participated.

But I also feel a sense of loyalty to Zahhn. My… *mate.*

I sigh and head for the corridor. I'm late for my shift in the mess hall, and it's probably not a good idea to make my coworkers worry, especially considering that I disappeared for two days recently.

Two weeks ago, my life wasn't complicated at all. I was happy-ish. I had the speakeasy and not a worry in the universe. Okay, maybe a few worries, but not a whole freaking list of them.

As I walk to the mess hall, my body protests every step. The area between my thighs aches terribly, and my muscles are throbbing. What I wouldn't give for a hot bath, but the water restrictions on the *Jansonna* would never allow that.

I start my shift and go through the motions, but I

can't help but wonder about Zahhn. Where is he? Why do I miss him so much?

My arms still tingle and itch, but I can't sense his presence or his thoughts, and after the intense connection we shared last night, the absence of him disturbs me. I pray he's okay.

Zahhn. Come find me.

Chapter 18

ZAHHN

My eyes open, and I immediately reach for Leona. But she's not there, and I'm in my own bed. On the *fluxxing Rorrsa*.

No. It couldn't have been a dream. It felt too real.

I toss the covers back and the scent of her arousal hits me. I glance down at my naked body. My naked body...

I'm not wearing sleeping shorts. Because I took them off and mated with Leona. But why am I not on the *Jansonna*? Why am I not in my mate's quarters aboard the human worldship?

I take a few deep breaths and try to calm my racing thoughts. But I struggle to answer any of the questions that plague me. I don't remember how I reached the *Jansonna*—whether I hitched a ride on a shuttle or stole one. It's a mystery.

Our mating session must've been real. My legs remain sticky with my dried seed, which makes sense considering she fell asleep in my arms with our legs tangled together. I'm also certain her dried essence is covering my shafts and thighs.

I lean down and take a deep inhale. Yes, that's Leona's arousal I detect. There could be no mistaking it. I could pick out that scent anywhere.

I jump to my feet and peer out the viewscreen of my quarters. Relief fills me when I see the *Jansonna*. It's still there, traveling within the hyperspace bubble with the Darrvason fleet.

Leona must be on the human worldship. It makes sense. It's where we copulated and became mates. Yet my presence on the *Rorrsa* defies explanation. I don't remember returning to my quarters. Furthermore, I would have never returned to the *Rorrsa* without Leona. She's my mate and we should not be parted.

I start getting dressed, only to realize I'm still covered in my seed and my human female's arousal. I can't walk around the *Rorrsa* smelling like I just copulated. Not when it's not common knowledge that I've claimed a mate.

Plus, the group of thirty females who were part of the first wave all currently reside on the *Haxxal* with their respective mates, so it would raise questions if I walked the corridors of the *Rorrsa* in my present condition.

My growl of frustration echoes off the walls as I enter the bathroom. I shower, making sure to scrub myself down thoroughly. I lather my body in soap four separate times and rinse off, cursing the heightened senses of my people the entire time. Then I hurriedly dress and storm through the corridors of the *Rorrsa*, determined to obtain answers.

On my way to the docking bay, I board an elevator. All I can think about is returning to the *Jansonna*. Returning to Leona. Even if I must steal a shuttle in order to reunite with my mate.

To my displeasure, on the way to the docking bay, the elevator stops to admit a passenger. The chief engineer of the *Rorrsa* steps inside the elevator and gives me a nod of acknowledgement.

"Doctor Zahhn," he says in an overly polite tone. "I am glad to encounter you this morning. Perhaps you could enlighten me. Are the rumors true?"

I turn to Chief Kameer, annoyed that he's speaking to me. What rumors is he talking about? Surely he's not aware that I've just entered an unsanctioned mating union with a human female. No one knows yet. I haven't told anyone. Unless… panic fills me.

Unless Leona has revealed the news to her people. Perhaps she woke up alone and told her friends, and somehow the authorities on the worldship learned of the news. I fight back my growing alarm as I stare at Chief Kameer.

I tilt my head to the side, effecting an undisturbed but curious expression. It's the sort of look I give my less intelligent colleagues after they misdiagnose a patient or make an error in a medical study. "I'm afraid I haven't heard any rumors lately. Perhaps *you* could enlighten *me*, Chief Kameer."

He presses a button to stop the elevator just before it reaches the deck that leads to the docking bay. I suppress a growl and endeavor to maintain my carefree aura. But my curiosity indeed mounts. If he's stopping the elevator, whatever rumor he's heard must be one of importance to our people.

Chief Kameer draws in a deep breath, and his red eyes brim with astonishment. "I am shocked that you haven't heard the news. But perhaps you have but you aren't allowed to talk about it." He steps closer, which of course makes my annoyance flare, and I struggle to hide how uncomfortable I'm becoming. "Heartbonds," he blurts. "Heartbonds are possible between humans and Darrvasons."

"What are you talking about?" I can scarcely get the words out because all the air has whooshed out of my chest.

"Admiral Tornn is currently experiencing the mating fever with his mate, a human female named Ellie that he first claimed about fourteen days ago. He came down with a fever, and it's reported that Ellie already has a few ancestral markings on her arms. I know someone who heard Doctor Groaa talking about it." Chief Kameer pauses, and his eyes gleam bright with excitement. "It's said that Doctor Groaa was called to Admiral Tornn's quarters after his mate appeared to have a rash on her arms. But, as you might imagine, it was no rash. It was the ancestral markings starting to form, the beginning of a heartbond."

For a moment, I'm so shocked that I cannot form words. I can barely take my next breath. If what he's saying is true, it changes everything. I give my head a shake and try to preserve an outward appearance of calm, though it isn't easy. "Where did you learn this information?" I can't call it a *rumor*, because I *fluxxing* know it's true. Just last night, I could hear Leona's thoughts. My ancestral markings also kept tingling in her presence. It can't be a coincidence.

Chief Kameer presses his lips together. "I can't reveal my source, though I promise he's a reliable male. But he obtained the information while eavesdropping on Doctor Groaa and one of his colleagues."

"Eavesdropping? Do you realize it would be very easy for me to learn the name of your source and have him detained for spreading rumors?"

The chief engineer's gaze suddenly turns so cold that it takes me aback. I'm not used to being glared at, especially with a look of violence. I'm used to my colleagues deferring to me and cozying up to my greatness. Yes, that might sound conceited, but it is the truth. Though I abhor attention, I am accustomed to being fawned over.

"And do you realize it would be very easy for me to help you meet your death in the elevator?" He displays a tight smile that doesn't reach his eyes. Then he gestures to the control panel. "All it would take is an *accident*. Faulty wiring. A random power surge."

A mirthful laugh erupts from my throat. I can't help it. Despite my initial annoyance, being threatened by the chief engineer of the *Rorrsa* is refreshing. The truth is, it's been ages since anyone has dared to challenge me.

"Is laughter your usual response to a death threat?" Chief Kameer asks.

My laughter finally fades, though I cannot wipe the smile from my face. I make the shape of a circle with my thumbs and pointer fingers, showing the chief that I mean no harm and take no offense to his threats. Finally, I allow my hands to fall to my sides and I lean back against the wall. "I don't say this to many people, Chief Kameer, but I think I might like you. Your arrogance perhaps matches my own, and I appreciate that you aren't licking my boots like half the males I encounter on this ship."

The tension appears to drain from the chief's body, and he also makes a circle with his fingers, then leans back against the opposite wall. "Awards and accomplishments don't impress me. Only character and work ethic will sway me. You might've saved our people from various ailments over the years, Doctor, but I have kept the *Rorrsa*—the oldest ship in our fleet—functioning at optimal levels. Oh, have I mentioned that I recently fixed a fatal mistake in the hyperdrive bubble's formation protocol? We would've all been incinerated during the next jump to hyperdrive had I not caught and fixed the error."

We exchange a genuinely cordial look, and despite my need to reach the *Jansonna* as soon as possible, I find myself relaxing in Chief Kameer's presence. He's shared a significant rumor with me, one that confirms my suspicions about the possibility of heartbonds with humans.

Another thought occurs to me. Perhaps the chief

could help me discover how I reached the *Jansonna* and returned without any memory of the travel. Surely he has access to the travel records between ships in the fleet. "Chief Kameer, I am not privy to any of the happenings on the *Haxxal* as of late. I've been solely focused on my emerging treatment for *forlonggsa*, a study that I'm conducting on the *Rorrsa*, and I must admit there are many messages awaiting me from my colleagues on the *Haxxal* that I simply haven't read yet. It's possible news of this development is included in those messages. I would be happy to share any information with you, though I must humble myself by asking for a favor at the same time." My tone is pompous as ever, but it seems I've found an almost-friend in Chief Kameer, because a thoughtful look comes over him, and he eventually smirks.

"Dare I dream? Have the Star Gods smiled upon me? Is the greatly esteemed and highly decorated Doctor Zahhn, legend among Darrvason males, asking *me* for a favor?"

I hold back a growl. "Even if I cannot find the information you're seeking in my unread messages, I am certain I'll be able to find out the details. All I must do is contact Doctor Groaa or another of my colleagues on the *Haxxal*. I will tell you what I learn in exchange for your kind assistance, Chief Kameer."

"It's a deal, Doctor Zahhn." He presses a button and the elevator resumes moving.

Chapter 19

LEONA

Nothing makes sense. I spend the day waiting for Zahhn to show up, but there's no sign of him. The absence of him feels like a gaping wound in my chest. It's alarming, not being able to sense his presence.

As I go about my day, I don't converse with many of my coworkers in the mess hall. But every time a Darrvason enters the mess hall for a meal, it takes all my self-control not to approach the male and ask if he knows anything about Zahhn's whereabouts.

What if I never see him again?

What if he woke up and changed his mind about keeping me as his mate?

I try to brush away the plunging sadness these worries bring, but it's not easy.

When I return to my quarters in the late afternoon, my father is in the kitchen with four men I don't recognize. All conversation halts as I enter the abode, and I can't help but shiver as I walk past the kitchen and down the hallway to my bedroom. No one speaks to me, not even my father. They simply glare as though I'm an inconvenience who's just interrupted their important business.

The stained sheets are no longer on my floor. Neither is Zahhn's underwear. I'm usually a tidy person, but I'm certain I left my room in shambles this morning when I departed for work. But my bed is freshly made with clean sheets and covers. Normally, there are four pillows on my bed, but only two remain. My face grows hot as I realize the missing pillows were likely defiled with Zahhn's seed or my arousal, or perhaps a combination of both.

Clearly, my father removed all evidence of a Darrvason visitor while I was at work. I perch on the edge of my bed and wrap my arms around my center, reeling with the events of the last two and a half weeks.

The hushed voices coming from the kitchen send a jolt of fear through me. Something terrible is about to happen. I just know it. I think about Commander Hampton's certainty that my father had a hand in the Deck Five Massacre twenty years ago and wonder if it's true.

Is he plotting something similar with the strange men in the kitchen? He rarely allows anyone in our quarters—from what I can tell, he prefers to do his secretive business elsewhere—which makes me think whatever meeting is being held in the kitchen is urgent. I pray it has nothing to do with Zahhn's visit last night.

I close my eyes and concentrate.

Zahhn. Zahhn, where are you?

There's no answer, and my heart sinks.

Maybe it's better this way. Better if I forget about the huge alien doctor. I don't want to leave the human worldship. Not until the Darrvasons succeed in guiding my people to a habitable planet, that is. I think about this term of the alliance and wonder if it'll ever come to pass. Finding a habitable planet that's not already occupied by an intelligent species has been a challenge for the leaders of the *Jansonna*. We've been traveling through space for decades without any luck.

There's also the glaring fact that the Darrvasons don't have a planet of their own. Their entire population resides on the fifteen ships in their fleet. According to the rumors I've heard, their homeworld was destroyed about twenty-five years ago while the Darrvasons were at war with another race of aliens. It was also during this war that they lost nearly all their females and children. If habitable planets were so easy to come by, wouldn't it reason that the Darrvasons would already be in possession of one?

I release a long sigh, then hop off the bed and head to the shower, thankful that it turns on without any issues. Normally, taking more than one shower a day wouldn't be possible, but the Darrvason engineers have already worked wonders on the *Jansonna*. The recirculated air smells fresher, and water and food rations have been increased. The lights in the corridors rarely flicker anymore, and ship-wide computer systems are running at near-optimum levels. Best of all, the ship is no longer freezing. I haven't seen my breath in over a week.

I hurry to get dressed in my casual evening clothes, donning a long blue skirt and a cozy sweater. I apply the faintest hint of eye makeup and then stand near the doorway, listening for the sounds of conversation.

My stomach flips. They're still talking in hushed tones, though on occasion, someone raises their voice in an urgent whisper-shout that reveals the seriousness of whatever topic they're discussing. I know it has something to do with the Darrvasons and the alliance.

I pray they're just a couple of old men venting about the current state of affairs. I pray they aren't truly plotting.

Does it suck that humankind must give over two thousand women to the Darrvasons? Yes, very much so. But I can't see an alternative. If we don't agree to the aliens' terms, I doubt they would help us out of the kindness in their hearts. We would remain stranded, dead in the water, with the worldship's systems on the verge of total failure.

Finally, I summon the courage to leave my room. When I reach the kitchen doorway, I pause in the hallway and face my father and his comrades.

"Whatever you're plotting, gentlemen, I suggest you stop." I meet my father's eyes. "I had a little run-in with Commander Hampton recently. He believes you're a criminal and that you've incited violence on the ship before. He also announced that your engineering skills wouldn't be needed for much longer, and he suggested that you might meet with an unfortunate accident. You should lie low and watch your back. Keep your damn nose clean so you aren't implicated in any more rebellions." I'm not on friendly terms with my father, but I don't want to see him jailed again, or worse. I think of the depressurization chambers that are used for executions and suppress a shudder.

My father stands and places a hand on the shoulder of the man seated next to him. "Geoffrey here just told me an interesting story. He says you were caught in the corridors after curfew and taken to the brig. That's why you disappeared for two days." He scoffs. "You thought I didn't notice you were gone, but I did. Geoffrey also says you were one of five women who were given to the Darrvasons for medical examinations, and you were released from the brig early as a reward for your *cooperation*." He points to an empty chair at the table. "Sit. I want to hear everything. All the details. Perhaps you learned something about the Darrvasons that will be useful."

Horror washes through me. Does he honestly expect me to help him? I want nothing to do with any rebellions on the worldship, big or small. I also don't want to reveal anything that happened during my examination. It feels too personal, my interactions with Zahhn too intimate to share with anyone.

I shake my head and back away. "No. I've got to go." I'm due at the speakeasy soon, but even so I have no wish to participate in my father's little meeting. Especially if it involves divulging information that might help harm the Darrvasons. I haven't forgotten that my father wants to kill Zahhn, and I'm grateful that he doesn't know his name.

"*Tell her,*" one of the men hisses.

"Tell me what?"

My father tilts his head, and his eyes spark with malicious glee. "The Darrvason you entertained last night doesn't appear to be on the *Jansonna.* We've been tracking and constantly verifying the locations of all the Darrvasons currently aboard the worldship. He must've departed early this morning on a shuttle. But, if he's returned to the *Haxxal,* which we believe he has, as all the Darrvasons who've visited the *Jansonna* have come from the lead ship in their fleet, he's already been *exposed.*"

My mouth goes dry. "Exposed to what?"

"A deadly virus brought aboard by one of the thirty women." My father smiles. "If he's not dead yet, he will be soon. The *Haxxal* and all the advanced technology it holds will belong to us. So will the *Jansonna.* Mark my words: Captain Warren's days are numbered."

The men chuckle darkly, and one of them adds, "In the single fucking digits, baby."

My trepidation increases, and I take a few more steps back. Worry for Zahhn consumes me. I must speak with him. I must warn him. But how could I possibly get a message to the *Haxxal,* assuming that's where he traveled this morning? I fight back the hurt that pierces my heart when I think about how he left without saying goodbye.

"You're all fools." I spin on my heel and flee into the corridor, ignoring the outraged shouts of my father.

Chapter 20

ZAHHN

I FEAR I'M GOING MAD. I STARE AT THE SCREEN displaying all inter-ship activity within the fleet during the last two days. No ships departed the *Rorrsa* for the *Jansonna* at any time. Furthermore, no vessels left the *Rorrsa* for the *Haxxal* or any other ships in the Darrvason fleet.

If Chief Kameer is curious about my reasons for wanting to see the departure logs, he doesn't reveal it. His face remains impassive as he leans against a desk in his private office.

"Are you certain no shuttles were stolen?" I turn to face him. "I have reason to believe someone from the *Rorrsa* visited the *Jansonna* last night but then returned to the *Rorrsa* undetected."

The chief engineer finally reveals a hint of surprise. His eyebrows lift slightly, and he glances at the screen with a mild semblance of curiosity. He clears his throat. "The logs are strictly maintained, and all shuttles not in use are kept secure. No unauthorized personnel can visit the docking bay, and the vessels are protected by a combination of secret passcodes that are constantly changed as well as a bio-identity check on any male attempting to pilot one."

I resist the urge to run my hand through my hair. I don't want the chief to know how frustrated I'm becoming, nor how desperate I am to find the answers I'm seeking. How in the *fluxx* did I visit the *Jansonna* undetected? It doesn't make sense, and I'm starting to wonder if maybe it never happened. Perhaps I had a very vivid dream about Leona and then imagined her scent covered me after I awoke. I haven't been able to stop thinking about her. Ever since the medical exam, she's occupied my thoughts so much that I've had trouble concentrating on my work. It's just as I feared—taking a mate would indeed distract me from my important research.

My responsibilities to the Darrvason Empire suddenly feel like a crushing weight on my shoulders. For the first time in my life, I find myself conflicted about what my true purpose is.

But I must continue my research, and I must proceed with the trials on the *Rorrsa*. I'm on the cusp of curing *forlonggsa* and I cannot abandon my work now.

A thought occurs to me, and I step closer to Chief Kameer. Though we're alone, I keep my voice low. "What about beaming technology? Has anyone on the *Rorrsa* been testing it?" Though we're aware of several alien races who use beaming technology, our people have avoided the glitchy technology that has been known to take lives. But perhaps a rogue scientist is testing it. Maybe that's how I reached the *Jansonna*, though if I did, wouldn't I have a memory of using it? *Fluxx*. I am grasping at flimsy conclusions in a futile effort to explain what happened to me last night.

Chief Kameer frowns. "I am aware of all scientific endeavors on this ship, and I can assure you that no unsanctioned research is taking place. If someone were testing beaming technology, I would know about it. Beaming signatures are difficult to miss, and part of the security protocols on every ship in our fleet include routine scans for use of the banned technology."

It's as though the floor has disappeared beneath my feet. I experience the sensation of falling fast, and I'm forced to place a hand on the desk to steady myself. What happened last night—traveling to the *Jansonna* and mating with Leona—defies explanation.

The most logical conclusion is that my memories are false. That I simply awoke after a vivid dream and imagined the state of my undress as well as the intimate bodily fluids covering me. If I hadn't already analyzed my DNA for a predisposition for *forlonggsa*, I would worry I was starting to show signs of the disease. But my DNA carries no marker for the great madness.

"If you would like me to track a specific individual's biosignature," Chief Kameer says in an overly casual tone, "I could do that for you."

"That's possible?"

He nods. "One of my colleagues recently developed

the technology." A knowing gleam enters his eyes. "Would you like me to track the location of *your* biosignature during the last two days, Doctor Zahhn? I'll be discreet. If we learn something interesting, I saw nothing, I know nothing. We never had this conversation."

"Do it." I draw in a deep breath. "Please."

Chief Kameer turns to a console and his hands fly over several screens so rapidly, I'm unable to see what he's doing. "One would think all Darrvasons would have the same, if not incredibly similar biosignatures. However, my colleague discovered how to track Darrvason males by searching for elements that are unique to each male's ancestral markings, almost like a tiny, incredibly faint transmitter embedded within our flesh that's so complicated to explain, I doubt even you would understand it. If you had any living relatives, however, we might run into some difficulties." He glances over his shoulder and his hands pause above the screens. "Do you have any living relatives?"

"No. All dead."

His fingers resume flying from screen to screen at the console. Then he retrieves a device from a drawer that's similar in appearance to a medical scanner. "I need to see your ancestral markings." He turns to me and holds up the scanner. "I promise this won't hurt."

I quickly tug the neckline of my shirt down, revealing my glowing blue ancestral markings. Chief Kameer scans the markings and turns back to his console. I watch as he uploads data to the screens, and my eyes widen when two schematics appear side by side —one of the *Rorrsa* and one of the *Jansonna.*

A flashing red dot shows my movements on the *Rorrsa*, and at first nothing is unusual. The dot moves from my quarters, down various corridors, remains in my temporary laboratory for a while, and also travels to various patients' rooms in the medical wing. Perfectly normal, however I take note of the time of day displayed next to the schematic. It's not showing my location last night and early this morning yet, and I hold my breath as I watch the time speeding up.

Then the dot disappears entirely. I step closer and glance at Chief Kameer. His brow is creased with confusion, and he reaches out to the screen, only for the dot to suddenly appear on the *Jansonna*.

Disbelief seizes me, and yet I cannot deny the truth that's staring me in the face. Somehow, by means I do not yet understand, I traveled to the *Jansonna* last night. My heart races faster, and I'm not certain whether I should be relieved by these findings or terrified.

I mated with a human female. *Leona*.

"What the *fluxx*?" The chief turns to me with questions brimming in his eyes. He looks partly horrified, but also curious. Then he snorts and says, "Of course, of course, of course. It makes sense, knowing what your father was."

"My father?" I take a menacing step toward him. "What does my father have to do with this?"

"He was a skilled assassin who took out many of our enemies during the great war. His body count is among the highest out of any Darrvason warrior who fought and died for the glory of the empire."

"I'm aware of my father's deeds. But I still don't

comprehend why his status as an assassin bears any importance on the fact that I suddenly appeared on the *Jansonna* last night." I gesture at the schematic of the human worldship. The red dot remains blinking over the area I assume is Leona's quarters. I make a mental note of the exact location on the ship.

"Ever hear about Project Xeera?"

"No. Explain."

Chief Kameer's eyes gleam with excitement, and I seriously consider punching him in the nose. He's staring at me like I'm a scientific curiosity and it pisses me the *fluxx* off. "Astral projection," he announces, and not for the first time today, I experience the abrupt sensation of falling. "Project Xeera was a classified experiment established by the former emperor during the war against the Yelltzins. Our brightest minds were able to pinpoint individuals with a predisposition for astral projection, and those males were recruited to become spies and assassins. The project was abandoned not long after the war."

I remain quiet for a long moment as his words slowly penetrate my consciousness. It all sounds too fantastic, yet I cannot surmise another explanation for the proof on the screens. "I must admit that I believed stories about astral projection were just that—stories. Also, if my soul projected to another ship, does that mean my physical body actually remained on the *Rorrsa*? Was it only my soul that traveled? How-how was I able to touch things while on the human worldship?" Well, I suppose the assassins like my father wouldn't have been very successful if they weren't able to physically touch objects or other individuals after astral projecting. But the very idea of it defies logic, and my mind struggles to grasp the science behind it.

Chief Kameer shrugs. "I must confess I don't know how it works, but it's obvious that an individual who's astral projecting can physically touch things, whether his body remains elsewhere. All evidence of Project Xeera's existence has been wiped from the Darrvason database. It's said a rogue scientist did it after worrying the former emperor was showing too much interest in the project after the war. As you know, the late emperor was experiencing the first signs of *forlonggsa* and many were worried that he would misuse the information and perhaps even use the remaining assassins against his dissenters."

How could my father keep such a secret? I'm not only taken aback by Chief Kameer's revelation, but I'm deeply shocked, so much that I'm now questioning if I ever really knew my father. He was a stoic male who believed in furthering the interests of the Darrvason Empire, though I had little contact with him after the war began. Eventually, not long after the destruction of our homeworld, I received news of his death.

"I am sure this information must come as a shock to you, Doctor Zahhn." Chief Kameer leans back on his desk and observes the blinking red dot, which remains stationary in Leona's quarters. "You probably don't want to answer this question, but I'll ask anyway. How did you spend your time while on the *Jansonna*? Did you interact with anyone? If you did and your unsanctioned presence was reported to the worldship's authorities or to Officer Brute, who is stationed on the *Jansonna*, your secret might not remain a secret for much longer."

I stare at the chief engineer, wondering if I can trust him. As I study his inquisitive expression, I decide he doesn't project an aura of trickery. Though I do not have any friends, perhaps aside from Emperor Radakk, I consider myself an expert on reading individuals. Years of treating patients and scientific observation have given me a talent for picking up the nuances that would indicate a deceitful temperament.

"I spent the duration of my time on the *Jansonna* in the company of a human female. I encountered no one else and I did not leave her bedroom. Therefore, I do not believe my presence on the worldship will be reported. I doubt the female will tell anyone." *Mate.* I feel a tug in my chest, and for the briefest moment, I sense her presence. But then it's gone and no matter how hard I try, I cannot reestablish the connection. The yearning to storm the corridors of the *Jansonna* until I find her is maddening.

But how could I possibly arrange to travel to the worldship?

"So, you astral projected onto the *Jansonna*, claimed a human female, then this morning you found yourself back on the *Rorrsa*?" The chief's visage fills with wonderment.

I swallow hard. "It would appear so."

"Amazing. Truly amazing." He huffs out a long breath. "Well, I suppose it's your turn. Time to uphold your end of the deal. Tell me what you've discovered about Darrvason-human heartbonds and whether the rumors about Admiral Tornn and his mate are true. I saw you checking messages on your wrist comm as we walked to my office. Surely you must've learned something."

"The rumors are true. A heartbond is indeed forming between Admiral Tornn and his human mate. He's three or four days into the mating fever, and yes, his ancestral markings have started to appear on his female's arms. Thus far, no other mating pairs have experienced a similar phenomenon, but Doctor Groaa believes it's only a matter of time before other couples are affected by the mating fever. I cannot yet explain it, but heartbonds are indeed possible between our people and humans. It's an extraordinary development, and I've been told Emperor Radakk is trying to keep the information a secret for now, as he fears some Darrvason males might attempt to steal human females from the *Jansonna*, particularly our engineers who are stationed on the worldship."

"Ah, because an unsanctioned mating union would be a direct violation of the Darrvason-human alliance." Chief Kameer's eyes twinkle. The bastard is actually teasing me.

"Yes, the emperor would prefer it remains a secret. At least until our engineers return from the *Jansonna*." I glare at the male as he smirks.

"Fear not, great doctor," he says. "I will keep your secret. Just please, if you astral project onto the *Jansonna* again, try not to let any security officers see you. I've been promised a mate, and I don't want anything to interrupt the next batch of human females we're set to receive. It's important that the alliance remains intact."

"I didn't astral project on purpose." I'm still reeling from the revelation of what I'm able to do. A talent that was passed down to me from my father. An ability that defies science. "Nevertheless, I will endeavor to avoid detection. I am eager to see the alliance succeed as well." But I don't admit that I'm contemplating loopholes that might allow me to claim Leona and bring her back to the *Haxxal* as my rightful mate.

Though Chief Kameer appears content to continue our conversation, I make an excuse to leave, and I hastily retreat to my temporary laboratory. I don't bother trying to reach the docking bay. Not when it's well-guarded and the shuttles wouldn't function for me even if I managed to sneak aboard one.

Tonight, I resolve.

I will attempt to astral project into Leona's quarters tonight.

It's only by sheer willpower that I'm able to focus on the study I'm conducting. I'm pleased to find the patients have improved markedly overnight. I bark orders at my assistants, and we resume the same treatments that we administered to the patients yesterday.

If I succeed in curing *forlonggsa*, will Emperor Radakk look the other way when I claim an unsanctioned human female? Would he help smooth over any upset my actions caused?

I work faster as I analyze the latest results of the study, determined to make progress.

Chapter 21

LEONA

THE SPEAKEASY IS EERILY EMPTY TONIGHT. ONLY A handful of patrons have turned up. There's no entertainment either. Jenny, as well as other musicians who sometimes visit to share their talents, are all strangely absent. Usually, at least one of them makes an appearance.

Angelo is standing near the entrance, and we exchange an uneasy look. A few of our volunteer workers failed to show up tonight as well.

There's no denying it. The atmosphere on the ship is becoming more and more tense as the days go by.

I glance at the clock. Almost closing time.

My stomach flips at the prospect of returning to the quarters I share with my father. A virus. I can scarcely believe it. He claims a human woman, one of the thirty, deployed a virus on the *Haxxal.*

Are Darrvasons getting sick? Are some of them dying?

Grief darkens my psyche. I've never felt more hopeless or helpless before. But what the fuck am I supposed to do? Report my father's crimes to the command team? My hands aren't exactly clean. I would implicate myself in the process.

Staying out after curfew.

Engaging in fornication.

Running an unsanctioned gathering place.

Brewing illegal substances.

Add up all my crimes, and there's a chance I would have a date with a depressurization chamber. Shivers rack my body and I wrap my arms around myself.

I can't return to my quarters. Not when I no longer trust my father. I'll have to sleep in the bar. I don't want to spend the night with a friend. What if a warrant is issued for my arrest? I don't want anyone I care about to be caught harboring me.

Lee-oon-ahh.

My breath catches, and hope rises in my chest. *Zahhn.* I peer around the bar, but he's nowhere to be seen. I close my eyes and concentrate.

Zahhn, I send down what I assume is our bond, *can you hear me?*

Yes, comes his reply, and I revel in the feel of his deep voice vibrating through me. *I can hear you. Thank the Star Gods. Are you all right?*

Yes, I tell him. *I am fine. Where are you? Why did you leave without waking me?*

I am on the Rorrsa. *I awoke this morning on the…*

His voice fades in my head. So does his presence.

I nearly scream in frustration. I still haven't decided whether I truly want to be his mate, but I'm desperate to have a conversation with him. I need to know if he's safe. I also need to warn him about the virus. He's a skilled doctor. Perhaps he can help devise a treatment.

A hand clamps down on my arm, and I yelp and tug away. My eyes shoot open, and I find myself staring at Angelo's concerned face.

"Hey, Boss, you okay?"

"I'm fine," I bark in a tone much harsher than intended. I sigh and soften my voice. "I'm fine, really. I, um, just spaced out for a while. My dad and I haven't been getting along. I was just thinking about our last argument." It's not a total lie.

"Why don't you spend the night in my quarters? As you know, we have plenty of room. My mom won't mind."

"That's very sweet of you to offer," I say, "but I'll be okay." I don't want to admit I would feel uncomfortable spending the night in Founder's quarters. Angelo is a descendant of Founders, though like Jenny, he tends to hang with the non-Founder crowd. His offer is truly touching, but if another Founder, one who believes in a separation of the classes, so to speak, witnesses me visiting his quarters at this late hour, it could spell trouble for both of us. I watch as the last of tonight's customers depart the speakeasy, then gaze up at Angelo and force a smile.

He sighs and drags a hand through his dark hair. "Well, let me help you clean this place up."

I cast a quick glance around the bar. "It's not that bad. It'll just take me a few minutes. Go home and get some sleep. I'll see you tomorrow."

"Are you sure?"

"Absolutely." I make a shooing motion toward the door. "Now go. Don't make me call a security officer on you."

He laughs and heads for the door. "Fine, fine. See you tomorrow, Boss."

I watch as he departs, then sink down on a stool at the bar. I drop my head in my hands as a shudder of exhaustion moves through my body. I'm mentally and physically drained, and somehow, I've become tangled in a mess I don't know how to escape.

I have a mate I'm not sure I want, despite my intense attraction to him.

My father is indeed involved with rebels who would like nothing more than to take over the command of the *Jansonna*. Apparently, they want to kill all the Darrvasons on the *Haxxal* and take ownership of that ship as well.

Zahhn claimed to be on the *Rorrsa*, but I don't know if he's visited the *Haxxal* recently, and I have no idea whether he or his comrades are falling ill. Unless our mind-connection starts working again, I have no way of contacting my mate to warn him.

Oh, and let's not forget that I run an illegal speakeasy and suddenly customers are scarce. My stomach flips when I consider why. The bar has been a place for rebels to congregate. Maybe business has slowed because my patrons are worried about a raid.

Fuck fuck fuck.

I groan aloud, a bit dramatically, then slip off the stool. I quickly clean up the bar and turn down the lights.

But I'm suddenly second guessing my decision not to return to my quarters tonight. What if Zahhn shows up and I'm not there? I don't want to see my father. Not only is he a rebel, but he's a would-be murderer. Thousands of Darrvasons call the *Haxxal* home, and he wants to kill as many as he can. While I can understand his misgivings about the alliance, I cannot condone his methods of protest.

In the end, I climb through the tubes to Deck Eleven, home sweet home, and slink through the shadows to my quarters. To my relief, I don't hear any voices when I enter. Nor do I see anyone. My father's bedroom door is cracked, and I peek inside to find it empty. Good. He's gone. Probably out engaging in criminal activity, but at least he's not here to try to convince me to help him.

I hurry to my bedroom and lock the door. Then I sit on my bed and hold vigil, waiting for Zahhn. Waiting for his arrival. Waiting for his voice in my head. Anything.

But no matter how hard I try to reach him, no matter how many thoughts I attempt to send his way, I receive no response. It's as though he's vanished from existence.

Worry clutches me. What if he was sick when he contacted me earlier in the night? What if his illness was the reason our conversation ended so abruptly?

I peer around my room, feeling trapped and useless.

I rack my brain for anyone aboard the *Jansonna* I might ask for help. But the only people who hold enough power to contact the Darrvasons are the most corrupt of all. Unless…

Nathan Gonlez. He's a security officer who was engaged to Jenny's sister. I don't know him well, but I know his face and I'm vaguely familiar with his work hours. I see him patrolling the corridors each day. Could he help me?

I huff and quickly push the idea aside. I don't know for certain where his loyalties lie. Approaching him might be too risky.

What about Officer Brute? Maybe I ought to approach the Darrvason security officer who has an interest in Jenny. It's been days since his visit to my bar, and he hasn't turned me in yet. Clearly, he's capable of keeping secrets.

Yes, I resolve, I'll try to track him down tomorrow. From what I've heard, he's been following poor Jenny around the ship lately. If I can't find him myself, I can always ask her for help in facilitating a conversation.

I prepare myself for bed and climb under the covers, trying not to think about why I have fresh sheets. I'm still mortified that my father heard *everything*, though why the opinion of a would-be murderer matters to me so much, I'm not sure.

At some point, I drift to sleep.

I awake in the morning to the beeping of my alarm, and I sit up in bed, weighed down with so much worry that it's difficult to breathe.

Zahhn didn't visit me last night. Not in person and not in my head.

I close my eyes and reach out with my thoughts, but nothing happens. I still can't feel him.

Zahhn. I'm sorry, but I don't want you as my mate. Forgive me, but I treasure the freedom I have on the Jansonna, *and I never planned to marry. I should have tried harder to push you away. I should have ignored my* urges. *But I still hope you're okay. Please don't be dead. Please, if you can hear me, let me know how you're faring.*

Chapter 22

ZAHHN

Days of terrifying silence pass. No matter how often I attempt to reach out, I'm unable to reestablish a conversation with Leona. I don't understand why our mind-connection has faded. Perhaps it's because I only rutted her once.

Typically, a heartbond between a Darrvason male and female takes about three moon cycles to fully form. It's unusual that it's already happening for Tornn and his mate, Ellie, just as it's not typical that Leona and I were able to share a connection, however briefly it lasted.

I sigh as I consider traditional Darrvason mating practices, which are no longer applicable, as there are no young Darrvason females left.

Shortly before a Darrvason female turned nineteen,

she would be relocated to a safe location, usually a locked room in her family's home, in anticipation of her first heat. Once her first heat occurred, she would be given to a mate, a male of her father's choosing, and the male would take her home and rut her until she was drenched in his scent.

If the female wasn't properly drenched in her mate's scent, she might encounter a ravenous unmated male when she ventured out in public. But if she was adequately covered in her mate's scent, or the heartbond had already formed and her mate's ancestral markings were glowing on her arms, she would be safe.

My people never believed it would be possible to share a heartbond with a human female. But now that we know it's possible, the rules have changed. Admiral Tornn and his mate are proof that the heartbonds will likely develop much sooner than three moon cycles' time.

I stand at the viewscreen in my quarters aboard the *Rorrsa*, staring at the *Jansonna*, wishing I could transport myself there in an instant. Well, I could, if I knew how to do it. But the first and only time I astral projected onto the human worldship, I did so by accident. Perhaps now I am trying too hard.

My attempts to search our database for information about Project Xeera have proved futile. Chief Kameer wasn't lying when he said all information about the secretive project had been wiped from our records.

If only my father had confided in me about his involvement with the project. Perhaps then I would know something useful, such as the technique he used for astral projection. I assume he achieved some sort of trance or vibrational state of mind that helped him send his spirit to whatever enemy ship or planet contained his target.

I'm one of the brightest minds in the history of the Darrvason Empire. Why can't I figure it out?

I curse and turn my back on the viewscreen. It's early morning, and I'm due in the laboratory soon. My assistants are probably awaiting my arrival so we might analyze yesterday's progress in our fight against *forlonggsa*.

But just as I head for the corridor, a brief shudder goes through the *Rorrsa*. A glance over my shoulder at the viewscreen shows we're no longer in a shared hyper-drive bubble. All fifteen ships in the Darrvason fleet, as well as the *Jansonna*, hold position in open space.

The lights go out, and a moment later, the emergency lights activate. A glance around my quarters shows no information screens are working. It would appear our systems are down.

I approach the viewscreen again and take notice of the other ships in the Darrvason fleet. The outer lights lining our vessels aren't illuminated as usual, indicating a fleet-wide power failure.

Alarm fills me when a beam of red shoots from the human worldship and impacts the *Haxxal*.

Star Gods, what is happening?

Not only does the red beam hit the lead ship in our fleet, but it appears damage has been done to the

Haxxal, which means shields are down. A second red beam soon impacts the *Haxxal*. I also witness twelve shuttles exit the human worldship's docking bay.

All twelve shuttles head for the *Haxxal*.

An attack. The humans have decided to attack us.

My thoughts immediately go to Leona.

Is she all right? Did she know about the attack ahead of time?

My worry for her deepens, and I bolt out of my quarters and head for the laboratory, which also contains a viewscreen where I can continue watching the attack unfold.

It's my hope that some of my colleagues might be privy to information that I don't yet know. Especially the security officers who guard the laboratory. Perhaps they can divulge the specifics of the attack.

I race through the corridors to the laboratory, where I join my assistants standing near the viewscreen. We watch in stunned silence as a beam of red shoots from the *Haxxal* and grazes the *Jansonna*.

"That must be a warning shot," someone says, and I agree. The *Haxxal* could've destroyed the *Jansonna* with one shot, yet they only grazed the starboard with a less powerful beam.

A security officer steps in from the corridor and clears his throat. We all turn to face the male, and it takes all my self-control not to shout at the officer to immediately reveal what he knows. He peers at his wrist comm, then says, "The attack is nearly over. Captain Warren of the human worldship has just yielded command of his vessel to Officer Brute. According to an initial report from engineering, the humans remotely hacked our systems using Xorrshanan technology, which was likely acquired at an outpost. Most of the humans who boarded the *Haxxal* are already dead, about two hundred of them. Those who remain alive will soon take their last breaths."

"Why did they attack us?" asks Doctor Yemm, one of my most valued assistants. "What was their end goal?"

The security officer focuses on his wrist comm again, squinting at the small screen. "The humans, a rebel group who call themselves The Saviors, apparently thought most Darrvasons aboard the *Haxxal* would be dead or dying of the virus they attempted to deploy using one of their females. Needless to say, they were in for a shock when they found all our males alive and ready for a fight. Some good news: No Darrvason casualties have been reported. Only a few minor injuries. It sounds like the humans tried to separate the *Haxxal* from the other ships in our fleet, but it didn't quite work, and all of our ships were pushed out of the hyperdrive bubble at the same time."

The overhead lights flicker back on, and all the screens in the laboratory instantly brighten and display various experiments-in-progress. I move to a console to assess any possible damage, and it's a relief to discover no data has been lost. Everything looks in order, and we are closer than ever to establishing a treatment for the great madness.

Leona. I back away from the console and glance out the viewscreen. The *Jansonna* remains intact. The warning shot that grazed the human worldship's starboard likely only caused a brief shudder, but I still find myself worrying about my mate.

But is she truly my mate?

Six days have passed since I astral projected into her bedroom, and it's been five days since we've communicated via our minds. My people mate for life, and I still have every compulsion to steal her away from the *Jansonna* and keep her as mine. It bothers me that I never got the chance to drench her in my scent.

The need to take possession of her, train her to be an obedient mate, and keep her forever burns in my soul.

But most of all, I want to make sure she's safe. The human attack on my people is worrying for a variety of reasons. What will this mean for the alliance? Will Emperor Radakk demand extra females in compensation? Will the humans try to back out of the treaty?

The uncertainty eats at me until I'm sick to my stomach and grumpy as *fluxx*. A growl rumbles from my chest as I survey the room and discover not a single one of my assistants has started their assigned work for the day.

I pound a fist on the nearest console. "The show is over. Get to work!" I appoint the more analytically minded doctors to study yesterday's data, while I gather the more personable doctors to join me in the secure wing of the *Rorrsa* that houses our patients suffering from *forlonggsa.*

Every time we walk by a viewscreen, I can't help but glance at the *Jansonna*. I also can't help but call Leona's name over and over in my head, trying to establish a mind-connection with the pretty human. Only silence greets me, as well as a gaping emptiness that causes my soul to ache.

Chapter 23

LEONA

I AWAKE TO A FAINT SHUDDER THAT COURSES THROUGH the worldship. Sitting up in bed, I listen carefully, but the steady hum that accompanies hyperdrive travel is absent. Hm. We must've left hyperdrive for some reason.

Perhaps the Darrvasons need to alter course again, like they did after supposedly discovering 58-Zallnanis, the planet they believe will be suitable for us to settle upon—a rumor I heard just yesterday that I suspect might be true.

Like I do every morning when I first awake, I try to contact Zahhn. But no matter how hard I concentrate as I reach out to him, there's no response. I chide myself for my original plan to hide my ability to hear his thoughts. I would give almost anything just to hear his voice one more time. Not because I want to become his mate—I've accepted it would be a mistake, and though

I'm loath to admit my father might be correct, it's probably true that I would be miserable living as a Darrvason bride—but because I want to ensure he's okay. That he hasn't been taken out by the virus.

A glance at the clock shows I'm running late. Shit. I forgot to set my alarm. I quickly get dressed and depart my bedroom. Relief spreads through me to find I'm alone.

I've only seen my father in passing since our last tense conversation, and he hasn't spoken a word to me. He's glared and grunted, but nothing more. I can sense his disappointment, and I hate that it guts me. I hate that I want his approval even though he's clearly lacking in morals.

Yeah, okay, I know why I want his approval. Because I've witnessed many of my friends grow up with loving fathers who delighted in spending time with them. I never had that, and I didn't realize until I was about eight years old that my dad wasn't like most fathers.

I cringe as I remember the years-long phase I went through during which I tried anything and everything to garner his attention and please him. But nothing worked, and it would appear now the only thing that would please him would be if I helped his rebel cause.

A cause that he hopes will result in the death of thousands of Darrvasons.

I haven't tracked down Officer Brute yet, nor have I seen Jenny lately. I resolve that I'll find the alien security officer today, even if I must approach a random Darrvason engineer and inquire about his whereabouts.

As I depart my quarters, I notice a flurry of activity

in the corridor. Dozens of people race by me, heading in the direction of an alcove. Curious foreboding fills me, and I find myself following the crowd.

My stomach drops to the floor when I finally glimpse what everyone is looking at. Though Deck Eleven's alcove is quite small, it's large enough to provide a view of what's going on. I swallow past the burning dryness in my throat.

Just as I suspected, we're no longer in a shared hyperdrive bubble. But something's not right. Most of the outer lights on all the Darrvason ships are not illuminated as they usually are.

Then it happens. A red beam shoots from the *Jansonna* toward the *Haxxal*. It makes impact and the alien ship rocks. My eyes widen. A few seconds later, another red beam hits the *Haxxal*.

"What the fuck is happening?" I whisper.

Suddenly, someone races down the corridor holding a blaster, and it's not a security officer. I recognize him as an engineer named Seth, an older man who's worked with my father for years. He holds the blaster high with a grin and runs faster. "To hell with the alliance!" he shouts.

More men follow him, though they are less enthusiastic. I reel with shock when I glimpse my father among them. He makes eye contact with me, but his expression isn't kind. A chill rushes down my back.

Where are they going? What are they planning?

The group of armed men board an elevator.

"Holy shit," a bystander says. "Look! Shuttles.

They're leaving our docking bay. Looks like about a dozen of them, and they're headed for the *Haxxal.*"

"Has to be rebels," a young woman says. "The command team wouldn't be stupid enough to attack the Darrvasons. The aliens haven't finished making repairs to our ship yet, nor have they guided us to a habitable planet."

I watch the shuttles zip toward the *Haxxal* and enter the lead alien vessel's docking bay. *No no no.* This can't be happening.

Then it hits me. The virus. The virus was likely deployed in order to weaken the aliens. Surely the Darrvasons possess weapons better than blasters that they could use against my people. But if they are sick and dying, humans will have a better chance at victory.

I feel sick to my stomach.

Zahhn. Zahhn, please answer me.

There's no response.

"Hey! The outer lights on the *Haxxal* just came back on!" someone shouts.

"Oh my God!" cries a young boy. "I think they're powering up weapons. Look right there. Do you see—"

A red beam emits from the *Haxxal* and strikes the *Jansonna*. The worldship rocks and the lights flicker. I lean against the wall to steady myself as a screeching static noise comes over the ship's speakers, and the multiple info screens lining the corridor suddenly flash blue.

I approach the nearest info screen and gasp when Captain Warren appears, and Officer Brute is standing with him. The captain is shaking, and Officer Brute abruptly grabs him by the scruff of his neck. Both males stare into the camera.

"Attention citizens of the *Jansonna*," Captain Warren says in a trembling voice. Perspiration trickles down his temple, and he pales further and winces. "Several minutes ago, a group of rebels launched an unprovoked attack on the Darrvason Empire. The attack has been thwarted and all the rebels who boarded the *Haxxal* are now dead. All two hundred of them. To demonstrate my horror over this most egregious attack, I have surrendered control of the *Jansonna* to Security Officer Brute. Please do not be alarmed. This is a temporary measure to ensure the peaceful continuation of the Darrvason-human alliance."

Officer Brute straightens and glares into the camera. "Effective immediately," he says, "there is a shelter-in-place order. If you are in the corridors, return to your quarters, a recreation room, or a mess hall—whichever location is nearest to you. Please rest assured that no human females aboard the *Haxxal* were harmed in any way during the attack. More information will be forthcoming as we investigate the rebel threat to the Darrvason Empire."

The screen goes blank, and there's a collective gasp in the corridor. For a few seconds, no one moves. We all exchange horrified glances. But eventually, several people take off down the corridor, and soon the entire group is dispersing.

I stand in front of the alcove, trying to decide whether to rush to the mess hall where I work or return to my quarters. If I go to the mess hall, I'll be among friends. But if I return to my quarters, I'll know if my father comes back in one piece.

I suspect the group of armed men, my father included, were still on the elevator when the captain gave his little speech. If the rebels were smart, they would've ditched their weapons and fled to their quarters immediately.

Two hundred human men… dead. I'm stunned that many people were able to cram onto the twelve shuttles.

The battle ended so quickly, I doubt many Darrvasons aboard the *Haxxal* were sick, if any were sick at all. Perhaps the virus didn't work in the way my father hoped it would.

I take a deep breath, send up a silent prayer for Zahhn's safety, then hurry to the mess hall.

Five of my coworkers are seated at a table in the back, sipping mugs of coffee. There are a few other people scattered around the mess hall too. I join my friends and gratefully accept a mug of coffee.

"Hey, ladies and gentlemen." I give a playful wink and sit casually in my chair, adopting the confident persona I habitually wear as armor. But my demeanor falters when Caroline's eyes suddenly brim with tears. I place a gentle hand on her shoulder. "Are you okay?"

Caroline covers her face and sobs.

I shoot a questioning look at the others, and Johnny finally speaks up.

"During the attack, she saw her father tackled by two security officers," he says with a frown. "They found a blaster poorly hidden under his shirt, which they confiscated, and they dragged him away while he screamed about a plan to assassinate Captain Warren."

"He's going to be executed now," Caroline sobs. "Traitors and murderers are always executed. What will I tell my mother? What about my baby sister? Oh God, they're going to be heartbroken." Her sobs deepen, and I rub her back in an effort to soothe her.

But she's not wrong. Traitors and murderers *are* always executed. Shit, even suspected traitors meet the same dark fate. Little proof is required.

I consider Officer Brute's words. *More information will be forthcoming as we investigate the rebel threat to the Darrvason Empire.*

I glance around the mess hall, going cold with trepidation as I half expect security officers to storm inside and arrest me.

While I've never been involved in a rebel plot, there's a good chance my father is about to be charged with treason. What if I'm implicated along with him? We share the same quarters, and it would reason that investigators might believe there's no way I wasn't privy to the rebel goings-on that occurred right under my nose.

Then there's the speakeasy to consider. More rebel activity directly under my watch. Yet I always pretended not to know. If I heard something suspicious, I would start humming loudly under my breath and walk away.

Caroline finally stops sobbing. She takes a few deep breaths, wipes her face with a napkin, and stands up. She glances at a nearby bench. "I think I'm going to lie down. I appreciate you guys, I really do, but I need some alone time. Maybe I'll get lucky and fall asleep." She approaches the bench, lies down, and curls up with her back facing us. Poor thing. My heart goes out to her.

But will I soon face the same grief as her?

A young woman approaches our table, and I'm so lost in my thoughts that I almost don't recognize her at first. But my spirits brighten when her identity registers in my mind. "Hey, Mandy, good to see you," I say. "Please join us."

"Thanks," she says, taking a seat next to Johnny. "I was on the other side of the mess hall and just noticed you sitting here. I don't want to be alone right now." She gives me a thin, watery smile, and she tucks her trembling hands onto her lap. "My poor mother. She's going to be so worried about me. I was on my way to the salon when the attack started."

"Why wasn't your mother with you?" I ask. "I thought you both normally worked at the same time." Mandy and her mother are beauticians who mostly serve Founders and their descendants, though both women have cut my hair a few times over the years.

A shadow crosses Mandy's face. "My sister isn't doing well. She can't even get out of bed today. I'd hoped the recent trip to the medical bay would help—we traded a favor with Captain Warren in exchange for the extra credits needed to visit a doctor—but sadly, Tasha's only gotten worse."

"What's wrong with her?" Johnny blurts, and I kick him under the table. He gives Mandy a sheepish look. "Sorry. I don't mean to pry."

Mandy shrugs. "We don't fucking know. Some days

she's fine, other days, her entire body becomes stiff, and she can't bend her legs or arms. She can barely open her mouth to take food and water. She also frequently develops high fevers, and her hair's falling out too."

I immediately think of Zahhn. Could he help Mandy's sister? I make a mental note to ask if I ever speak with him again. Surely the Darrvasons possess superior medical technology compared to us. But after our attack on their lead ship, will they be willing to share?

"Wow, that sounds bad," Johnny says. "I'm really sorry."

"I'm sorry too." I aim a comforting smile at Mandy and pray her sister will make a full recovery soon.

"How long do you guys think the shelter-in-place will last?" Johnny asks, clearly eager to change the subject.

"Probably until the Darrvasons and the command team finish rounding up the remaining rebels, however long that takes," Mandy says. "Two hundred human men were killed on the *Haxxal* today, rebels, all of them, but surely some of their comrades stayed behind. I mean, who hacked our systems and fired at the *Haxxal* not once but twice?"

She makes a point, though I already knew some rebels stayed behind. A vision of my armed father boarding an elevator flashes in my mind. I glance toward the entrance of the mess hall, my heart in my throat.

A dark thought creeps into my head. The thought that maybe he deserves to die. If he was truly part of a plot to kill thousands of Darrvsons with a virus, that's fucking messed up. I never believed him to be an overly kind man, but I never viewed him as cruel either. A bit cold and unfeeling, yes. But cruel? No.

Suddenly, chaos erupts. Over a dozen security officers storm into the mess hall, weapons held high. Gasps and screams fill the large room, and some people hide under tables. I brace myself for a possible confrontation.

The officers break off in pairs, and they start scanning the palms of every person in the room. They shout at people hiding under tables, and the trembling regular citizens emerge and hold out their palms. The officers even force the teenagers present to stand still while their palms are scanned, but thankfully the younger children are left alone. Also thankfully, none of the teenagers are taken into custody.

I can't say the same for the adults, however. By the time a pair of security officers approaches our table, they've already arrested three middle-aged men. The charge? Treason. I try to fight back a chill as the officers stare us down.

"Hold out your palms, citizens," the shortest one orders. "Comply or face arrest."

One by one, we all hold out our palms. As it so happens, they scan my palm last, and the moment the scanner emits a low-pitched beep, my heart plunges to my feet.

"Ah, Leona Zimmerman," the taller officer says as he peers at the identity scanner. "We've been looking for you. We just arrested your father a few minutes ago." He withdraws manacles from his belt. "Leona Zimmerman, you are under arrest for the crime of treason. You will be taken to the brig and given a swift trial."

I don't resist. What's the point? They'll shoot me dead if I put up a fight. I slowly stand up, then turn and place my hands behind my back.

The officers are quick to put the manacles on me. I gaze at my friends with tears in my eyes. Johnny appears incensed, and I give a slight shake of my head, silently begging him not to interfere. This is my fight. Not his.

I smile through my tears. "See you later, guys. I love you all. Caroline, I'll keep an eye out for your father. Mandy, I'll pray for your sister. Johnny, try not to be an asshole to everyone." I make similar comments to the others at the table, and I'm grateful that the officers don't drag me away until I'm finished speaking.

As they guide me to the nearest elevator, I know I won't be released from the brig this time. Treason. My teeth chatter with the chill that's descended upon me. Or maybe it's shock. Yes, I think I'm going into shock. Not only are my teeth chattering, but breathing becomes difficult and I feel so lightheaded that I fear I might pass out.

When the elevator reaches the deck that houses the brig, my knees practically buckle. Somehow, I remain upright and manage to walk down the dim corridor leading to the brig.

Treason. I've been charged with treason.

Do I deserve it? Maybe. If I'd blabbed to the command team and confessed that my father was plotting something, perhaps the attack on the *Haxxal* could've been stopped.

But no. Even if the attack was thwarted and all the rebels involved in the scheme were rounded up, a rash of executions would've taken place. The two hundred human men would've still died, though they would've met their ends in a depressurization chamber rather than perish at the hands of the Darrvasons.

This realization helps alleviate my guilt somewhat.

I'm going to die. I'm going to be executed.

By the time I'm placed in a dark cell, I'm trembling so hard I can no longer stand. The officers drag me into the cell, deposit me on the cold, hard floor, and lock me inside.

Sobs and shouts echo throughout the brig, but the sounds eventually fade into the background. Lying on the floor, I hug my knees to my chest and try to regulate my breathing.

I'm going to die.

Chapter 24

ZAHHN

It takes three days to arrange a video comm call with Officer Brute. I'm pacing my quarters in a heightened state of agitation when his call finally comes through. I rush to the video comm console, sit down, and accept the call.

"Doctor Zahhn," he says. "I received your message a few days ago, but as you might imagine, things have been busy on the *Jansonna* and I haven't been able to reply until now. Your message indicated you wished to confirm the wellbeing of one of your former *patients*. A human female named Leona." His eyes gleam with mild curiosity.

I draw in a deep breath. "Yes. What can you tell me about her?"

"She's alive and in good health, however she is currently in the brig. Unfortunately, she was one of the seventy members of The Saviors who stayed behind on the *Jansonna* during the attack."

No. Despair rips through me, and I abruptly stand and walk to the door, as though I intend to storm the docking bay, steal a shuttle, and head to the *Jansonna* in search of my female. But I soon freeze in my steps and curse as reason takes over.

Fluxx. I'm not authorized to travel to the human worldship at this time. I'm stationed on the *Rorrsa* and if I try to travel to the *Jansonna*, I'll be stopped and questioned.

If I told the truth, would anyone believe me?

Did Leona have a hand in the attack on my people? It's a daunting thought. The Saviors were responsible for the virus that would've killed thousands of my people had it worked. All because they wanted to break the alliance, *rescue* the thirty human females living aboard the *Haxxal*, and take possession of the *Haxxal* and its advanced technology.

Is Leona capable of that level of coldblooded, ruthless deceit? I am still fiercely drawn to her, and I still yearn to keep her as mine. But if she despises my people so much that she would risk her life in order to murder thousands of Darrvasons, I fear any possible mating union between us would be doomed.

Dark thoughts enter my mind. Deliciously tempting dark thoughts. I could force her. I could lock her up until she comes to her senses.

I could claim her over and over, drenching her in my seed until a heartbond finishes forming between us. I could conquer her completely, and I could train her to serve and obey. I could reform her until she forgets about her ill-fated rebellion and her only waking thoughts revolve around how to best please me.

Suppressing a growl, I glance at the video comm screen. Officer Brute is waiting patiently. I summon patience of my own and resume my seat. "What will happen to her?" I'm unable to hide the worry from my voice.

A hint of compassion enters Officer Brute's eyes, making me suspect he's aware of my true motives. Surely he must realize my interest in Leona goes far beyond her status as my former patient. I examined her *once*, over twenty days ago, and my reasons for doing so certainly weren't to provide medical treatment.

"Captain Warren wanted to execute the remaining seventy members of The Saviors, including the women," Officer Brute says with a frown, "but I made a deal with him to save the ten females who are among the rebels."

Relief suffuses me. "Thank you for arranging that. Females, even those guilty of treason, should not be executed."

"I agree, and I've made arrangements for the women to be released from the brig and taken into Darrvason custody. This will occur when the next wave of females are given to us, after our engineers finish repairs on the *Jansonna*. It's estimated that will occur in approximately two moon cycles."

"Taken into Darrvason custody?" Foreboding spreads through me. I hope the women aren't being released from the human worldship's brig only to be imprisoned again. Females, even guilty ones, should not be wasted. Jailing them isn't logical when we have a dire need to procreate. Using them for breeding purposes would be the smartest option. I hold my breath as I await Officer Brute's reply.

"As I previously stated, there are ten females from the rebel group in custody. Five are within the nineteen to twenty-five age bracket, and those five will be officially included in the group of one hundred. The other five, the older females, will not be imprisoned, not exactly, though we will attempt to find a use for them. Perhaps they'll make adequate servants." He glances at his wrist comm and releases a low growl. "The emperor would like to speak with me. I must go. I hope I've answered your questions regarding your former patient."

"Wait!" I move to the edge of my seat. "Is Leona being mistreated in the brig? Is she warm enough? Is she being given nutritious food and clean water?"

Officer Brute's eyes widen slightly. He clears his throat and leans forward. "I am personally seeing to the welfare of the females in the brig, Doctor Zahhn. They're being housed together in a heated cell that contains enough beds for everyone. They're also being served nutritious meals three times a day, and there is a water station located within the cell. I promise you, Doctor, the females are faring well. Physically, at least." He glances at his wrist comm again. "I must go."

"Thank you for your assistance, Officer Brute. I am indebted to you."

He gives me a polite nod, then the screen goes blank.

It's late in the evening, and after preparing for bed, I resume my mental exercises in hopes that I can contact Leona. Though I still haven't managed to find any information in the Darrvason database about Project Xeera, I recently tracked down a former assassin from the days of the war. The elderly male divulged several mind tricks he once used to achieve astral projection, and I'm determined to continue practicing until I find myself on the *Jansonna* at Leona's side.

I imagine her scent first, and I take slow, deep breaths. Next, I picture her face and the contours of her body, painting a picture in my mind. Step one is visualizing something—a person or place—that you desire to reach. Once I'm certain I've fulfilled the first step, I move beyond Leona and imagine her surroundings. A cell in the brig that contains ten beds, a water station, and nine females in addition to her.

Then I clear my mind and hum deep in my throat, a vibration that spreads outward and fills the air. Initially, I don't believe it's working, but I suddenly feel weightless and cold.

Star Gods, please let this work.

Falling. Now, I'm falling. But I don't impact upon a hard surface. My descent slows and I eventually find myself seated on a bed in a dark room. I blink as my vision adjusts to the dim lighting, and when I glance down at the bed, I notice a small form huddled beneath the covers.

Dark wavy hair obscures the female's face, and I reach down to tuck the locks behind her ear. My pulse skitters. It's Leona. My female. My little rebel who may or may not have wished me dead along with thousands more of my people.

A quick glance around the cell shows the other women are sleeping, tucked in their beds. The cell is warm, just as Officer Brute promised, and I'm relieved when I notice the water station as well as the beginnings of a small kitchen. Leona might be a prisoner, but she's not languishing in a cold cell. She's not being starved or mistreated, and for that I am thankful.

I continue stroking her hair. She turns over on her back and peers at me with wide eyes.

"Zahhn? Is that you?" she whispers. Her gaze brims with moisture and she starts blinking fast.

I caress the side of her face. "Yes, human female. It's me."

She glances at the cell's locked door. "How did you get here? It's the middle of the night, and even so, we aren't allowed visitors."

"I am projecting my soul here, and my body, in a way. But I am not certain how long I'll be able to remain with you." I assist her as she sits up, and I cannot resist leaning down to smell her hair. Her familiarity washes over me, and some of the tension drains from my body.

"I don't understand." She places a hand on my chest, and for the first time in days, my ancestral markings begin to tingle.

"I'm projecting myself here, temporarily, so I might visit you. It's a trait that apparently runs in families. It's a skill my father possessed, and it would appear I'm capable of astral projection too." I stroke her hair and delight in the softness of her dark locks. "Why did you do it?" I ask, and I cannot keep the biting accusation from my voice. "Why did you participate in a plot against my people? Did you truly wish to kill thousands of Darrvasons?"

She shakes her head. "It's not what you think. I-I shouldn't be here. Well, maybe I should, but I'm not part of The Saviors, I swear it."

I want to believe her. I truly do. But I know virtually nothing about her life. All that exists—or existed—between us is sexual attraction. Well, perhaps more than sexual attraction. At least on my end. Beyond my burning desire for her, I harbor a fervent need to protect her. To keep her as my possession, my mate, until she's coated in my scent. Until she's wearing my ancestral markings on her arms.

A heartbond. If a heartbond finishes forming between us, I'll be able to read her thoughts with ease. I'll know the truth about her involvement with The Saviors, or non-involvement as she claims.

But what if I don't like what I find?

What if we become heartbonded and I feel her hatred?

"My people assisted in the investigation into The Saviors' activities. I doubt you were arrested without cause." It's impossible to fight back my agitation. How dare she deny her part in the attack?

After days of yearning to be reunited with the female I've technically claimed as my mate, I'm taken aback by how furious I am with her. I suppress the urge to grab her and shake her hard.

Fluxx. I'm tempted to turn her over my knee and

thrash her until she makes a full confession. Until she sinks to her knees and begs for forgiveness. But we aren't alone. If I punish her, the commotion would wake her fellow prisoners and alert the guards to my presence.

She shakes her head and says something, but her image is fading, and I can no longer hear her voice. I blink, and suddenly I'm back in my temporary quarters aboard the *Rorrsa*.

But I did it. I intentionally transported myself to the *Haxxal's* brig to visit Leona, and I'm confident that with more practice, I'll manage to do it again and stay for a longer visit next time.

Lee-oon-ahh. I will find you again.

Though I don't hear her reply in my head, I sense her presence, and my ancestral markings are still tingling. When I inhale deeply, I swear I catch a hint of her arousal in the air. I place a hand on my chest and touch the markings. *Lee-oon-ahh. I will make you pay for what you've done.*

Chapter 25

LEONA

A FEW DAYS AFTER MY ARREST, I AWAKE WITH A HEAVY heart.

It's execution day.

I sit up in bed and exchange worried glances with the other women. Thankfully, we've been saved. But the sixty males who were arrested and charged with treason? Their hours are numbered. At intervals throughout the day, they'll be taken to the depressurization chamber in groups of five, their deaths broadcast on every info screen in the worldship.

My father is among them. So are many of his friends, but that's no surprise. I blink back tears and feel a surge of anger. I'd promised myself I wouldn't cry. The Saviors' crimes are abominable. The terms of the alliance aren't perfect, and yes even I think the aliens are getting the better end of the deal, but that's no excuse to plot the deaths of thousands.

It hurts realizing that I never really knew my father. He kept so many secrets. And while he tried to protect me sometimes, like when he paid off security officers to pretend they didn't know about the speakeasy, in the end he attempted to recruit my help with his rebel cause. I'll never forget that he wanted Zahhn dead.

The info screen in our cell flashes blue, then I hear Captain Warren's voice as he narrates a text alert that scrolls by.

Attention citizens of the Jansonna*:*

I have joyous news to share. Our Darrvason friends have recently located a planet called 58-Zallnanis that will be perfect for humankind. It's sixty-eight percent water, has breathable air, and contains several large continents that are brimming with life. We will reach the planet in about five months. Another joyous development—the Darrvasons have also decided to settle on 58-Zallnanis, though they do not plan to live on the same continent as humankind.

Truly, today is a day for rejoicing. Let us not forget that if The Saviors had succeeded in overthrowing the Darrvasons and gaining control of the Jansonna, *all would be lost and we wouldn't be mere months away from a brand-new life on a beautiful world. Let us rejoice in the justice that is about to prevail.*

Be well and be kind to one another.

The captain's message repeats several times before the info screen goes dark.

So the rumors are true. The Darrvasons have indeed located a habitable planet for us to settle upon. I'm not sure how I feel about the aliens joining us.

But what does it matter? I won't spend the rest of my days on a continent settled by humans. I swallow hard. I'll be taken to the Darrvason settlement on 58-Z. Whether as a bride or a slave, I am not certain.

All I know is that Officer Brute negotiated for our lives. A security officer who took pity on us shared this news recently, and he claimed the female prisoners between the ages of nineteen and twenty-five would be included in the next handover of one hundred women, but the older women like me would be given to the aliens *for free.* As compensation for the trouble brought by The Saviors.

What the Darrvasons plan to do with us, I'm not certain. But I doubt I'll enjoy it. I might trade one cell for another, but I'll always be a prisoner.

The last thing Zahhn said sends a shiver through me, and I can't stop thinking about it.

Lee-oon-ahh. I will make you pay for what you've done.

The screen flashes blue again, and I immediately turn my back to it. I climb under the covers and press my fingers in my ears. I don't want to hear the screams of The Saviors as they're executed. Executions are always broadcast ship-wide, and I've witnessed too many to count over the years.

I remain in bed for hours, trembling and crying with my fingers pressed in my ears. Maybe it makes me a coward for not watching, but I don't care. I just want today to be over.

My thoughts stray to Zahhn. I'm not sure where we stand. When he last visited me—when he somehow temporarily projected himself into the worldship's brig

—he seemed bent on vengeance. He thinks I was involved in the rebel plot against his people, and he didn't stay long enough to hear me out.

I will make you pay for what you've done.

I shiver again.

Silent tears soak my pillow as I consider all I've lost. My entire life has been upended, and all the plans I had for the future have turned to dust. I used to dream about opening my own restaurant on whatever planet humankind finally settled upon—with a secret bar in the back, of course.

Growing up, I always felt so alone. So rejected. Having an absentee father will do that to a person. Especially when your mother's long dead and you have no other living family members.

My speakeasy not only kept me busy and helped occupy my mind, but it gave me the opportunity to assemble a tight-knit friend group. A chosen family. Even when Ellen, Angelo, and Michaela weren't around, I still had plenty of friendly people surrounding me at the bar. Because of the speakeasy, I never lacked for companionship.

In addition to my selfish reasons for establishing the bar, I believe I did a good thing by providing a gathering place for regular citizens of the *Jansonna* to hang out and unwind. A place for people to socialize without worrying about a fucking morality officer breathing down their neck.

Maybe I should've kept rebels from congregating in my bar, but how was I to know they were planning to mass murder the Darrvasons, take out the command team, and assume leadership of the *Jansonna*?

The truth is, I never believed they would succeed in overthrowing Captain Warren. Over the years, several rebel groups have tried and failed. All who were caught paid with their lives.

I dig my fingers deeper in my ears, determined not to hear anything. If I hear a single scream or gasp of pain coming from the info screen, I'll wonder if it's my father, then I'll probably end up checking.

A heavy, warm hand runs up and down my back. I startle and turn over, but no one is there. As I check to see who touched me, I'm careful not to glance at the info screen or remove my fingers from my ears. How very strange. A glance around the cell shows my fellow prisoners are seated on their beds.

Again, I feel a hand caressing my back in a comforting manner. Then I detect Zahhn's familiar masculine scent in the air, and I can't help but take a huge lungful of it.

He's *here*. He's here but he's… not.

Not physically, anyway.

I suppose he doesn't want to fully project himself into the cell in the middle of the day. Not when my cellmates are awake and the guards patrolling the corridors walk by every few minutes.

Though our last conversation was a tense one, and I'm not sure whether he truly plans to seek retribution against me for my alleged involvement in The Saviors' foiled plot, I can't help but take comfort in his touch.

Tears burn in my eyes. Today is one of the darkest

days of my life, but Zahhn is here with me, offering me the gift of his presence. Offering me comfort. I breathe deep of his scent and sigh softly as he continues rubbing my back.

Are you going to hurt me? I ask. *When I'm handed over to your people in two moon cycles, will you hurt me?*

There's a long pause. Then his voice finally rumbles through my head. *I haven't decided yet, human female.*

He keeps gently rubbing my back.

Chapter 26

ZAHHN

I'M BACK ON THE *HAXXAL* WITH ANOTHER SCIENTIFIC achievement to my name, probably my greatest yet. The trials on the *Rorrsa* were a huge success, and a treatment for *forlonngsa* now exists. All the patients who've been treated thus far have made full recoveries.

As I peer around my laboratory, the sense of pride I'd expected to feel at this moment doesn't come. Not fully. All I can think about is Leona. In a matter of days, she'll be given to my people. Also in a matter of days, I plan to take ownership of her.

Though I've spoken with Officer Brute a few times recently, he is not yet certain what will happen to the five females who aren't in the nineteen to twenty-five age range. He's suggested that perhaps they'll be used as servants, but I cannot fathom how that will work.

Because those five women won't be drenched in the

scent of a mate, which means, through no fault of their own, they'll be a temptation to unmated Darrvason males who might encounter them. Perhaps Officer Brute doesn't want to admit it, but those five females will have to be kept in a secure location. Like the brig.

But that will not happen to Leona.

I will not allow it.

My wrist comm buzzes and beeps with a message from Emperor Radakk. *Fluxx*. I drag a hand through my hair. I've barely had time to settle back into my old laboratory, yet he's on his way for a visit. Not only that, but he's bringing his mate along. Empress Thalia.

I hurry to pull up the information on the screens that I know the emperor is seeking. He's not just visiting to thank me for curing *forlonggsa*, he wants to know if he's a candidate for the treatment.

Once the correct information is on display, I straighten my shirt and turn to the doorway, awaiting their arrival while praying they don't linger for long.

Emperor Radakk soon escorts his female into my laboratory, and I immediately avert my eyes from his mate. Tradition dictates I cannot interact with her in any way until he formally introduces us, but I'm pleased when he's quick to do so. Because it indicates he trusts me and values our friendship. Given that I'm planning to claim an unsanctioned female during the next few days, I am pleased by this outcome.

"Doctor Zahhn, this is my mate, Thalia."

I finally lift my eyes to the female and incline my head. "Good morning, Empress."

"Good morning, Doctor Zahhn," she says with a faint smile.

I clear my throat and gesture at a nearby screen. "As you are aware, Emperor Radakk, I decided to re-sequence your genes after noticing some anomalies in your most recent blood sample."

"And? Am I a candidate for the same treatment you used on the *Rorrsa*?"

"You're not a candidate for the treatment," I say, "because it'll never be needed. The markers that indicate an increased risk for *forlonggsa* are now missing from your genetic makeup."

"How is that possible?" he asks.

Excitement fills me, and I feel as though I'm bouncing with energy even though I'm standing perfectly still. I gesture at a second screen. "The same thing happened to Officer Tannall. He possessed an even larger risk than you, and the markers are now missing from his genetic makeup as well. The common factor, of course, is that you both recently mated and developed a heartbond with a human female."

The emperor and empress exchange a hopeful look.

"I'm still running tests to discover the science behind it," I continue, "but it appears a heartbond with a human can alter the genetic makeup of a Darrvason male. It's an amazing development."

"This is wonderful news." Emperor Radakk flashes a rare smile, an expression so joyful I'm almost taken aback. "Thank you for making the discovery, Doctor Zahhn, and thank you for developing the treatment that's helped my uncle and so many others. I've said it before, and I'll say it again—your service to the Darrvason Empire has been invaluable. I hope perhaps this development will encourage you to consider the offer I made you recently."

My mood immediately darkens. *Fluxx*. I'm tempted to specifically request Leona, but then I stop myself. Because what if Emperor Radakk refuses my request? No, I must follow through with my original plan. Even if I must face harsh consequences in the aftermath of my crimes. My thievery. My violence. Yes, I will battle my own people if I must in order to obtain Leona.

"Perhaps, Emperor," I eventually force out. "I am still debating the matter." Lies. I'll say anything to make him drop the subject.

After Emperor Radakk and his mate depart the laboratory, an idea occurs to me. One that I feel foolish for not thinking of before. I hastily move about my laboratory, setting up the same test I used to analyze Emperor Radakk and Officer Tannall's genetic makeup. I extract a sample of my own blood and get to work.

The results are so shocking, I gape stupidly at the screens for a long moment, not quite believing what I'm seeing.

My genetic makeup is altered in several locations. Not as many as Emperor Radakk and Officer Tannall's, but it's enough to give me hope.

Hope that perhaps I'm no longer sterile. Or, if I still am, I won't be for long. If I stake my claim on Leona and rut her until a heartbond forms between us, perhaps I'll eventually be able to sire offspring.

Optimism continues to swell inside me, but then I

quickly tamp it down. *Fool. You don't possess all the information yet.*

My sudden growl reverberates around the laboratory. I shouldn't allow myself to become hopeful when I am not entirely certain it will work.

Furthermore, there's the glaring fact that Leona was involved in a rebel plot against my people. If she continues to harbor hatred for my kind, having a child with her is likely a terrible idea.

But I cannot fathom the idea of her rotting in a brig. Nor can I stand the prospect of her becoming a mated pair's servant, for that would be the only way she could serve in a household—if the male was already heart-bonded to another female.

Lee-oon-ahh. I plan to visit you tonight.

Zahhn? Her voice echoes in my head, and my ancestral markings immediately start tingling. I revel in the sensation even though I'm not yet certain of her true feelings for me.

Leona. Your obedience training begins tonight. I will see you soon.

I detect her nervousness through the… *bond?* Whatever it is that links our emotions on occasion. Then the connection goes silent, and I'm no longer able to sense her presence. But I will see her tonight, and it will be an interaction that pushes her limits.

Chapter 27

LEONA

I LIE AWAKE, ANTICIPATING ZAHHN'S ARRIVAL. IT'S THE middle of the night and I'm fairly certain my cellmates are fast asleep. We'll have a little privacy, though we'll have to remain quiet. Of course, we can simply communicate telepathically.

Nerves flitter in my stomach, and my breaths become shallow and fast. When I heard Zahhn's voice in my head earlier, he didn't sound pleased. He sounded stern and authoritative.

Your obedience training begins tonight.

A shiver rushes through me. What did he mean by that?

Given my status as a prisoner, and the fact that I'm older than twenty-five, I don't think he'll be able to rightfully claim me as his mate. Never mind that we already copulated once.

I sigh, wishing I knew more about Darrvason laws and customs.

The truth is, I don't know what to expect when I'm handed over to the aliens. All I know is that I won't be free. I'll never be free again. I'll spend the rest of my life in captivity.

My nervousness increases.

Does Zahhn intend to keep me as his… *slave?*

In our recent communications, he mentioned retribution. He mentioned training me to be obedient. Neither of those things sounds very pleasant.

Oh, how I wish I could escape.

If I could somehow reach a bustling trading outpost, I could disappear into the crowd. I could change my name, take a menial job on a departing vessel, and simply vanish. If only.

But there's no escaping the brig. There's only one way out and it remains heavily guarded. And it's not like I could steal a shuttle. The docking bay is as heavily guarded as the brig.

My breath catches as awareness skitters through me. I sense Zahhn's masculine presence, though I don't see him yet. I sit up and glance around the cell. A few minutes pass, and then…

He appears out of thin air.

I blink fast a few times, astonished by what I just witnessed. He steps closer and delves a hand into my hair.

A look of reverence fills his eyes as he caresses his long fingers through my locks.

But his visage soon becomes stern, causing nerves to clench in my stomach.

I focus on the tether between us, which feels strongest when he's near. *I'm not a rebel*, I send down the bond. *I had nothing to do with The Saviors' attack on your people.*

He looks skeptical. *I read the investigators' reports. Your father was one of the most involved members of the rebel group.*

Annoyance flares within me. *And what did the investigators' reports say about me? If I'm as guilty as you seem to believe, what specific role did I play in the attack?*

The hand that's stroking my hair suddenly tightens in my tresses, and I wince at the pain. *According to the investigators*, he sends down the bond, *you were fully aware of your father's plotting. You were also present in your quarters when a final meeting to plan the attack was held in that very location. And let's not forget that you founded Leona's Speakeasy, an illegal meeting place that's been used by rebels for clandestine operations for years.*

I was horrified by my father's scheming, especially his plans to kill Darrvasons! The thought erupts from me before I can stop it. So much for convincing Zahhn of my innocence. *Once I learned about the virus, which I only found out days before the attack, I wanted to warn someone. But I wasn't able to contact you at the time. I tried but received no reply. I considered warning Officer Brute, but I couldn't find him. Then the attack happened, and I've had over two months in the brig to regret my actions.*

And do you regret your actions? he asks. *Or rather, your lack of action?*

Is that what you want to hear? That I regret not trying to warn someone? Well, I'm not sure if I do. Because what difference would it have made? If I warned someone, the worldship's command team would've tracked down The Saviors and executed every last one of them. No matter what choice I made, people would've still died. But I never imagined they might use strange technology to disable your ships and attack the Haxxal. *The plan… the virus… I didn't truly comprehend what was happening until it was too late.*

His eyes darken, and his grip remains tight in my hair. *Were you truly horrified by your father's plans to kill Darrvasons?*

Of course I was. I inhale a shaky breath, wishing he would release my hair. My scalp is really starting to hurt. *Just because your people got the better end of the alliance doesn't mean I want you dead.*

The better end of the alliance? He scoffs. *Is that honestly what you believe? We are saving humankind. Without us, you would all be dead.* Jansonna's *systems would've completely shut down. No more water. No more breathable air. No artificial gravity. You should consider yourselves lucky that we struck a deal with you rather than storm your ship and steal all your females. We could've easily just taken what we wanted without giving you anything in return.*

My throat burns with emotion, and frustration singes what's left of my patience. I don't like fighting with Zahhn. Partly because, goddammit, his argument is well-founded.

Two thousand one hundred and thirty is a big fucking number, I send down the bond. *Plus five, apparently. Do you have any idea what such a loss will do to my people? Families are going to be torn apart. People will lose their daughters, sisters, and friends.*

We're all settling on planet 58-Zallnanis. I am certain visita-

tion between our people will take place, even if we live on different continents. He lets go of my hair, then sinks down on the bed next to me. His thigh touches mine. Despite myself, his nearness sends a quiver of desire through me. The huge alien doctor infuriates me, and yet I cannot help but crave him.

Perhaps we should agree to disagree. I peer up at him, lost in the depths of his glowing purple eyes. *I don't believe your arrogance would allow you to lose an argument.*

I hear him chuckle inside my head, and there's something about our telepathic communication that feels special. Intimate.

Since our argument appears to be over, human female, and it would seem I have emerged the victor, I believe it is time to begin.

My heart races. *Time to begin what?*

He places a hand on my thigh and squeezes. *Your obedience training.*

I don't need obedience training. I try to pull away, but he tightens his hold on my leg, digging his fingers into my flesh. A whimper leaves my throat, and I quickly glance around to make sure everyone's still sleeping. Only deep, steady breathing and soft snores greet me. No one appears restless or on the verge of waking up. I exhale with relief.

You are too rebellious, Leona. Too proud. You must be humbled. You must be made to surrender. He suddenly covers my mouth with his hand and guides me back on the pillows. It takes all my self-control not to whimper or make a noise of protest. Finally, he retracts his hand from my mouth.

What's going to happen to me when I'm handed over to your

people? Tremors jolt my body, a mix of fear and quaking arousal. I wish I could shut him out. I wish I didn't find him so handsome and captivating despite his domineering ways.

He hovers over me and leans down to take a long inhale of my hair. The warmth of his body soaks into mine, and his closeness sends a wave of longing to the depths of my soul. I want to ask if he still considers me his mate, but I'm terrified of the answer. But maybe if he reveals what will happen after I'm given to his people, my question will be answered in a roundabout way.

He pulls back to stare down at me, and heat flares in his eyes. His lips twist in a somewhat cruel expression, and I feel very much at his mercy. He strokes a hand lazily down my stomach, then delves inside my prison-issue pajama pants. Oh God. His fingers immediately seek out my clit, and it's agony to endure the bliss in silence.

What's going to happen to me when I'm handed over to your people? I send down the bond again, unable to keep the impatience from my tone.

His eyes glitter in the dim light of the brig, and a mocking smile dances over his features. *You'll get what you deserve*, he finally replies, then he abandons my clit to shove three thick fingers in my core. Or maybe it's his whole goddamn hand. All I know is that it's huge and unexpected and I'm trying very hard not to scream.

You'll get what you deserve, he repeats. He commences pounding me with his massive fingers, driving in and out as I tremble and writhe on the bed. His dark chuckle reverberates in my head.

I was already wet for him when he shoved inside, but as he thrusts faster and deeper, I practically gush moisture. I feel the slickness coating my inner thighs.

He takes a long inhale, and I hear him growl with pleasure. Telepathically, of course. He hasn't made an audible sound since his appearance in the brig. I imagine he's a vengeful phantom come to seek retribution.

Without warning, he pulls his fingers from my core. He holds them in front of my face, and I flush when I notice the gleam of my arousal coating his digits.

You will suck your arousal off my fingers, human female. His voice is a sharp command, and though I don't understand why, I'm compelled to obey. There's a softness that flows through me, a boundless yearning to please him.

I part my lips on a gasp, and he drives his fingers into my mouth, creating a slow sensual plunging motion. The taste of my essence surprises me, sweet and tangy, and I flush when I remember how much Zahhn enjoyed licking me *down there* on the night he appeared in my bedroom.

Then I recall the way he tastes. My temperature rises, the ache in my core deepens, and I become so breathless that dark spots swirl in my vision. His essence is sweet, like an iced pastry, and a whimper builds in my throat as I visualize the act of kneeling to take him in my mouth.

His breath hisses inward, the only real sound he's made since his arrival, and a knowing look enters his eyes. He withdraws his fingers from between my lips and smirks. *I saw that,* he sends down the tether that links our minds. *That naughty thought you just had. What a vivid imagination you possess, human female.*

I almost retort that if he can catch glimpses of carnal thoughts, perhaps he should search my mind for the truth about my involvement, or non-involvement, with The Saviors. But I don't want to start another argument, and the pleasure quaking in my core is making it difficult to think clearly, so I push the idea aside.

Later. Perhaps later he can search my mind for the truth, though my stomach flips when I consider what else he might find.

Knowing that he can pick up stray thoughts and images from my consciousness even when I'm not intentionally sending him the thought makes me curious. Perhaps I can do the same to him. But before I get the chance, he guides me off the bed and forces me to kneel on the floor. He arranges me between his spread thighs, and I can't help but glance at the enormous bulge in his pants.

He places a finger beneath my chin, forcing my gaze to his. His eyes blaze with heat and a bit of sternness, and before he even speaks, I know he's about to give me another order. He unfastens the front of his pants, moves a strip of leathery fabric aside, and his dual appendages spring out, long and thick and massively erect. To my great mortification, my mouth waters as I anticipate tasting him.

Get to work, Leona. He drops his hand from my chin and leans back. *Suck, swallow, and repeat.*

Chapter 28

ZAHHN

LEONA PEERS WIDE-EYED AT MY SWOLLEN COCKS, THEN she casts an uneasy glance around the cell.

They're all asleep, I assure her. *If anyone wakes, I will know.*

And then what will you do? she asks. *Disappear?*

A smile tugs at my lips. *Precisely. Now get to work. You are not as quick to obey as I would prefer. As I've said before, you are in need of training.*

I fail to see how sucking your appendages qualifies as 'obedience training.' A hint of defiance dances in her eyes, and she shifts on her knees, clearly uncomfortable in her position on the hard floor.

I could show her mercy and place a pillow beneath her knees, but I won't. Not this time.

Leaning forward, I grab the front of her shirt, then I tear the fabric in a quick but fairly quiet motion. Her breasts spill out, and her mouth falls open as her eyes brim with fury.

How dare you? she seethes.

I trace one of her nipples, then give it a firm pinch, squeezing so hard it brings tears to her eyes. She covers her mouth with one hand as her face twists with agony. With her other hand, she grabs hold of my wrist and tries to wrench it away from her bosom.

I can't take you over my knee and give you a thrashing right now, human female. Not without waking the whole cell block, I send down the bond. *So, the methods of punishment I use when you are insubordinate will have to be quiet ones. I highly recommend obedience, Leona, or you are in for a night of extreme pain and humiliation.*

Even in the dim light, I can see her face turning a bright shade of red. I sense her fury, but also her shame. A moment later, a pulsating wave of her arousal hits me, and I savor a deep inhale. I pinch her nipple harder and twist, drawing a faint whimper from her. A single tear cascades down her cheek, and she blinks faster.

Finally, I release her nipple. A look of immense relief steals over her, and she immediately rubs the punished area. Her entire body is now trembling hard. Through the bond, I sense a wave of reluctant surrender coming from her. I send back a surge of power, and she dips her head in a show of submission so lovely that it causes a pang of warmth in my chest.

Good little female. I gesture to my fully erect shafts. *Now, obey.*

She lowers her head to my crotch, and I watch to see which of my shafts she will suck first. She goes for my upper appendage. I'm shocked when she curls a tiny hand around the base of this shaft without any prompting, and it takes a great deal of control to keep from growling aloud.

Her hand is so small that she cannot curl it all the way around my cock, but as she tries and squeezes, the pleasure cascades through me and both my appendages lurch upward. She gasps, startled by the movement, but she doesn't release her hold on my upper length.

Stop gasping and whimpering, Leona. If you wake your cellmates, I will be very displeased with you.

Sorry. Her gaze flicks to mine briefly, then she refocuses her attention on the shaft she's about to suck. Anticipation mounts inside me, a quaking euphoric heat, as she parts her lips and leans down.

Then she takes me in her mouth. She runs her tongue up and down the side of my shaft, and I sense her uncertainty through the bond. When she last took me in her mouth, I held her head in place and pounded her face, not allowing her much freedom during the act. She had no choice but to remain on her knees with her lips parted while I plunged in and out, slamming into the back of her throat while she gagged and whimpered. Desire sizzles through me at the memory.

But there's a certain appeal to watching her fumble her way through a cock sucking session. A nourishment session. Not for the first time in her presence, I experience the overwhelming urge to spurt my essence down her throat in order to nourish her, to fill her stomach with my highly nutritious seed.

Fluxx. She's moving too slow. She's being obedient,

but Star Gods, she is moving too slow. Is she teasing me on purpose?

I'm on the verge of taking control when she suddenly increases her pace and starts bobbing her head forward and back over my rigid member. *Yes. Perfect. Good little female.* Whether I actually send my praise to her, I am not sure. The pleasure becomes so intense, it's difficult to concentrate. *Your pretty mouth feels so good.*

As she continues her work, she keeps the base of my shaft gripped tightly in her tiny hand. She manages to take almost the full length of my shaft in her mouth, but always withdraws the moment the tip hits the back of her throat. I suspect she's trying not to gag. Observing her somewhat clumsy efforts causes another wave of affection to flow through me, and before I realize what I'm doing, I'm sending that wave of tenderness straight down the bond to her.

Am I a bastard for questioning her tonight? I want to believe she had nothing to do with the attack, but she admitted she suspected something was about to happen. She knew her father and his comrades were plotting.

When she spoke of her horror over her father's plan to take Darrvason lives, however, she seemed genuine, and I sensed her honesty. Perhaps when the bond we share becomes stronger, I will learn the full truth.

I suppress a groan as she swirls her tongue over the tip of my shaft. *Star Gods. Fluxx.* I press my eyes shut and revel in the feel of her mouth on my upper appendage. I reach out, seeking her emotions, searching for the heart and soul that will soon belong to me.

I sense a wide range of emotions in varying degrees.

Desire, anticipation, shame, worry, uncertainty, guilt. Desire and anticipation are the strongest, which pleases me greatly. She's aching for a release, and her center is drenched in her arousal. She's slick and eager to be pounded with my shafts.

Will I fuck her in the middle of the brig?

Probably not.

I long to bury my cocks in her mating orifice, one after the other, but I do not believe I can do so without growling and moaning and waking up the occupants of the brig. While I don't care if anyone witnesses me claiming my female, I have no wish for guards to come running. I would be forced to disappear and return to the *Haxxal*.

I'm not ready to leave Leona yet, never mind that she'll belong to me in mere days. A thrill rushes through me when I imagine the moment she'll officially belong to me by the laws of my people.

I stroke a hand through her hair as she continues sucking my appendage. My scrotum vibrates faster as I visualize the moment I'll steal away with her. I've already discovered she'll be brought to the *Haxxal*, along with the other female prisoners, and I know the names of the guards who will be escorting the women to their temporary quarters.

Thinking about my plan to steal her, to remove her from one form of captivity to another, causes my desire to spike. Waves of ecstasy descend and my cock pulses in Leona's sweet mouth. I climax down her throat in rapid spurts, and I tighten my fingers in her hair as she endeavors to swallow all that I give her.

She succeeds in gulping down every last drop, and I send a flash of praising warmth down the bond. She pulls away from my shaft and attempts to catch her breath. I reach out to touch the nipple I tormented earlier, but this time I simply give it a soft caress. She shivers at my touch and her hips jolt forward. Her arousal thickens in the air.

I grasp the base of my lower appendage and give her an expectant look. Her eyes widen and she hesitates. She's still breathing hard, however, and she also shifts uncomfortably on her knees. At first, I think she's going to argue or plead tiredness, but she eventually leans down to accept my unspent cock in her mouth.

Good little female. Keep sucking.

Chapter 29

LEONA

By the time my *nourishment session* is over, after sucking each of his cocks twice, I'm deliriously fatigued and can no longer remain in position on my knees. I wince in pain and fall forward just as I swallow the last spurt of Zahhn's seed.

The huge alien male catches me. He lifts me in his arms and cradles me in his lap, and I desperately seek out waves of tenderness and reassurance from him.

After I'm remanded in Darrvason custody, will I see him again? I'm tempted to ask, but I fear his answer. He's evasive whenever I ask about the specifics of what's going to happen. *You'll get what you deserve.*

I fight back a shiver wrought from fear of the unknown, and I strive to relax in his embrace. His muscular arms are huge and strong, and when I lean closer to his chest, I hear the rapid beating of his heart.

Though he just erupted in my mouth, multiple times, his shafts are already swollen and large beneath me. The steady vibration of his scrotum causes pangs of heat in my core.

My face grows warm as I shift on his lap. Wet. I'm so immensely wet, I've soaked through my panties and pajama bottoms. Laundry service comes once a week. For the remainder of my stay, I'll have to sleep in one of my prison uniforms.

He presses his forehead to mine, and I nearly break into a sob at the affection that flows from him. Is it real? Does he truly care about me?

I don't send him a wave of tenderness back. I can't bring myself to do it. A little voice in the back of my mind keeps whispering that I should keep my guard up. I want to trust Zahhn, but I don't yet know if I can.

He's already admitted he's not sure if he'll hurt me after I'm handed over to his people. Whether that means I'll have contact with him, I'm not certain. Maybe he hasn't yet decided.

Will his people forever view me as the enemy? It's possible Zahhn will view me as tainted, and he might not want anyone to know he's claimed me. My spirits darken under a cloud of uncertainty.

I remind myself that I've been treated surprisingly well during my incarceration. From what I've heard, prisoners in *Jansonna's* brig usually sleep on the floor. They aren't given blankets or clean clothes, and they aren't fed regularly or provided with an endless supply of clean water.

Officer Brute, the Darrvason who's infatuated with

Jenny, has personally seen to our welfare. He's visited the brig numerous times, and I've witnessed him scolding the guards when we didn't have enough blankets or our meals were delivered late, among other reasons.

Maybe it's a sign. A sign that we won't be tormented after the aliens take possession of us. I close my eyes and revel in the warmth of Zahhn's arms.

It soon becomes difficult to remain still in his embrace, however, because the aching in my core won't abate. I flush, knowing Zahhn can detect my arousal. I'm still shocked by how drenched I became as I sucked his appendages. My clit throbs as I squirm in place, desperate for his touch, and my pussy clenches as I recall the feel of his three massive fingers plunging in and out.

Still holding me in his arms, Zahhn straightens and rises to his feet. He sets me down facing the bed, then guides me to bend over it. A shuddering breath escapes me, and my whole body trembles with need.

I remind myself that the lights are dim enough that even if my cellmates awake, they likely won't see much in the darkness. Hopefully they'll think they're dreaming and simply roll over and go back to sleep. If Zahhn is discovered and forced to disappear before he brings me to pleasure, I'll spend the remainder of the night tossing and turning, restless and frustrated.

Don't worry, human female, he tells me in a chiding tone. *You're about to get what you want—what you're craving. But you must remember to be quiet.*

Pressing my lips tightly together, I hold back a whimper.

He yanks my pajama pants and panties down in one

swift movement, baring me to his gaze. Despite the darkness in the brig, I suspect he has better vision than the typical human. My suspicions are confirmed when he sends me a clear image of his current viewpoint—a vision of me bent over with my thighs slightly parted to reveal my plump, gleaming folds.

His cocks are still freed from his pants, and he stands behind me and presses his engorged members to my center, dragging them up and down through my slick folds. My head falls to the side and my mouth opens on a soundless cry. *Oh God. Yes. Keep going. Oh God, oh God.*

Yes, that's right, Leona. I am your god. I'm going to be your everything, whether you like it or not, he sends down the bond. *You will serve me, and you will obey me. You will kneel before me in supplication.*

Raw, masculine power emanates from him. Though I'm bent over the bed in a vulnerable position, I still find myself tucking my chin down as the urge to submit to his authority courses through me.

He grasps my buttocks, taking one cheek in each hand, and spreads me wide apart. He steps closer, rearranges his grip in order to keep me spread using only one hand, and drags two fingers through my moisture. When he drives those fingers into my aching center, I rise on my toes and my mouth parts on another soundless cry.

My pussy clamps down on his plunging digits, so large and huge inside me. Oh God. My hips undulate, and my clit throbs in a steady, urgent pulse.

Be a good little female for this next part, comes his ominous warning, and then he withdraws from my center and nudges his two lubricated fingers at my anus. I grip the covers as he breaches my pucker. I want to cry out and beg him not to plunge his huge digits into my ass, but I fear his retribution if I make a noise and wake my cellmates. Furthermore, despite my current discomfort, I'm not yet ready for him to leave.

He pushes more forcefully, shoving his fingers in my bottom hole. The fullness steals my breath, and I wince at the slight pain even as fresh pangs of desire reverberate in my core, causing my hips to undulate once again.

Beautiful. This puckering hole of yours could easily accommodate a cock. Look at how you can stretch around my fingers. He sends me another image from his point of view, and I flush at the sight of his two digits fully submerged in my ass.

I blink and the vision fades, but the fullness in my bottom doesn't. I struggle to remain silent as he presses one of his appendages to my slick, aching pussy. Oh God. Is he going to penetrate both my holes at the same time? I recall how difficult it was to accept a double-intrusion during my medical exam.

He'd only used one finger in my ass during the exam, however, and the metallic phalluses he'd shoved in my core were smaller than either of his appendages. My heart races and I clutch the covers tighter. How will I endure?

His mocking chuckle echoes in my head. *You will survive, Leona. Now be a good female and take it.* Then he shoves his massive lower shaft—I'm certain he's using the bigger one, the insufferable bastard—into my core, impaling me in one rapid drive.

I writhe underneath him and claw at the covers, trying to pull myself up so I might escape. He's too big. It's too much. And yet… and yet the pleasure is overwhelming, and his vibrating scrotum is pressed directly over my clit. He holds me in place and withdraws from my center, only to slam inside. He repeats this motion over and over, pumping his huge appendage in and out of my tight core, all the while keeping his thick fingers buried in my ass.

I close my eyes and see an explosion of light, and then the pleasure descends in powerful quaking waves, an assault of bliss unlike anything I've ever known.

The climax steals my breath, and I become lightheaded as the release continues pummeling me. My hips jerk in place and when I think I'm about to cry out, I shove a fist in my mouth and bite down until I taste blood. Tears coat my face. Not being able to make a noise is sheer agony.

I remain bent over the bed while Zahhn continues plunging in and out. At some point, he withdraws his lower appendage from my core and impales me with his upper one, even though he hasn't spurted inside me yet.

He doesn't remove his digits from my ass, and accepting the intrusion in my most private place gradually becomes easier. A slight sting remains, but it no longer hurts enough for me to beg him for mercy.

He alternates claiming me with his upper and lower appendages, switching back and forth with rapid speed. The constant in and out, accompanied by the firm press of his vibrating scrotum to my clit, soon sends me over the edge of bliss again. While this release is intense, it doesn't last as long as the previous one. It's deliciously forceful, but the final vestiges of the climax soon fade. Yet my need quickly mounts again, and it doesn't take long for my clit to start throbbing under fresh pangs of desire.

Good female. Very good. Keep coming on my shafts, he sends down the bond, and I melt at his praising tone.

Sore. I'm starting to become sore. I wince as he drives his largest appendage deep in my center. Perspiration trickles down my temple, merging with the tears that keep escaping. The urge to moan aloud is so strong, I'm not sure how much more silence I can withstand.

I know you're getting sore, human female, he says. *But I'm not finished with you yet. Keep holding position and remain quiet as I pound you.*

Chapter 30

ZAHHN

My shafts are throbbing hard and I'm aching for a release, but I strive to maintain control for a bit longer. I continue alternating plunges with my cocks, and I don't withdraw my fingers from her ass.

The capitulation I sense flowing from her through the bond is bringing out my more beastly side. I'm succeeding in my quest to conquer her, to make her crave my authority and guidance.

Should I tell her I plan to steal her? Should I admit I have a plan in place to kidnap her and rut her repeatedly until a heartbond finishes forming between us?

Before I can reach a decision, her pussy clamps down on my lower appendage and I finally lose control. As the first pulsing spurt of seed fills her, I suppress a growl and grasp the base of my upper shaft.

Then I erupt simultaneously, my essence releasing

from both my cocks at once. The seed from my upper shaft hits her lower back, bathing her in the proof of my ownership.

My blood heats further and my vision swirls. Her center clamps down on my plunging shaft as she reaches yet another climax of her own, and I revel in the feel of her asshole clenching on my fingers. The smallest whimper escapes her.

Quiet, I command through the bond.

Though I sense a flash of annoyance from her, she settles and falls silent. I release my cock and stroke a hand down her back. Slowly, I withdraw my lower appendage from her slick chasm. Next, I pull my digits from her ass.

Relief and fatigue flow outward from her. She'll probably have little difficulty falling asleep once I leave. She's gone limp over the bed, her hands no longer gripping the covers, her hips no longer undulating. The only movement is the rapid rise and fall of her back as she attempts to catch her breath.

I glance toward the bathroom, but I know using the shower or the sink to clean up will likely wake her cellmates, so I remove my shirt and use it to wipe my essence from her back. Then I cleanse the area between her thighs.

Without meaning to, I send affection down the bond, a surge of pulsing warmth that I imagine feels like an embrace. But I don't retract the tenderness. Instead, I marvel at it, how natural it feels. How perfectly right.

I note that she doesn't send me any warmth in return. Will the heartbond finish developing anyway? If

I keep spilling my seed inside her, will the bond form even if she tries to resist it?

I cannot deny that there are aspects of the heart-bond, even between two full-blooded Darrvasons, that defy scientific explanation. The heartbonds that formed between the thirty human females and their respective mates all developed a bit differently. Some quickly and without much warning, like Admiral Tornn's, and others more slowly, like Emperor Radakk's, which took nearly three moon cycles to complete.

I ball up my shirt, place it on the floor, and tuck my shafts back into my pants. Then I lift Leona in my arms and peer into her eyes, wishing our connection could be easier, less fraught with conflict.

Many times, I have felt her pushing me away. I have sensed her resistance.

Trust. When our heartbond finally forms, there will be trust between us. I will know her secrets, and she will know mine.

I place her on the bed and tuck her under the covers.

Goodnight, Leona.

She stares at me but doesn't offer a reply. Her inner turmoil is evident, but the hour is late and I must leave. I know she has questions, and she's frustrated I haven't provided the answers she's seeking, but I do not think it wise to give her advance warning of my plans to steal her.

What if she tells someone? Perhaps one of her cell-mates? A guard might overhear the conversation, and if my people learn of my plans, stealing her will be more difficult.

I press a kiss to her forehead, and even though I doubt she will return my affections, I send her a pulsing wave of tenderness.

I retrieve my shirt from the floor, stand tall, and close my eyes. Humming low in my throat, I strive for the trance that will facilitate a return to the *Haxxal*.

Coldness surrounds me and I'm falling, falling, falling…

I open my eyes to find myself standing in my quarters aboard the *Haxxal*. Alone. Alone, but not for much longer.

Leona. Soon, she will belong to me.

I set about finalizing my preparations. I check to ensure the mini-blasters I've acquired are functioning properly, all set to stun. Though I'm prepared to commit violence in order to acquire the pretty human, I would prefer not to kill one of my own people unless it's my only option.

I'm pleased that the mini-blasters are easy to conceal in my pockets and underneath my shirt. Though I'm a male of science and I've spent my entire adult life healing the wounded, curing the sick, and conducting important medical research, I completed the requisite Darrvason warrior training years ago, and I know how to use most types of weapons.

Once I verify the mini-blasters are fully charged, I conceal over a hundred shooting stars in the seams of the clothing I intend to wear during the heist. Normally, shooting stars, which are tiny metallic throwing blades, contain a nerve agent embedded within them that kills a foe almost instantaneously. However, I have modified these shooting stars with a compound that won't cause any permanent damage to those who are struck, but it will render them paralyzed for a full day.

I gather several other small weapons that are easy to conceal in my clothing, then double and triple check to make sure everything is working. There will be no room for mistakes.

Then I pull up a comm screen and start typing a message to the team of guards who are scheduled to escort Leona, as well as the other four females who share in her predicament, to temporary holding quarters until someone in command determines the best use for them.

Guard Team Alpha 12,

As you are probably aware, I have been tasked with developing strict protocols to follow when the next wave of females arrive, an event that is only days away. It's important that we ensure another virus doesn't find its way to any of our ships, or another sort of weapon.

Please remember that no female from this wave is permitted to bring any personal belongings with her. No bags or suitcases of any kind, small or large. None. Furthermore, all Darrvason males who claim a mate from the second wave are required to strip search their females immediately after bringing them aboard their respective ships. There will be no exceptions. Please remind the males of their duty to protect the Darrvason Empire by confirming that their females are unarmed.

Lastly, extra precautions must be taken around the five females from The Saviors who are above the age of twenty-five. I will personally accompany your team as you escort the females to their holding quarters, and I will help verify that none are armed or in possession of any dangerous substances.

-Doctor Zahhn

I transmit the message to the guard team, then lean back in my chair, feeling quite pleased with myself. I glance at my outfit that contains the concealed shooting stars, as well as the mini-blasters sitting next to it.

Surely I can incapacitate the five guards who will be providing escort. I'll be taking them by surprise. Before they realize they're under attack, they will all be lying on the floor, unable to do much more than blink.

Fortunately, my quarters reside on the same deck as the females' holding quarters, which will make getting Leona alone that much easier. I've also outfitted my quarters with force field technology that will ensure we have plenty of privacy while I'm rutting her.

I pray the heartbond will be quick to form between us.

Sighing, I drag a hand through my hair, then I turn to peer out the viewscreen. The *Jansonna* resides in its normal position in the fleet, so close to the *Haxxal* that I can glimpse the deck lights on the upper levels that contain numerous viewscreens. It's my understanding that the wealthier residents of the human worldship reside on the upper decks. Leona lives—*lived*—on Deck Eleven, in cramped quarters that revealed a lower status among her people.

I resolve that she'll want for nothing when she lives with me. I'll commission gowns in the softest, sheerest fabric for her. I'll deck her in jewels and buy her any trinket her heart desires when the fleet visits an outpost.

On planet 58-Z, I will make sure our house is built with her comfort in mind, as well as her preference in style. Though I once told Emperor Radakk I would like a grand house in an elevated location with a majestic view of the landscape, I now find that I care little for such details. All that matters is that I have Leona with me and she is comfortable in her new life.

I move to the viewscreen, and though I suspect she's sleeping, I send her torrents of affection down the bond. *Lee-oon-ahh.*

Chapter 31

LEONA

Shouts echo throughout the corridors of the brig, as well as blaster fire. I'm huddled in the bathroom for safety with my nine cellmates. None of us have a clue what's going on, but it seems reasonable to hide behind a closed door, even if the door lacks a lock.

Hopefully the lock on the cell will keep any villain from entering.

Zahhn. Zahhn, what's happening?

He doesn't answer. My worry increases, and my heart sinks. He's visited me frequently during the past few days. Most of the time, I'm able to sense his presence. I think our bond is growing stronger. But why can't I hear him or sense him now?

"It's probably another rebel group," someone says, and I don't bother looking up to see who's speaking. "Or maybe members of The Saviors that they failed to arrest. Not that I would know anything about that." The woman gives a discreet cough.

"It's certainly possible," adds someone else. "Maybe we're being rescued. Oh, I hope so. I don't want to belong to a Darrvason male."

"Quiet," the woman next to me barks. "I thought I just heard footsteps, but you idiots won't stop blabbering."

The screams that keep echoing down the corridor sound agonizing, making me wonder what kind of weapons are being used.

Are the Darrvasons aware of the attack? Will they help us?

"Listen," I whisper. "The hum that accompanies hyperdive is gone. We're no longer traveling in hyperspace."

The sounds of battle come closer, and I'm tempted to leave the bathroom so I can get a better look. But I don't want to put the other women in danger, so I stay put.

Lee-oon-ahh, comes a familiar masculine voice in my head, and I almost sob with relief.

Zahhn! What's happening? I hold my breath as I await his response.

Grozznolan mercenaries, he sends down the bond. *They've knocked the Jansonna, as well as the entire Darrvason fleet, out of the shared hyperdrive bubble. Are you hiding in the bathroom? I do not see you in your cell.*

Yes, we're all in the bathroom. I long to rush back into the cell and search for him, but I can barely move with the other women pressed up against me. If I open the door, we'll all go tumbling out. *Are you in the cell or in the corridor?*

I am in the corridor. Do not be afraid, he says. *I am well armed, and I will destroy any Grozznolan mercenary who sets foot in this cell block. Your people are fighting back against them, as are the Darrvason engineers who are stationed on this ship. Only a few mercenaries remain alive.*

Mercenaries… who hired them? I ask. *Why are they attacking us?*

According to the chatter on my wrist comm, an unnamed but wealthy group from the Jansonna *hired them to destroy my people and dispose of Captain Warren and his command team. They were not only paid a handsome sum, but they were promised every ship in the Darrvason fleet aside from the* Haxxal, *which the wealthy rebel group wants to keep for its technology. While we possess superior firepower to the Grozznolans, they believed they would be victorious if they beamed to our vessels and faced us in combat. But they did not anticipate the shields our ships possess, and they were only able to beam to the* Jansonna.

Thank you for coming, Zahhn. My throat burns with emotion. He's putting himself in danger to ensure my safety. Perhaps it means he truly cares for me, and perhaps it means my life as a Darrvason captive won't be so terrible.

The Grozznolan ships were just destroyed, he informs me. *Only a few of the creatures remain alive on the* Jansonna.

Savage snarls reverberate down the corridor, and while I can still sense Zahhn's presence, I no longer feel our mind-connection. Sick with worry, I press a hand to my stomach and close my eyes. For the first time in a long fucking time, I pray. I pray to whoever's listening, the human god or the Darrvasons' Star Gods, that no harm will come to Zahhn. *Please keep him safe. Please please please.*

Then I glimpse a vision so awful, I cannot restrain a gasp. My legs give out, and I sink to the floor. I feel hands on me and hear concerned inquiries as my fellow prisoners attempt to help. But they don't know what I just saw. They don't know how terrible the Grozznolans are. Zahhn referred to them as creatures, and now I know why.

Another image flashes in my mind, and I don't think Zahhn's doing it on purpose. He's in the thick of battle, fighting an enemy that's worse than anything I could've ever imagined. The creature possesses two heads, two mouths dripping with saliva, and razor-sharp teeth within each of those awful mouths. It's freakishly muscular, and long tentacles stretch from the lower half of its body.

Shudders rack me as I continue praying for Zahhn's safety. The fight is taking place just outside the cell, and I can only imagine what the Grozznolan mercenary would've done to us if it managed to breach our cell. Dead. We'd likely all be dead.

I glimpse flashes of something tiny and metallic that Zahhn keeps throwing at the creature, and I also see flashes of red. A blaster. Zahhn has a blaster.

Blood oozes from several wounds on the mercenary. Its movements become slower and its heads droop. The beast's mouths hang open and slimy drool continues running down its neck. Nausea rises in my gut as the graphic images keep flashing in my mind.

At last, Zahhn inflicts a fatal blow—he throws a tiny metallic weapon into one of the creature's open mouths, which causes it to gag and flop to the floor. Its tentacles rise and fall with a thump.

A few seconds pass, and there's no movement. It's dead. The mercenary is dead and Zahhn is alive. I send up prayers of thanks to whatever deity answered my call.

I jump out of the huddle of women and open the door, ignoring their cries for me to stop. Zahhn is standing outside the cell, panting breathlessly as he looms over the dead Grozznolan mercenary.

There's a commotion at the end of the corridor, then I hear running. But there are no more screams, and I sense the danger is over. Zahhn confirms my suspicions when his voice echoes in my head.

All is well, human female, he says with a glance at his wrist comm. *The very last mercenary was just slain.* His eyes bore into mine, and he takes a step closer. But the approaching footsteps grow louder, and then… Zahhn disappears into thin air.

A collective gasp sounds behind me, and I glance over my shoulder to find all nine of my cellmates staring wide-eyed at the dead Grozznolan mercenary.

Human security officers, along with two Darrvason engineers arrive on our cell block. They rush down the corridor to ensure the creature is dead. Then they each grab a tentacle and drag it away.

"What's going on?" someone asks, grasping my arm.

I turn to face my cellmates, trying to figure out how to best explain what I know and how I acquired the knowledge. Telling them I have a telepathic connection with the Darrvarson doctor who examined me, who also happens to possess the ability to astral project himself at will, sounds a bit fantastic. If I were in their shoes, I would probably think I was full of shit.

So, I simply shrug and say, "I'm not entirely sure, but I think the danger is over. Don't be scared."

But just as we all get settled on our beds and start to relax, the info screen in the cell turns on. It flashes blue and then… I see a view of the stage at my speakeasy. It's a recording. Jenny is on stage playing the keyboard and singing one of her most popular rebellious songs while the crowd chants along. Oh God. This is bad.

We all jump off our beds and approach the info screen. The song continues playing for way too long. Poor Jenny. She's been exposed. I doubt she's the person responsible for the broadcast. What will happen to her? Will the big Darrvason who follows her around protect her from Captain Warren's wrath? I really hope so.

Suddenly, there's a moment of static and the screen goes blank. Then Angelo… mostly sweet but sometimes hotheaded Angelo, one of my best friends in the whole universe, appears on the screen. But he doesn't look the way I remember. He seems… deranged. Sweat runs down his face as he glares at the camera. I catch a glimpse of his mother in the background and realize he must be in his quarters.

"Citizens of the *Jansonna*," he says. "Rise up. Fight back. Follow the words of Captain Warren's niece. Rise up and fight back. Do whatever you can to break the alliance with the Darrvasons. Kill the Darrvasons if you can." He raises a fist. "Resistance!" He staggers backward, and his mother collapses on the floor.

Jenny's performance resumes.

I fall to my knees. Angelo. Jenny.

They're both as good as dead.

Chapter 32

ZAHHN

I'm standing in the command room where Emperor Radakk and his advisors hold their classified meetings, trying to maintain my composure. It's the morning of the handover, and I am anxious to meet the group of guards I will accompany to the *Haxxal.* I have no wish to join whatever meeting is about to occur, and I cannot imagine why my presence would be required. The fleeting idea that perhaps the emperor plans to ask me to become an advisor dances through my mind, but I quickly dash it away. No, that would not make sense.

When a familiar Darrvason engineer enters the room, I narrow my eyes and glare at the male. I suddenly have a very good idea why I've been summoned. Unfortunately, I didn't disappear from *Jannsonna's* brig before I was spotted by one of my own people, and it would appear he's a snitch. I hold back a growl as all the muscles in my body tense. The urge to pummel this male in the face grows stronger by the moment.

Several advisors file into the room, along with Admiral Tornn and Emperor Radakk. I feel as though I'm about to be put on trial, though I keep telling myself I didn't do anything wrong. As far as I'm concerned, they ought to be thanking me. Not only did I protect the human females in the worldship's brig, but I slaughtered a Grozznolan mercenary.

"Doctor Zahhn, please have a seat," Admiral Tornn says as he exchanges a look with the emperor.

I sink into a chair and peer from face to face, waiting for the verbal lashing to commence. I'm ready to argue my case, of course, but I resolve not to speak until I obtain a better understanding of their version of events. Whether they know about my obsession with Leona, I am uncertain.

I remind myself that Officer Brute and Chief Kameer are likely the only males who are aware of my interest in Leona, but they aren't present in the command room. I silently commend them for not being snitches like this other male.

"I am sure you're wondering why you've been summoned to the command room, Doctor Zahhn," the emperor says, "so I will get straight to the point." He glances at the engineer. "We have reason to believe you astral projected aboard the *Jansonna* during the Grozznolan attack. More specifically, you transported yourself to the worldship's brig."

I shrug. "Well, I am a very talented individual."

Admiral Tornn grunts. "Doctor Zahhn, we did not summon you to the command room to charge you with a crime. I highly suggest you are more forthcoming during this meeting. Now, answer the emperor's question."

I lift my eyebrows. "Technically, Emperor Radakk didn't ask me a question. However, if you insist, Admiral Tornn, I will tell you what happened." My gaze sweeps around the table as I attempt to stall. What the *fluxx* should I say? I draw in a long breath. "As soon as I realized there was danger aboard the *Jansonna*, I strapped on some weapons that I happened to have lying around my quarters, then I astral projected to the worldship's brig, risked my life to protect the female prisoners, chivalrous male that I am, and single-handedly brought down a Grozznolan mercenary." I display a wide grin as I take particular enjoyment in the stunned silence that falls.

Advisor Bemment clears his throat. "Doctor Zahhn's father possessed the ability to astral project, so we should've seen this coming. We need to compile a thorough list of all the descendants of the assassins who were part of Project Xeera. Under stable leadership," he says with a nod at Emperor Radakk, "such abilities should be encouraged, if for no other reason than to keep the empire strong. The doctor's skills would be very useful in a battle."

The advisors converse for a while, and I lean back in my chair, feigning a look of boredom. Eventually, they vote and agree that Project Xeera should be reinstated. The snitching engineer is dismissed from the command room, and eventually the advisors are as well, leaving me alone with Emperor Radakk and Admiral Tornn.

"I suspect there is more to the story you told us, Doctor Zahhn," the admiral says. "However, we are due to collect the next batch of human females soon, so a full explanation will have to wait." He rises to his feet, nods at the emperor, and departs the command room.

"Ah, just the two of us," I say with a grin.

Emperor Radakk gives me a pointed look. "Are you aware that Doctor Ammdox requested a specific female from today's batch to become his mate?"

I tense. "No, I was not aware. I haven't spoken to Doctor Ammdox in some time. We have differing interests."

The emperor stands and faces the viewscreen that overlooks the fleet. "Yes, he requested a former patient of yours, as it happens. A human female named Leona Zimmerman."

Fury consumes me, a searing rush of violence. I quickly rise to my feet. "That is very interesting," I force out, but there's no hiding the anger in my voice.

Emperor Radakk turns to me. "Unfortunately, Doctor Ammdox's contributions to the Darrvason Empire are not quite grand enough to warrant the reward of a mate. Not from this batch of females, anyway."

My rage cools somewhat, and I exhale a long breath. Thank the Star Gods. The prospect of Doctor Ammdox or any other male touching Leona—my mate by all rights—is enough to make me murderous.

"The ten females who were part of The Saviors

have presented us with a dilemma," the emperor says. "It's my hope that the five who are between the ages of nineteen and twenty-five will be quickly tamed and bred by their new mates. As for the five older females, well, I have decided it would be best to assign each of them to an older male. Males who I think could use the companionship and perhaps the challenge of a rebellious female."

My pulse accelerates as Emperor Radakk's meaning sets in. I swallow past the dryness in my mouth, hopeful and terrified of what he will say next.

"Doctor Zahhn," he says in a severe tone, "I am assigning Leona Zimmerman to you. You will become her mate, and you will ensure she adheres to our customs."

Disbelief cascades over me, and for a long moment all I can do is stare at the leader of the Darrvason Empire. "How-how did you know?" I finally ask.

Amusement flickers in his eyes, warring with the serious set of his jaw. He is trying to be the high and mighty emperor he's supposed to be, but there are times his demeanor slips. He blinks and the humor fades. "I didn't. Not for certain until just now. But I heard that you nearly pushed Doctor Ammdox out of the way just to claim Leona as your patient. After I realized you'd astral projected to the cell block where Leona was being housed, I started to become suspicious."

I straighten. "I will claim the mate assigned to me, Emperor, and I will make sure she stays out of trouble and adheres to our customs. I give you my word."

"Go and claim your bride, Zahhn," he says, using

my name without a title preceding it, and I marvel at the friendship he's once again showing me. He nods toward the door. "The shuttles depart soon."

Though I've never dared to address him by anything but his title, I say, "Thank you, *Radakk*," in an earnest tone.

His lips turn up in a thoughtful smile, and he gives me a nod of thanks in return, clearly approving of my use of his name.

I depart the command room and nearly break into a run once I reach the main corridor. I hurry to the docking bay and find the guard team. There are four additional males waiting, and I soon realize they too have been assigned one of the five females.

We board the shuttle and wait for takeoff. The one hundred brides are being split among the fifteen ships in our fleet, and several shuttles are traveling to the *Jansonna* to retrieve those brides. At last, we zip away from the *Haxxal*. Moments later, we land in *Jansonna's* docking bay.

I hurry to open the hatch, eager to claim the mate who's been assigned to me. *Leona*.

Chapter 33

LEONA

A STERN-FACED HUMAN SECURITY OFFICER ENTERS THE cell. I lift my chin, trying to be brave, but inside I'm trembling. Today is the day we'll be handed over to the Darrvasons. Prisoners for life. At least that's how I view it.

The officer holds up a tablet and starts reading off the names of the younger women, those who will be included in the group of one hundred. Those who will be claimed as mates. My heart goes out to them. God, I hope they'll be okay.

"If you just heard your name," the officer says, "exit the cell and you'll be escorted to the docking bay."

The young women reluctantly file out of the cell. A group of guards is waiting in the corridor to provide an escort. Once they're gone, the security officer peers at us intently. "The five of you have each been assigned to a Darrvason male."

"As slaves?" a woman asks in a fearful tone.

"As *mates*," the security officer clarifies. "Apparently, Emperor Radakk himself made the assignments. From what I hear, he wished to reward some of the older Darrvason males he believes are deserving of a mate." He steps toward the cell door. "Follow me."

Shock fills me. I've been assigned a mate. And the emperor made the assignments to reward specific Darrvason males who live on the *Haxxal*. I don't dare let myself hope I'll be assigned to Zahhn. Oh God, what will happen? Will I be forced to mate with a strange alien I don't know despite the intimacies I've shared with Zahhn?

With a heavy heart, I follow the security officer outside the cell. A second group of guards escorts us to *Jansonna's* docking bay. As we step into the huge area, which I've never visited before, I almost back away. I consider running. Then I look at the empty shuttles and wonder if I could possibly steal one. Not that I have any idea how to pilot one…

I glance around the docking bay. This is it. One hundred human women are being given to the Darrvasons in exchange for their assistance in repairing the *Jansonna*. One hundred plus five, that is.

Trepidation skitters through me when I notice the assembly of Darrvason males. They're all standing around various shuttles, expectant looks on their faces. My heart lodges in my throat and I exchange worried glances with the other four women in my group.

I'm shocked to my core when I see Officer Brute escorting Jenny toward a vessel. She's alive! I almost run over to her, but I quickly stop myself. Later. I will talk to her later and discover how she survived her ordeal. I still can't believe Angelo used a recording of her in an attempt to incite a rebellion.

Angelo… He's gone. Dead. He and his mother took their own lives before they could be arrested, or so a friendly guard recently whispered to me through the cell door. The guard also informed me that Angelo was one of five wealthy Founders who paid the Grozznolan mercenaries to attack the fleet. I sigh and push thoughts of him from my mind. His betrayal and the loss of him is simply too painful to contemplate right now.

I refocus my attention on Jenny, and I notice glowing green markings on her arms. Hm. The markings are similar in appearance to the blue markings that cover Zahhn's chest. How very strange. I can't help but wonder if she got those Darrvason-style tattoos willingly, or if Officer Brute forced her.

My stomach drops. Will my assigned mate force me to get tattoos on my arms? Is it considered a mark of ownership?

I watch as Jenny boards a small vessel with Officer Brute, then I notice an older woman following her inside. Her mother, Margo. Whoa. It appears her mother has a mate as well, and I can't help but wonder how that happened. An older engineer I've seen in the mess hall a few times escorts Margo onto the ship, and to my surprise they look… happy. Joyful, even.

As I'm pondering how this situation came about, I

glimpse a familiar face in the docking bay. *Zahhn.* He's disembarking a Darrvason vessel. When our eyes meet, he releases what sounds like a triumphant growl.

I freeze in place, my knees so weak I can't take another step. My anxiety intensifies, because what if he's not my assigned mate? He's not exactly my friend, but he's not my enemy. We share a connection, and he saved my life as well as the lives of my cellmates. If I'm to belong to anyone, I want it to be him.

He strides up to me and takes my hands in his. I peer at him in question, my throat too clogged with emotion to speak.

Leona, he says down the bond. He releases one of my hands and reaches for my cheek. I lean into his touch, soaking up his nearness. *Leona, I fear I have some terrible news to deliver.*

My stomach plummets to the floor. *What is it?* I hold my breath, waiting for his response.

His eyes twinkle, and he steps closer. *You are my assigned mate.*

I exhale quickly. *You ass*, I send down the bond, not caring if he punishes me for it later. *That wasn't funny.*

A mix of relief, shock, and trepidation fills me.

I'm going to belong to Zahhn. He's my assigned mate.

He wraps an arm around my shoulders and guides me toward the craft he just disembarked. We're the first couple to board the shuttle.

What happens now? I ask.

He helps me into a seat and fastens the buckle. His gaze bores into mine with so much intensity that I almost look away. Power emanates from him, the aura of dominance that always surrounds him seeming larger than ever. He tucks a lock of hair behind my ear and leans close. *Now I take you back to the* Haxxal *and rut you until you're sore between your thighs and dripping with my seed. I claim you over and over until a heartbond forms between us. And I train you to be an obedient mate.*

My hands tremble in my lap, and the trepidation I'd felt earlier starts to return. *Heartbond?* I ask.

A permanent bond that links our hearts and souls, he answers, and his response renders me lightheaded. *I believe it is already starting to form between us. That is why we can hear one another's thoughts sometimes. But the heartbond is not complete until we experience the mating fever, during which time we'll be consumed with lust for one another. Mating fever typically lasts for five days, though sometimes it's shorter, sometimes longer. Darrvason-human heartbonds seem to form atypically, so there is no telling exactly how long it will take. Once the heartbond has finished forming, my ancestral markings will have appeared on your arms, marking you as mine forever.*

A heartbond. Permanent. Mating fever. Ancestral markings. It's almost too much information to take in, and the gravity of his statement leaves me reeling with uncertainty. For someone who never planned to marry, the idea of a heartbond is frightening indeed.

Another couple boards the vessel, and Zahhn moves out of their way and sits next to me. As I process the significance of a heartbond, I keep one eye on the newcomers.

Other Darrvason-human pairs board the vessel, and Zahhn keeps a proprietary hand on my thigh. Whenever another male walks by our seats, he glares at them and appears on edge, never mind that they're escorting females of their own. Possessive, much?

I felt possessive of you the moment I first saw you, Leona. His voice reverberates in my head, a deep comforting rumble that makes me want to lean closer to him.

Stop reading my thoughts. I give him a sharp look.

I cannot help it, human female. He squeezes my thigh. *I am so curious about you that I find I'm always listening. Always hoping for a stray thought or feeling from you. You belong to me, and I want to know everything about you.*

He's curious about me? Why does that make me flush with warmth? I inhale a shaky breath, and I try to suppress the sudden achiness that's building in my core. But I can't help it. It's hitting me that in mere minutes, we'll be alone together in his quarters. I'll be at his mercy. He'll be able to do whatever he wants to me, and I won't be able to stop him.

The hatch closes, and a slight shudder runs through the vessel as the engines activate.

I'm leaving the *Jansonna.*

A brief moment of panic strikes me. I was born on the human worldship, and I've never even set foot on a trading outpost in space, let alone visited an alien spaceship or a planet. In a few months, three to be exact, we'll be settling on a planet known as 58-Zallnanis. It's a lot of change to come to terms with, especially when I take Zahhn into consideration.

I'll be his mate, and he's made it no secret that he expects my obedience. Will I have any freedoms? Or will he keep me locked away in his quarters?

He releases a dramatic sigh. *Yes, I will keep you locked up for a while. But only until the heartbond forms between us. Once the bond is fully formed, and you're drenched in my scent, and you're wearing my ancestral markings on your arms, I will allow you* some *freedoms.*

But why? I turn to face him. *Why must I remain locked in your quarters until the heartbond is fully formed?*

His nostrils flare, and his eyes take on a fierce glow. *Because I do not want to risk another male attempting to claim you. There are thousands of unmated Darrvason males on the* Haxxal *that are eager for a female of their own. I will not risk any harm coming to you, and I will not risk the chance you'll be stolen from me. You're mine, Leona. Mine.*

Chapter 34

ZAHHN

Anticipation builds inside me as I escort Leona down the corridor that leads to my quarters. I cannot wait to get her alone. But just as we round a corner, a familiar male blocks our path. I growl.

Doctor Ammdox.

Before I open my mouth to speak, he points a blaster directly at my head. "Hand over the female. She was supposed to be mine!"

I step in front of Leona, shielding her with my body, even if she's not Doctor Ammdox's intended target. "Emperor Radakk assigned Leona to become my mate, not yours. Perhaps you will receive a female from the next batch, the group of two thousand."

He peers around me, looking at Leona. "I want that one. I like the way she smells, and you dishonored me when you prevented me from claiming her as my patient three moon cycles ago." His eyes cloud with swirling darkness, dimming the usual glow, a sign that he's recently taken an illicit substance.

"You're not feeling well, Doctor Ammdox." I slowly reach out a hand. "Give me the weapon and I'll help you."

He snarls and moves closer, the blaster still pointed at my head.

Listen to me carefully, Leona, I say down the bond. *Slowly, very slowly, take a step back, then another, and keep going until you're safely around the corner.*

What about you? she asks.

Do it. Obey. I will protect you. I promise.

I feel her acquiesce, and I sense when she takes a step back. To my relief, the crazed male doesn't seem to notice her retreat.

I eye the blaster in Doctor Ammdox's hand, trying to determine its model. Until very recently, my people were not in possession of blasters. We prefer to use shooting stars and knives during battle. But one of our traders recently acquired a huge stock of blasters from an outpost, and the weapons were, perhaps unwisely, distributed throughout our vessels. Unlike the blasters used by humans, these newer ones can penetrate the thick texture of a Darrvason's skin. Which means I *fluxxing* hope this bastard doesn't shoot me.

As I stare at the weapon in Doctor Ammdox's hand, I realize it's one of the deadlier models, and I resolve that I must keep him from firing the blaster near Leona.

I sense my mate take another step back, then another, and I'm relieved when I realize she's close to rounding the corner. I stare at the crazed male, then I peer beyond him with the most horrified expression I can muster. A silly trick? Perhaps. But it works. His eyes widen and he spins around with the blaster held high, obviously expecting to meet a foe. But there's no one there.

I tackle Doctor Ammdox and we tumble to the floor. I wrench the weapon from his hand and throw it as far as I can. It clatters somewhere at the end of the corridor.

He growls and thrashes in my hold, and I reach for one of the shooting stars or a mini-blaster concealed in my clothing, which I plan to use to temporarily paralyze him, only to realize I'm wearing the wrong outfit. *Fluxx.* I'd intended to change into my armed clothing after the meeting in the command room, but after learning Leona was assigned to me, I never bothered.

Doctor Ammdox punches me in the jaw, and I growl as I launch myself on top of him. I'm larger, and the impact of my weight is surely crushing. He gasps and flails, unable to get up.

Then I grab his head and slam it to the floor. He immediately loses consciousness. Rage pumps through me as I stare down at him. How dare he attempt to steal my mate? I could kill him where he lies, but he did not officially challenge me to *lahhkda*—a battle to the death for a mate.

Banishment. That's the sentence he'll receive for his crimes today. Banishment from the Darrvason Empire. Even if he lives, he'll never pose a threat to Leona again.

I sigh and lift my wrist comm to my mouth. "This is

Doctor Zahhn. I'm requesting security officers and a medical team to Deck Twenty-Five."

I stand up and rush to Leona. When I see her peek around the corner, I shoot her a stern look even as I hurry to take her in my arms.

I meant for you to remain hidden and safe, I tell her.

Sorry. She gives me a sheepish look. *I just wanted to make sure you were okay. Are you?*

I am fine. I touch my jaw. *He got one punch in, but I will live.*

She stands on her toes, takes my face in her hands, and presses a kiss to my jaw. Then, for the first time, she purposefully sends me a wave of affection through the bond. It's warm and bright and soothing.

It's everything I never knew I needed.

I growl and scoop her up in my arms. As I carry her down the corridor, we pass the security and medical officers. I pause only long enough to explain what happened.

I carry Leona into my quarters and call out a verbal command to lock the door. And even though I didn't have to steal her, I still activate the force field in front of the door.

No one can enter, and no one can leave.

Leona peers around my living space, but I don't pause to give her a tour. I carry her straight to my bedroom and place her on her feet. She blushes as she glances at the bed, and as she fidgets in place, I notice she's pressing her thighs tightly together. Aching. She's aching to be filled up. Aching to be bent over the bed and pounded with ruthless vigor.

My cocks harden and my scrotum commences a rapid vibration. I'm about to rip her clothes off and sink inside her, until I remember the new safety protocols all Darrvason males must follow as we acquire our new mates, protocols I was charged to develop.

Poor innocent Leona. She has no idea what's about to happen to her. How thorough I'll be as I perform a strip search to ensure she's not hiding any weapons or contraband. I will delight in searching her tight orifices. Her slick pussy. Her shy bottom hole.

Her eyes widen, making me suspect she's picked up a few of my more recent thoughts.

"No," she says in a pleading tone. "Absolutely not. I'm not hiding anything. You don't need to search me. Please don't."

My dual appendages thicken further, and I savor the scent of her growing arousal. She might be averse to a strip search, but she's quivering with arousal whether she wants to admit it or not. There's no denying the sweetness of her feminine essence in the air.

"I like it when you beg, human female."

"Seriously, you don't need to search my… *orifices*." She whispers the last word as though it's highly scandalous, and her face turns a darker shade of pink. I don't believe I've ever seen her blush so hard. As she peers up at me, she starts scratching her right arm.

"Give me your arm!" I step closer and snatch her arm. Shock resounds within me as I gaze at a faintly glowing blue mark on her flesh. My breath catches, and I look up to meet her eyes.

"Is that an ancestral marking?" she asks in a tone of sheer disbelief.

"It is." Relief fills me. It's happening. The heartbond is happening. Sure enough, my blood immediately heats, and I start sweltering in my clothing. Pure savage need for my female pulses in my veins, and I snarl as my swollen appendages press painfully against the front of my pants. "I'm afraid your body cavity search will have to be quicker than I was originally planning. I am ravenous to claim you. My female. My mate. Lee-oon-ahh."

Chapter 35

LEONA

STRIPPED OF ALL MY CLOTHING, I STAND IN THE MIDDLE of the bedroom, waiting for Zahhn to begin my body cavity search. Nerves dance in my stomach even as warmth quakes in my center. I watch as he inspects my clothing, running his fingers carefully along all the seams, apparently searching for non-existent weapons and contraband.

"I told you I don't have anything on me. You're wasting your time."

He glares at me and tosses the clothing aside. I swallow hard as he closes the distance between us. He's still completely dressed, which makes me feel extra vulnerable and exposed. I glance at the bedcovers, tempted to grab them so I might shield my nudity from him.

If you attempt to cover up, human female, he sends down

the bond in a warning tone, *I won't allow you to wear clothing for an entire moon cycle.*

His threat causes a pang of heat in my center, and I press my legs together as I wait for him to get started.

He nods at the bed. "Bend over and spread your legs."

I tremble as I approach the bed and assume the ordered position. Breathless and achy, I'm eager for his touch, but I'm still nervous about a body cavity search. Will he shove especially deep in my orifices?

God, my arms. They won't stop itching. It's a struggle to remain in position because I'm desperate to scratch. I glance at my left arm, the one that itches the most, and I gasp at the sight. Three more markings have appeared. When I hear Zahhn's quick intake of breath, I know he sees it too.

He sinks down next to me and examines my arms, tracing the glowing markings. He meets my eyes, then takes his shirt off. I glance from the markings on my arm to those that cover his chest. They're exactly the same. A perfect match.

He leans down and kisses my arm, and I can't help but melt. Affection flows from him straight to my heart, an emotion so strong it brings tears to my eyes. I attempt to return the same level of warmth, and I hear his appreciative growl in response.

"Beautiful," he whispers in my ear. "So beautiful. I never thought..." His voice trails off for a moment. "I never believed I would have a mate. And now I do, and a heartbond is forming between us. You're wearing my ancestral markings. Praise be to the Star Gods." He strokes a hand down my back before he rises and moves to stand behind me.

My stomach flips. He's going to search me now.

Be a good female and hold still, he sends down the bond. *The more cooperative you are, the quicker this will be.*

I will try, I answer. My legs tremble and I can't catch my breath. Heated pulses affect my core, and my inner thighs are already coated in my wetness.

I hear a snapping noise, and I glance over my shoulder to find he's just donned a protective glove on his right hand. My pussy spasms.

Trembling and aching, I remain bent over as I await the invasion of his long alien fingers.

He nudges his gloved hand between my legs, prodding my slick entrance. A finger brushes over my clit, but not for long. He soon focuses on spreading moisture from my core over my bottom hole. I whimper, knowing he's about to push inside the snug orifice.

He places a hand on my lower back, then breaches my anus with one thick finger.

"Oh!" To my mortification, my hips undulate in a wanton manner, and more arousal escapes onto my inner thighs. I blink as perspiration runs in my eyes, and suddenly I'm burning up.

He presses further into my bottom hole, and my clit throbs and throbs. He pokes and prods, twisting his digit this way and that, until finally he withdraws from my ass.

I heave a sigh of relief, and when I glance over my shoulder again, I witness him removing the glove.

He wastes no time in checking my pussy for contraband. Stepping close, he nudges two fingers into my slick center. I brace myself as he shoves so very deep, and a cry escapes my lips when he curls his fingers inside my channel as he continues his inspection.

Good little female. It appears you were telling the truth. You are not in possession of weapons or contraband. But he doesn't withdraw his fingers. Instead, he places a thumb to my clit and swirls moisture over the sensitive bit of flesh.

Oh God. *Oh yes.* He brings me to a release quickly, and I writhe over the bed, my thighs still parted wide, as he expertly strokes me to a climax that leaves me gasping for breath. Shudders afflict me in the aftermath of the quaking pleasure, and I summon the energy to peek over my shoulder when I feel him step away.

My desires heighten when I see he's removing the remainder of his clothing. His hugely muscular body gleams in the overhead lights, and for a few seconds, I forget how to breathe.

He approaches me with his lower shaft, his largest appendage, in his hand while he gently strokes the base. He observes the area between my legs and a lusty growl emits from his chest.

What happens next is frantic and almost violent.

He claims me hard, over and over, mounting me from behind and pounding me with his shafts. He plunges into my slick center with one appendage, fills me with his seed, and then immediately drives his unspent shaft inside me.

The process repeats until I'm so sore, I doubt I could stand on my own. And yet I don't wish for him to stop. The more he ruts me, the more at peace I feel.

Ancestral markings keep appearing on my arms. Each time the itchiness spikes, I glance at my arms to find another one.

With each spurt of Zahhn's seed inside me, I'm able to better sense his thoughts and emotions. I even learn some of his secrets—he was originally planning to steal me today, but at the last minute, he learned I was his assigned mate. Also, he's been sterile for years, but he believes the heartbond might help change that.

He pauses in his thrusts and his fingers dig into my hips. I sense his sudden surprise, and I turn my head to meet his gaze as I attempt to decipher his latest thoughts. But his voice soon echoes in my head.

I can see the complicated situation you found yourself in, human female, with your father and your bar and all the happenings on the worldship. He caresses my back and sends me a wave of affection. *I know that you wanted to warn someone about your suspicions, but you didn't have any good options. Not without implicating yourself, and not without being the cause of a mass execution.*

I exhale with relief. *I was so worried when I didn't hear from you for a few days,* I send down the tether. *The thought of you being sick or dying… it terrified me. I was so happy when I learned you were safe. I was happy when I realized The Saviors' plan to deploy a virus on the* Haxxal *failed. I never wanted any part of a rebellion. I never wanted anyone to die.*

We communicate for a long time, mind-to-mind, while his huge stiff lower cock remains submerged in my core. His balls also keep vibrating against my clit, a blissful sensation that's somewhat distracting, but I don't wish for him to withdraw from my center. I like having him close.

He shares his findings about heartbonds altering a Darrvason male's genetic makeup, and the hopefulness that radiates from him touches my heart. Children. There's a chance we might have children together. Just a few days ago, such a prospect would've scared the hell out of me. But the developing heartbond allows me to sense his integrity, his true character, and I find myself hoping for a miracle.

He readjusts his grip on my hips and rides me to another completion. We climax at the same time, and after we catch our breath, he cradles me on his lap. He strokes my hair and peers into my eyes, his gaze brimming with devotion. Devotion *for me.*

Our telepathic secret sharing session continues as we piece together the events of the last three months. Misunderstandings are resolved. Apologies are issued. Promises are made.

After he glimpses the day of my arrest, combing through my mind to acquire every little detail, not only does he show concern for Mandy's sister, but he insists he'll visit the *Jansonna* to help her soon. He also says I can accompany him, as the last of his ancestral markings have just appeared on my arms.

As it turns out, he won't have to keep me locked up out of fear that another male will attempt to claim me. I shiver as I push away thoughts of the unpleasant encounter with Doctor Ammdox, and I'm grateful the heartbond has finished forming between us so quickly.

I stare at the glowing markings on my upper arms,

then look at his chest. I also notice his flesh is cooler to the touch than it was an hour ago. His mating fever must be abating. Considering how many times he mounted me and erupted in my depths, I'm not surprised.

A smile tugs at my lips as I recall how this all started. The dreams. The dreams about glowing purple eyes set in a face obscured by shadows. I hold his gaze as my soul does a little dance.

My precious mate. He presses his forehead to mine and tightens his arms around me. I bask in the comfort of his embrace, and as I drift to sleep, I hear him whisper, "Mine. My sweet Lee-oon-ahh."

About Sue Lyndon

USA TODAY BESTSELLING AUTHOR SUE LYNDON writes naughty, heartfelt romance filled with sexy discipline, breathless surrender, and scorching hot passion. Hard alpha males, strict husbands, fierce alien warriors, and stern daddy-doms make her go weak in the knees. She's a #1 Amazon bestseller in multiple categories, including Sci-Fi Romance, Historical Romance, BDSM Erotica, and Fantasy Romance. She also writes vanilla sci-fi romance under the name Sue Mercury—but no matter the genre or pen name, her books always have a swoon-worthy happily ever after.

WWW.SUELYNDON.COM

****Get FREE reads when you sign up for Sue's newsletter—and be the first to hear about freebies, sales, and new releases:** https://www.suelyndon.com/newsletter-sign-up ******